Empower

Publishing

Also by Percy D. Kepfer

*The Homeless Veteran*

*Symbiosis*

*The Smell of Power*

# The Daughter of the General

a Novel

By

# Percy D. Kepfer, M.D.

Empower Publishing
Winston-Salem

# Empower

# Publishing

Empower Publishing
302 Ricks Drive
Winston-Salem, NC 27103

First Empower Publishing Books edition published
January, 2024
Empower Publishing, Feather Pen, and all production design are trademarks.

For information regarding bulk purchases of this book, digital purchase and special discounts, please contact the publisher at publish.empower.now@gmail.com

Cover design by Pan Morelli

Manufactured in the United States of America
ISBN 978-1-63066-569-2

# THE DAUGHTER OF THE GENERAL
## CAST OF CHARACTERS

1) Tanya. AKA: Lily Marie Kruger Beltran, the general's daughter
2) Doña Maria Beltran de Kruger, Tanya's mum
3) General Guillermo C. Kruger Larrave. father of Tanya
4) Captain Mario Guillermo Kruger Beltran, Tanya's brother
5) Melchior: AKA Carlos, Guerrilla fighter
6) Maria, Guerrilla fighter and Tanya's best friend
7) Camilo, Guerrilla fighter
8) Efrain, Guerrilla fighter
9) Ricardo, Guerrilla fighter
10) Don Rafa, chief of the dissection lab at the Medical School
11) Tom Hopeland, freelance American reporter
12) Juan, bartender at Camino Real hotel
13) Doctor K, physician
14) John Gordon Mein, USA ambassador
15) Mrs. Gordon Mein, ambassador's wife
16) Colonel Ricardo Oliva, frenemy of General Kruger
17) Richard M. Helms, Director of the CIA
18) Agent Smith, CIA operative
19) Dr. Williams, Washington DC Coroner
20) Tony Benedetti, free-lance assassin works for the CIA
21) General Ramiro Zelaya
22) General Mario Camacho
23) Colonel Benito Benitez
24) Richard Morton, acting US Ambassador
25) Claudia Gonzalez, alcoholic beggar
26) Captain Jaime Garcia, MD, same as Tony Benedetti
27) Octavio, Guerrilla fighter and sniper

THE DAUGHTER OF THE GENERAL is a fictional story, very, very loosely related to real events, however most of the characters and situations are totally fiction and entirely the product of the fantasy and imagination of the author. Therefore, any similitude with persons living or deceased (other than those of historic significance), are pure coincidence.

This book is dedicated to the country of my birth, Guatemala, and to all those who fought and perish there and elsewhere, pursuing the impossible dreams of freedom, equality, peace, the end of poverty, and true independence for their countries.

—Percy D. Kepfer, MD
July 3, 2022

# ONE

## The Year: 1963
## The Country Guatemala
## The City Guatemala City
## Guatemala's Club

She said that her name was Tanya.

Of course, I knew that was not her real name, as I had met her seven or eight years earlier when she went by her real name Lily…Lily Marie Kruger- Beltran

I also believe that I fell in love when I first laid my eyes on her.

She was a young and beautiful socialite, the daughter of an army General, who was very close to the president and part of his inner circle.

I met her that first time at the Club Guatemala, an exclusive and elegant Members only, social Club located at the corner of 7$^{th}$ avenue and 13$^{th}$ Street Zona1, which was the center of the city back then.

It happened when my buddies and I crashed her lavish *"Quinceañera"* party.

She was sitting at the main table, between her parents, the then Colonel Guillermo Cesar Kruger-Larrave, her mother, Doña Maria Beltran de Kruger, her brother Mario Guillermo Kruger – Beltran and her elderly grandmother.

The Beltran family name was a well-known name, a very wealthy name, the name of a family that owned the most famous and popular rum and spirits distillery in the Country.

And considering that Guatemalan people consume alcoholic beverages, in significant quantities, since well before adolescence, the family's income was vast and enormous.

To my middle-class eyes, She and her family looked, like the

1

royals in the painting of a famous artist from bygone historic times.

General Kruger, Her father, was in full gala uniform, with several medals hanging from his chest; he was tall, slender and muscular; his hair was blondish with graying at the sides, cut short, military style, and his eyes were brownish, appearing at times to be green, like her daughter's but lacked the sweetness of hers, in fact, his, eyes had an expression of resolve, perhaps even cruelty, his mouth was small and lascivious. He smiled rarely and when he did, gave the impression that it was a forced, fake smile.

The General's wife, Doña Maria, on the other hand, was as beautiful as her daughter, had similar black hair, cut, and combed in the way it was the fashion in the fifties, she had the same sensual lips as Lily Marie had, although some wrinkles had started to appear at the corner of her mouth. Her eyes were green, or greener than her daughter's, almost turquoise, but gave the impression that they were about to burst into tears at any moment.

Doña Maria must once have had a splendid body, but now her body was extremely thin, almost pathologically slender. She was wearing a long dark blue gown, with the top part adorned with a few sequins of lighter blue and dark red, resembling the wings of a bird, her only ornament was a gold medal engraved with the image of the Virgin Mary, about the size of quarter, dangling from her neck and a pair of small gold earrings.

The fourth and fifth family members at their table were her older brother Mario Guillermo, who was a student at the Military Academy of Guatemala and who was wearing the elegant, and somewhat sumptuous gala uniform of the "Caballeros Cadets"; Mario Guillermo was also tall and handsome, blondish, like his father but also had the mother's green eyes, minus the sadness that she had on hers.

Grandmother, Doña Luisa was a woman in her seventies or late sixties.

She was the perfect example of a woman belonging to the old Spanish aristocracy: thin, erect, svelte, elegant, and imposing, she had White hair that she proudly refused to dye and that she wore somewhat short for the fashion of the times; Doña Luisa was also wearing a long gown, of dark green color, no ornament, except for earrings of two real pearls.

From her neck hung a simple gold cross with two tiny emeralds, one at the crown and another at the feet of Jesus. The emeralds dangling from her neck, were a perfect match to the color of her dress, and that was her only other ornament.

Lily was gracious enough to share a dance with me, probably only because it was customary for the "*Quinceañera*" to dance with all her guests, but otherwise, she would not have given me the time of the day for the rest of the night or thereafter...Lily Marie was gorgeous at fifteen and became more beautiful over the years, as she matured into a woman. Her long, curly black hair gave her an air of sensuality, even at fifteen, and her sleepy green eyes gave her an air of nostalgic sadness; her nose was fine and perfect, her lips red as roses, even without lipstick, her face was oval and perfect, her skin was ivory white and her body, barely blossomed under the long *Quinceañera* dress. Her whole figure was like that of a Greek statue—at least under my testosterone-fueled twenty years old imagination.

After that evening, I dreamed of her several weeks in a row until gradually she faded into the fog of time, helped by work, school, and the love of other women…

Yet I do not think that I ever totally forgot her.

Then, one day, years later, as I was completing my last year of Medical School and waiting at the Dean's office to pay the dues for some of my last remaining tests, I saw her again, more beautiful than the last time, even though she was clad in a simple black and white blouse, blue jeans, and tennis shoes.

I learned that she was enrolling in the medical school.

I felt then the urge to tell her to beware, that she who looked to me like a beautiful, innocent sheep was getting into a place full of hungry wolves, but as I tried to start a conversation, she cut me off and went into Dean's office.

Although apparently, she was a brilliant student, a few months after I graduated, I learned that she had quit and dropped out of school, entirely shortly after starting only her second year.

Thereafter I heard rumors that she was "living la Vida Loca," drinking, doing drugs, and becoming quite famous for her promiscuity…So much for an innocent sheep.

Upon hearing that, I felt sorry for her, almost to the point of crying.

And she was back in my dreams again.

# "Hospital General San Juan de Dios"

### 1968, late February

Several months later, I learned the reason for such wild behavior and dissipation from Lily Marie.

By that time, I was a doctor and a surgical resident at the Hospital General San Juan de Dios, a public, free for all, overpopulated, understaffed, undersupplied, very old Hospital located in the Northwest of the city.

One day, a man was dropped off at the Emergency Room by an unknown person; he had suffered a gunshot wound, an event that was not unusual in those days, especially considering that the Country had been fighting a civil war for several years and that such war was getting worse, bloodier, spreading to the Urban areas and closer to everyone.

This man had sustained a very serious gunshot wound to his abdomen and we could barely operate him on time to save his life, after which he had a rather complicated post-operatory period.

I made rounds on him twice daily, sometimes three times, before he started the process of recovery, which, most unfortunately, he would have to complete elsewhere, because, as a member of the FAR guerrilla group, every day he spent in the hospital was a new risk to his life.

If the secret police, the army, or the "Mano Blanca" ("the white hand) an extreme right-wing paramilitary group), learned of his identity, he would be arrested, tortured, and killed.

Eventually, I gained his confidence, and we became friends. At some point, during my visits to his bed, he related the story of how he had been wounded and how he had landed at our emergency room.

He told me that he was a veteran of "Las FAR"—Fuerzas Armadas Rebeldes—(Rebel Armed Forces), having been a member since he was a kid of about 11, living in a small town in the Countryside, both his parents and his siblings had been killed during an army raid on his village, a raid from which he escaped by rubbing the blood of his mom on his face and pretending to be dead.

Days later, after walking alone in the jungle, without food or water, he was found by a FAR group, fed, clothed, and sheltered. He was taught how to read, write, and, more importantly, fight. Therefore, he became one of them.

To me, he was still a kid, two and a half years younger than me, but hardened by the life in the mountains, the hardships of war and the killing of men.

His real name was Melchior, but he went by the more common name of "Carlos."

Carlos said that he was used to fighting in the mountains, and in the jungle, and that this time he had been sent to the city to meet with the urban FAR and coordinate some "actions" but was not supposed to participate in any operations while in the city. Yet he could not resist the temptation, when the local group was planning to rob a central bank, and he insisted on participating,

Carlos had never been wounded before, and his youth and testosterone made him think he was invincible.

Only four people, in one car, were to participate in the robbery.

The commander of the group was a very, very, beautiful woman who went by the name of Tanya, who was also the driver of the getaway car, and the only one in the group who did not cover her face during the assault.

Carlos said that they parked the car right in front of the bank, and three of them got into be bank lobby, after disarming the policeman guarding the front door; one of them fired a shot to

5

the ceiling and shouted to the costumers to lie down and be quiet while instructing the tellers to put all the cash in plastic bags.

Everything was going ok, till Carlos saw the tip of a rifle coming out of the bank's vault.

Carlos jumped over the teller's counter and fired in that direction.

Carlos was an excellent shot, but the man in the vault was sheltered by the heavy metal door, so Carlos rolled on the floor while continued shooting and, although eventually got the guy, and his partner, who was also holding a shotgun, he was wounded in the process.

Carlos felt the impact of a bullet and the penetration of it in his abdomen.

The other two men on his team tried to drag him out of the bank and into the car but only were able to carry him to the middle of the lobby, as he was telling them to leave him, take the money and run.

Police sirens were being heard in the distance.

Thereafter he was not sure what had happened. Either Tanya was out of the car, and coming to their aid, as she heard the shots, or the guys told her what happened, and then she may have ordered them to go back to fetch him.

Carlos only remembered being dragged again from the lobby and put in the back of the car.

He regained consciousness four days later and was informed, in some secret way, that it had been Tanya the one who commanded, at gunpoint, the other two guys to go back and fetch him.

"As far, as I know she went in with them, and she then drove me to the hospital, and let you save my life.

Moreover, she has been to visit me couple of times, and she will arrange for me to leave from here, and to a safe house as soon as you say it is OK."

I asked him to describe Tanya for me, and he did more than that as it turned out that he was quite good at drawing people's faces, so he did a very good sketch of her.

I recognized her immediately, and to say that I was surprised would be an understatement, I was totally and completely taken aback.

I could not believe my eyes.

Tanya, the bank robber, the guerrilla group commander, was no other than Lily Marie Kruger Beltran, the beautiful socialite whose Fifteen Birthday party my buddies and I had crashed years earlier and whose image had stayed in my mind all those years.

Tanya was now her "nom de guerre," the one she chose after becoming a guerrilla fighter, a guerrilla cell leader, but why would a rich spoiled socialite and a straight "A" Medical student choose to switch her life around so drastically and dramatically?

I would learn her reasons a lot sooner than I would have wanted.

As Carlos was recovering more and more as the days passed and because we were always short of beds at the hospital, I informed him that he would be released within a day or two and suggested planning to find a place to go to.

He told me not to worry about that because his comrades would handle it.

Sure enough, a day later, as I walked out of the hospital. A red Mustang convertible, with the top down, pulled by the curve alongside me.

I was being driven by none less than Lily Marie Kruger.

I was surprised and confused as I said: "Whoa, is that you? Hello Miss Kruger."

Beautiful, as always, wearing jeans, a red blouse, and her black hair covered by a pink scarf, she smiled and said:

"Why are you calling me by that name? Perhaps such would have been my name in another life. My name now is Tanya."

And she continued as it she did not remember ever seeing me before in her life:

"I understand that you are the physician in charge of the treatment of one of my men, Carlos, and I also understand that you think he is ready to be discharged. Is that correct Doctor? I want to confirm that is this true, because Carlos is very anxious to get out of the hospital, so he may be altering the facts to his like and frankly I can blame him for that because, as you may realize, each day that he is in there his life is at risk".

"Yes, I realize that and no, Carlos is not lying, he is telling the truth. But he still needs time to recover, and I am worried of where is he going to go for that".

"Let me worry about that, Doctor". She said and drove away.

When I went to make rounds on Carlos the following day, I saw that this bed was empty and somebody else was occupying it. When I asked what had happened, the nurses told me that, following my orders Carlos had been discharged.

They did not know that he was in the military, but a young army Captain came to fetch him, accompanied by a private, an provided the patient Carlos with a Sargent's uniform after which they sat him on a wheelchair and walked out of the hospital.

The nurses were surprised to be tipped twenty-five Quetzales a piece, by the young officer and made a point to say that the officer was not only very young but extremely cute.

I suspected who the officer was, and I prayed to God to never see Carlos or that cute young officer ever again for the rest of my life.

Unfortunately, the Lord was going to ignore my prayers.

# TWO

## August 10, 1968
## Hotel Camino Real
## Guatemala City
## 3.30 pm

Guatemala City and most towns in the country are divided into districts or *zonas*. Each zona has avenues going north to south and streets (*calles*) going east to west. Each avenue and street with few exceptions, like *Carretera Roosevelt, Paseo La Reforma, Avene Elina,* etc.) are labeled with a number. There are 21 zonas in Guatemala City today. There were fourteen in 1968.

At that time, Zona 1 was the center of the city, the place where the National Palace, the cathedral, most of the government offices, banks, big retailers, theaters, and restaurants were. Zonas 9, 10, and 14 were the ritzy areas where the villas and mansions of the rich, the foreign embassies and the elegant clubs, and hotels were located.

The bar of the lobby at the elegant Hotel "Camino Real", in the "Zona 10"; one of the plush and expensive area of the city, had been deserted but it was slowly beginning to fill, as the rush hour approached.

Tom Hopeland, a freelance American reporter, and photographer had been sitting for over one hour, at a table at the far end of the bar, a table that the waiter, courteously but firmly, had insisted on sitting him at.

Tom was a patient man, but, as he was nursing his third "cerveza Gallo", the local, and most popular brand of beer in the country, he was beginning to think that the person he was so

9

anxious to interview, was not going to show up for a date that she, herself had arranged.

He did not had lunch yet and the Guatemalan beer had more alcohol than American beers, so he was beginning to get a bit lightheaded and quite hungry; especially since he had had breakfast very early that morning.

The "boquitas" (snacks) that came with the beers were not enough to fill his stomach, as he was a big guy.

Indeed, he was, Tom stood at 6 feet 2 inches, slender and muscular, curly, bushy, rebel, black hair, brown eyes, and a stubbed half-grown beard, which hid his perfect teeth and smallmouth at thirty-eight, although he looked older due to the thick glasses that he had to wear because he almost lost his right eye after he was hit by shrapnel from a mortar fire, while fighting in Vietnam.

Vietnam was a war he did not believe in, or care about, but a war into which, by his bad luck, he had been drafted in to fight.

Tom had been less than six months in the rice fields of Nam when his platoon came under mortar fire, and he was hit in the right side of the face by shrapnel, shattering the orbit and damaging the eye, which he almost lost.

Tom eventually recovered from his wounds, and, fortunately, he did not lose his vision, but he was forced to wear those thick glasses in order to see and perform his job as a reporter and writer.

Of course, after few weeks in the hospital he got honorably discharged from The Army and sent home, where he enrolled at Berkley, studied journalism, and eventually became a professor. Later, he resigned from his tenure, preferring to travel all over the world in search of the latest news and adventures as a reporter and photographer.

Tom had credentials from and received a stipend, albeit small, from National Geographic and Time Magazine, but he also had columns published by the New York Times, The Miami Herald, and the San Francisco Chronicle, among others.

He dreamed and prayed to one day have a regular syndicated column in any or all those publications, so perhaps the interview he was expecting today would allow him to achieve that dream.

After all, they say that God works in very mysterious ways.!

Suddenly, appearing out of nowhere, she stood before him.

"Hello, I am Tanya; you must be Mr. Hopeland. Correct?" she said in perfect English.

Tom stood up awkwardly, tipping the bottle and spilling what was left of his beer on the table and the floor, thus making her smile, him to blush and the waiter to arrive, fast as a bullet, to clean the mess and prevent the beer from spilling into the chair where the woman was supposed to sit, a task he very skillfully accomplished being rewarded by a glorious smile and a "gracias Juan", coming from her beautiful mouth.

The woman was totally gorgeous, one of the most beautiful Tom had ever interviewed, and those included rock stars and movie actresses.

Long, slightly curly black hair and green eyes; she was dressed simply, in a white dress with tiny red and yellow flowers coming down to just about an inch above her knee; on her legs, she wore long leather boots covering about three-quarters of her perfectly shaped lower extremities.

Tom Hopeland was calm and almost always in control of himself kind of guy, but in front of that beautiful woman, he lost all composure and awkwardly managed to say – "Are you sure you are Tanya, the guerrilla girl?".

And after a short pause, he continued: "I was sure that you did not exist, that you were only an urban legend.

Anyway, thank you for coming; please have a seat."

She remained standing while saying:" would you mind switching seats with me? I much prefer to seat with my back towards the wall and my eyes on the entrances…for obvious reasons… of course."

"Of course, "he said and got up, giving his chair to her.

Not soon, she sat as Juan came solicitous asking her what she wanted to drink,

"The usual Juan, thank you", was her answer. - "Rum Zacapa Centenario, on the rocks and a Diet Pepsi on the side, Mr. Hopeland may want another Gallo since I spilled his last one".

She smiled mischievously as she said that and added: "And please bring us a menu from the main dining room; we are going to have lunch right here. I am famished, and believe Mr. Hopeland is also very hungry."

She ordered a blackened salmon, a small Cesar salad, and a baked potato,

He ordered a 6-ounce sirloin steak, medium, pink at the center, also a Cesar Salad, and a baked potato. They talked as they ate; Tom was surprised, not only at her youth and beauty but also about her calm.

Was this beautiful woman really Tanya, the guerrilla woman about whom he had heard so much and had such a difficult time getting an interview with?

No question that he had he been very lucky.

She looked perfectly at ease, if she was nervous or afraid, she did not show the last bit of it. Perhaps for the first time in his life, Tom felt awkward, and felt stupid when the only thing he could ask her again was:

"Are you really Tanya, the guerrilla fighter? I thought that you were a myth, an urban legend. I never really expected that you materialized here, today."

Hesitating, as if he could not yet believe that the gorgeous specimen of humanity in front on him, was who she said she was, he he asked awkwardly again:" Do you carry a weapon, Miss Tanya; do you have weapons on you?"

She laughed and responded, "Only two at the moment, one in my purse, a 9mm Smith & Wesson, and a small one, a 380 Ruger, in my boot.

"Why? Are you afraid of weapons Mr. Hopeland?"

"No, I am not afraid of weapons, I was in the military. But I may be afraid of women with weapons.

Besides, it is just that you do not fit the type of an Amazon; I am having difficulty imagining you are actually a guerrilla fighter."

She laughed again, became serious, and said: "Never judge a book by its cover Mr. Hopeland".

"And speaking of books let me ask you how much do you know about the history of my country Mr. Hopeland; how much do you know about the history of Guatemala?"

Tom regained his composure and responded, "What is this history test? I am not bragging but I know something about history, after all, I write for *National Geographic Magazine*."

"Do not be offended, Mr. Hopeland, I would just like to know how much you know about our country. If you do, you can understand the reasons for this war or, if not, I should tell you the history of this war from the very beginning.

Although I know that you are more interested in my personal life and story. That may come later, or not at all; it depends. So, you go ahead, tell me."

"Depends on what Ms., Tanya? "

"Depends on you gaining my trust, Mr. Hopeland, and I warn you that I trust no one"

"Fair enough, but since I imagine that there is no last name attached to Tanya, and also that Tanya is not your real name, why don't we drop the formalities and start calling me Tom."

"Ok, Tom, start with the Mayas."

"You would like me to start with the Mayans that is way far back, Miss Tanya??"

"Yes Tom, start with the Mayas."

"Ok, here it goes: The Maya civilization was developed by the indigenous people of this area, but they did not call themselves Mayas. It was us, the white men, who later called them Maya.

The Mayans were noted for their most sophisticated and highly developed writing system in pre-Hispanic America. They were also known for art, architecture, mathematics, calendar, and astronomical systems.

The Maya civilization developed in the area that today comprises southeastern Mexico, all of Guatemala and Belize, and the western portions of Honduras and El Salvador. It

13

included the Yucatán Peninsula and the Mexican state of Chiapas.

Once again. "Maya" is a modern term likely developed by the Caucasians, and currently used to refer collectively to the various peoples that inhabited this area.

They did not call themselves "Maya" or have a sense of common or political identity.

Nevertheless, the people we now call Maya are an old civilization and their evolution can be separated into different periods.

Before 2000 BC, the Archaic period saw the first developments in agriculture and the earliest villages.

The Pre-classic period (c. 2000 BC to 250 AD) saw the establishment of the first complex societies in the Maya region, and the cultivation of the staple crops of the Maya diet, including maize, beans, squashes, and chili peppers.

The first big Maya cities developed around 750 BC, and by 500 BC these cities possessed monumental architecture, including large temples with elaborate stucco façades.

Those large cities developed in the Petén Basin, and the city of Tikal and of Kaminaljuyu rose to prominence in the Guatemalan Highlands.

Hieroglyphic writing was being used in the Maya region by the 3rd century BC.

Beginning around 250 AD, the Classic period is largely defined as when the Maya were raising sculpted monuments with sculpted dates.

This period saw the Maya civilization develop many city-states linked by a complex trade network.

In the Maya Lowlands, two great rivals, the cities of Tikal and Calakmul, became powerful.

The Classic period also saw the intrusive intervention of the central Mexican city of Teotihuacan in Maya dynastic politics.

In the 9th century, there was a widespread political collapse in the central Maya region, resulting in intertribal warfare, the abandonment of cities, and a northward shift of population.

The Post classic period saw the rise of Chichen Itza in the north, and the expansion of the aggressive Kiche' kingdom in the Guatemalan Highlands.

In the 16th century, the Spanish Empire colonized the Mesoamerican region, and a lengthy series of campaigns saw the fall of Nojpetén, the last Maya city, in 1697."

"Whoa, Whoa, whoa! I see you know the pre-columbine history, Professor Tom Hopeland what happened next?

"Professor? Why do you give me such title, Tanya?'

"Weren't you a professor at Berkley, at some time>?"

"I supposed I was. For a couple of years. How do you know that?

"I may tell you that later. I am sorry for the interruption, Tom, please go ahead, continue."

"Ok, then the Spanish conquistadores came killed most of the natives and made slaves of the rest, all in the name of God and King they plundered and burned their cities and their books, raped their women and eventually they settled as rulers of the New World considering the natives, who they called Indians, (because as you remember Columbus thought that he had reached India).

Nevertheless, the Spaniards considered them savages and henceforth third or fourth class citizens considering them as inferior to the white man, and in need to be submitted to obedience, and to convert to Catholicism, by whatever means necessary."

Tanya interrupted: "and such condition has persisted even after we became independent from Spain, and pretty much to this day and age that is why we are fighting today, Mr. Professor Tom Hopeland. at some point we became voluntarily part of Mexico, although it was for a short time, and we had to fight to split off from them, in the process we lost big chunks of our territory; this was followed, or preceded—I am not sure—by the split of the Povincias Unidas de Centro America, in to five small republics, which, at one time or another were ruled by ruthless dictators, usually military ."

"Sorry I interrupted you, Tom, there is no doubt that you are well versed in Mayan history, and I am sure you are an expert in colonial and post-colonial history as well, because I know that you taught history of the Americas at Berkley, unfortunately, although I am enjoying very much the lunch, drinks and company, we are wasting time on that, so let's jump to the years 1944 to 1957, what is your take of that period of our history?"

"How do you know that? I only did teach there for a year and a half or so."

"Why did you quit Tom, you did not like teaching?"

"I did like teaching Ms. Tanya, but I guess that I am too restless to be confined to a classroom "

"I heard one of your lectures, when I was a student at Berkley, you were very good. I thought your conference was excellent "

"You were at Berkley..., when?

"That is classified Mr. Hopeland, and perhaps would be discussed again, later at our next interview" ...and she added, in a somewhat somber way." if I am still around and able to give you a next interview.

So, Please Professor Hopeland; indulge me with your version of the Guatemalan history during those dark years."

"Very well, Tanya, let me see" ... President Jorge Ubico, a Dictator for almost fifteen years, was deposed about October 1944 by a popular Revolution, leaded by both the Military and University students and his departure was followed by General or Colonel, Federico Ponce Vides assuming the Presidency.

Ponce Vaides was a minion of Ubico; therefore he did not last but a few weeks and was replaced by a Junta made by the leaders of the October Revolution; two Colonels, Jacobo Arbenz Guzman, Francisco Javier Arana and a civilian, Jorge Toriello Garrido.

The Junta called for elections and an exiled philosophist by the Name of Juan Jose Arevalo Bermejo, who had been living in exile in Argentina, during most of the Ubico years, was overwhelmingly elected President. "

"How am I doing so far?"

16

"You are a showoff professor, but so far, so good."

"Ok, it seems that President Arevalo had to suffocate several small rebellions, against him, mainly from the Military, but he was a popular with the people of Guatemala, having created many good social  programs , among them the Guatemalan Institute of Social Security, which was not similar to the USA social Security Program but a health care program, initially to care for workers suffering work related injuries but witch, in later years, after the end of his administration actually expanded to care for all kinds of illness, and included pregnancy care,  for both workers and families.

President Arevalo was succeeded by Colonel Jacobo Arbenz Guzman, who, like Arevalo, was overwhelmingly elected on a free election.

However, both Arevalo and Arbenz had communist ideas and tendencies,

Arevalo not only allowed the creation of workers unions, which became increasingly powerful, but also allowed the foundation of a Communist party, and both fell under the Soviet influence, leading to the possible establishing of Soviet bases in Guatemala.

It did not help Arbenz, that he had been accused of having been implicated in the assassination of his fellow officer, and possible rival candidate for the presidency, Colonel Francisco Javier Arana in 1949

With the anticommunist McCarthy's paranoia being rampant in the US, our government had no choice but to intervene and therefore commissioned the CIA to depose Arbenz and they did this by finding a willing person to lead an invasion from outside the country.

The CIA got funding for an invasion and selected for their leader an ambitious but poorly known Army Colonel, one Carlos Castillo Armas, who had been imprisoned by the Arevalo government for attempting a cue, and who had made a spectacular escape from prison.

Then, with an army of defectors and peasants, plus some air support by CIA pilots and airplanes the people of Guatemala

17

were able to depose Arbenz, after only a few squirmiest and the threat of US Marines coming to the aid of the rebels.

The Rebels called themselves "The Movimiento de Liberacion Nacional", which became simply known as "La LIberacion" (The Liberation); so, with the help of the US ambassador, and I am sure many bribes to military officers, the Guatemalan army surrendered to the so called "liberators" July 2, 1954

I would add that the Guatemalan Catholic church, lead by the Archbishop of the Dioceses of Guatemala, one Monsignor Mariano Rossell y Arellano, who was an ardent anticommunist, supported "the Liberacion" to the point of organizing nationwide processions carrying the statue of the most revered by Guatemalans, Christ of Esquipulas, -who had never before been removed from his temple- in a tour around the Country, as the way that the Archbishop choose to cement the people's support for the "Liberacion".

I may be wrong, but I believe that he later named the statue of the Holy Christ of Esquipulas, "the Christ of La Liberacion."

Of course, this and the overwhelming propaganda machine displayed before and after the July "victory" most of the country rallied behind the new "liberators".

However, that support was short lived, as apparently the Liberators committed excesses, jailed, and killed many supposed to be communists, exiled many people, including refugees from the Spanish civil war, who had lived in your country for years.

So, eventually Carlos Castillo Armas was assassinated by a communist sympathizer, a soldier, member of his own guard in July 1957; allegedly, as revenge for the murder of his father committed by the Liberation army years earlier.

He was briefly succeeded by Luis Arturo Gonzalez Lopez and Oscar Mendoza Azurdia, and Guillermo Flores Avendaño all of them military, and eventually by Miguel Ydigoras Fuentes, a General who was popularly elected and presided the country from 1958 to 1963 but whose government was plagued with corruption and a severe economic decline, as well as the beginning of a Civil war, which started with the uprising of the garrison of Puerto Barrios under the leadership of an officer known as "el Chino Yong Sosa".

The garrison was rapidly submitted but Yong Sosa, with a bunch of soldiers and few civilians fled to the mountains, where, to this day he or his successors conduct guerrilla warfare.

So, surprise surprise, Ydigoras was overthrown by another military Enrique Peralta Azurdia in 1963, about a year and a half before ending his constitutional mandate of Six years. Peralta called for elections and in 1966, your current president, the first civilian since Juan Jose Arevalo, is to this day, so far, still in power.

How am I doing so far, are my facts correct?"

"Whoa, you are really impressing Professor Hopeland, you have a fabulous memory."

"Actually, I have been told that I do have photographic memory, it is one of my many flaws, but please, I ask you again to call me Tom, the title of professor makes me feel old and wishing to grow a longer beard.     Plus, I have not been teaching in years."

"Ok Tom, I am sorry, but you have many parts of your historic facts all wrong."

"Is that so Tanya?  Then, do please enlighten me."

And so, Tanya began telling Tom Hopeland the correct version of the story of Guatemala, as she had seen it, and partially lived it:

"Ok, I am supposing that you know who Joseph Goebbels was?"

"Sure, Joseph Goebbels was Adolf Hitler minister of propaganda, but what that anything to do with Guatemala?"

"Have you ever heard of Edward L. Bernays?"

"Yes, Tanya; I know who Edward L. Bernays was, the so-called king of public relations but what has it to do with your revolution?"

Tanya's beautiful face show a smirk of satisfaction, over the ignorance, of at least this fact by Professor Thomas Hopeland, as she continued:

"OK professor, first let me state that the history of our struggle is closely tied to the history of the giant foreign corporations, mainly the United Fruit Company and the International railway Company."

"Ok Tanya, go on and correct my story."

"You may know, Tom that the United Fruit Company was founded, in 1899, by Minor C. Keith, a Boston entrepreneur, who was mainly in to building railroads, and went to Costa Rica, where some of his relatives were already working in building a railroad.

The construction of the train was delayed due to financial difficulties from both the government of Costa Rica and Mr. Keith, so in the meantime he grew bananas and started exporting them."

When the railroad was finished, some nineteen years later, Keith found that it was not profitable to just carry passengers, so he carried bananas in the trains, and that proved to be so profitable that his company bought all its competitors in the banana trade, and so, the United Fruit Company was born.

Among those competitors was the "Cuyamel Fruit Company" owned by none other than Sam Zemuray, who also became a partner and shareholder.

In 1933, Zemuray staged a hostile takeover of the company and became the head honcho of the United Fruit Company.

Meanwhile Minor Keith was called to Guatemala by the government and contracted to manage the Postal Services.

Keith did more than that in Guatemala, he managed the railroads and created also the "Tropical Radio and Telegraph Company" literally controlling all the communications systems in the Country.

Plus, he continued being a shareholder of United Fruit.

However, there was a problem with the way the United Fruit company was viewed in Latin America and the rest of the world, specifically after the Colombian "Banana Massacre" on December 6, 1928, on which the Colombian army gunned down over one thousand peasants working for the banana Company who were just asking for better salaries and working conditions.

The United Fruit Company was known Worldwide then as "The Octopus."

So Zemuray contacted and contracted Bernays to improve the image of the United Fruit Company, and, of course, to promote the consumption of bananas in the United States.

"Edward L. Bernays was the Joseph Goebbels of Guatemala, or rather, of the United Fruit Company and he was amazingly good at what he did.

Bernays was born in New York, the son of wealthy Jewish immigrants and nephew of Sigmund Freud.

This is the same Bernays, that as you correctly stated, was called in his obituary "The father of Public Relations."

Barnays had written several books, one called "Crystallizing Public Opinion" and another called "Propaganda", exalting the value of advertising, public relations and publicity as a powerful political weapon to influence and to control de masses and because of that he draw the attention of Samuel Zemurray.

At the time the United Fruit Company was the most powerful fruit Company in the world owning land in all the Central American and most Caribbean Countries.

In Guatemala alone, the United Fruit Company owned 41% of the land, although they barely cultivated 15% of it and, most important, they did not have to pay taxes, the company initially had forced the workers to work grueling hours for pitiful salaries, and when they tried to protest or form unions the Company bribed the local governments and used the army to control the workers, as it happened in Colombia

The United Fruit Company did not pay taxes in the Countries it operated and when governments tried to levy taxes on them they were deposed by a coup, as it happened in Honduras where Zemurray with a small group of hired mercenaries and few ships, pretending to be part of a larger invading US army battalion, he deposed the then president and put a stooge, in his place, who rapidly re-established the no tax rule.

I do not think that Zemurray, was part of the United Fruit Company when the Colombian Massacre occurred, but the Company had a very bad reputation. Mostly because of that.

Barnays did more than propaganda and public relations; he could foresee future problems and saw one coming upon the arrival of Juan Jose Arevalo to the Presidency of Guatemala, who some rumored was a communist sympathizer.

Although Barnays did rule out that President Arevalo, or the people surrounding him where communists, and that the only Russians who had visited the Country were himself and Sam Zemurray (he had been born in Russia), he nevertheless, detected a threat to the United Fruit Company by Arevalo's Presidency

The threat was that Arevalo was a progressist and a Democrat and wanted to make Guatemala a nation that functioned like the United States.

In addition to the Social Security health services you mentioned, he established the minimal wage, and taxed the big companies.

Arevalo allowed workers to form Unions, and yes, he allowed the formation of political parties of all kinds, including the Communist party, witch on the best of its days, only had a handful of members who actually knew what the word Communism really meant.

Nevertheless, all that was unacceptable to the interest of the United Fruit Company. Those changes meant taxation, meant lower profits, workers' unions, and education for the masses, all of which meant potential problems that would be a burden, at best, and at worst, could mean the end of the United Fruit Company as they knew it.

So, the propaganda machine started working, here, as well as in the United States, and it was easy, as the time was ripe, because those were the years of the McCarty anti-communist paranoia.

In addition, the brothers Dulles, had an enormous deal of power during the administration of President Eisenhower, John Foster Dulles was then Secretary of State, and his brother Allen was the Director of the CIA, and both men were in the board of Directors of the United Fruit Company.

Arevalo had indeed been able to suffocate several rebellions and cue attempts, caused, in not small way, because he took away some of the privileges of the Military, mainly abolishing the rank of General and limiting the officers' rights to free imports of expensive goods, including automobiles.

Yet Arevalo's presidency survived, and he was succeeded by Colonel Jacobo

Arbenz, who was freely elected but also was even more bold and progressive than his predecessor.

Arbenz taxed the landlords, including the United Fruit Company, proposed, and had had approved by congress a swiping land reform, on which the Government would buy the idle lands, and sell them to the peasants, at very low interest and long-term payments.

Arbenz also started building the road to the ports of the Atlantic, which at that point, could only be reached by railroad.

A railroad, of course, owned and operated by the United Fruit Company or a subsidiary.

Arbenz also started building the Jurun-Marinala, electric generating plant, who would generate electricity, thus competing with the Electric Company, which was also foreign, owned.

So, the propaganda machine intensified, and public opinion was bombarded with "news" about the Communist regime of Guatemala and the possibility of Russian bases being established.

So convincing and strong was the propaganda that not only the Guatemalan population, but the Catholic Church and the people of the USA, including the CIA swallowed the hook, sink, lure, and reel believing the big lie of the communist Guatemala and the Soviet Invasion.

Of course, it did not help the cause of Guatemala the fact that the Dulles brothers occupied key, important positions in the Eisenhower cabinet.

So, although the CIA knew well that there were no communists or Soviets in Guatemala, they realized that the financial interests of the United Fruit Company and the financial interests of the Dulles brothers were in jeopardy, therefore the wheels of the powerful CIA machine started moving.

The First step was to abscond Castillo Armas from prison.

They did this by staging a fake escape from the penitentiary pretending that he escaped through a tunnel and a hole in the wall of the prison, when in fact he walked out of their front door and was driven away in a CIA vehicle.

This in fact was the first step in making Castillo Armas look as a hero in the eyes of the gullible population of Guatemala thereafter using him as a stooge to lead the invasion they called "*La Liberacion*".

*La Liberacion* did not depose Arbenz, with an armed struggle.

The Arbenz government was toppled by a small bunch of cowards, corrupt, traitors and easy to bribe Military Officers, which were bought and scared by your ambassador, one John Puerifoy and the archbishop Rossell, who, to this day I am not sure if really believed in the whole communist plot or was also a patsy brainwashed or bought by Puerifoy.

As a soldier, can you believe Tom that 780, poorly trained and poorly motivated foreign mercenaries, would have been able to defeat, the Guatemalan army?. Castillo Armas certainly was not Leonidas, and his men were not Spartans.

In fact, the "Liberators" were defeated in the only two contacts they had with the army on which a total of 173 mercenaries were captured.

Can you believe Tom, that we had an small air force who actually had more and much modern planes that those flown by the CIA "liberators", but the Guatemalan Air force did not attempt, not even once, to take to the air and fight the "Sulfatos" (which is the name of a very strong, popular and common laxative) and which was the nickname given by the people of Guatemala to the CIA planes, because they made our flamboyant military officers shit in their pants.

No, the army did not fight. And the air force did not fly, so, after those two battles, there was no more fights and a deal was made in Guatemala City by the, so called, friends and colleagues of President Jacobo Arbenz Guzman and CIA representatives.

You know the rest, except that Castillo Armas was not killed by that poor little soldier who was blamed for it, and likely assassinated as well.

"Cara de Hacha" ("Ax face"), as Castillo Armas was popularly known, was killed by members of his own staff who put the blame on Romeo Vasquez Sanchez, an ignorant soldier who barely could write and read and who supposedly wrote a poetic dairy confessing to the murder,

The CIA, with the help of our military, the Catholic Archbishop, and the US ambassador, succeeded in overthrowing the Arbenz government and helped the so called, Liberators to kill or jail as many as 70,000, mostly innocent Guatemalan citizens.

Considering that the total population of Guatemala at the time was slightly over 3 and half millions, 70,000 that was then about 2% of the total population of the Country.

The "liberators" completed the show by setting up an exhibit of pictures, in the National Palace, showing gruesome photos of the victims who supposedly had been killed by the Arbenz government during his last days in power.

We know now that those photos were most likely photos of killings done by the "liberators," or simply poor souls killed during those brief skirmishes with our few decent militaries.

So, the United Fruit Company succeeded in deposing Arbenz, the land was never taken from them, the company was never taxed, the Unions were dissolved, the political parties banned, the "Comite de the Defensa contra El comunismo"- (Committee of Defense Against Communism) another repressive government agency, was created and in general the lights of freedom and progress were turned off in Guatemala.

The new government bought the aging railroad from the International Railroad Company, a subsidiary of the United Fruit at a very inflated price... and everyone did not live happily ever after.

25

Except for the rich, the landlords and the almighty United Fruit Company

Yet, the CIA failed miserably politically, not only here but in most Latin America and the Caribbean, because many countries as in response to the Guatemalan experience, turned towards the left and deposed old dictators or are in the process of doing so.

Here, in Guatemala, we had had a succession of military cues and military governments, the last being General Miguel Ydigoras Fuentes.

Now, we have elected one civilian, the current, President Julio Cesar Mendez Montenegro, a Lawyer, whose Vice-President: Clemente Marroquin Rojas, is a columnist and newspaper owner, both civilians and relatively decent people but controlled 100% by the military.

The people had great hopes on them, but in order to allow them to assume the Presidency, the military Officers forced the President and Vice-president to agree to give free hand to the Military to control the security of the Country, which really meant they had free hand to do as they pleased, to whom they pleased.

The Guatemalan military is a monster, Tom, a monster, that since the days of Peralta Azurdia, has massacred people from entire villages and has created Para-military forces to kidnap, torture and assassinate people, especially union leaders, university students, politicians, and anybody who opposes or simply criticizes them.

The press is not free, as reporters, including women reporters, like Irma Flaker, and even celebrities like Miss Guatemala Rogelia Cruz Wer were kidnapped, tortured, and ultimately murdered.

Of course, the foreign companies are not the only ones to blame for the miseries of our country. The main culprits are the homegrown oligarchs, our very rich for which the military establishment, for a price, of course, is the enforcer, the armed hand, the protectors of the interests of these one percent who own ninety percent of the wealth of this nation. The military and the rich have been in cahoots for centuries. They sold themselves to your CIA, declined to even pretend that they had tried to stop Castillo Armas and his fake "*Liberacion*" and they have done nothing before or after but be the armed enforcer of the interests of the oligarchs.

And yet, to this very day, a sizable group of old very religious ladies and some old politicians, but mostly the rich, praise these criminals and still light votive candles in front of pictures of the Traitor Castillo Armas, who, if there is a just God, should be burning in hell as we speak.

Of course, Ydigoras, being a general himself, did not want to be degraded and therefore reinstated the rank of general, promoted several Colonels to that rank and restored the privileges of the military.

All these while the majority of the population is hungry, malnourished, sick, or homeless.

So, Tom, that is why we are here, that is why we are fighting, that is why we are dying.

Please do not insult my intelligence by telling me that there are other ways. Guatemalans have tried all, since the day we thought that we were free by gaining independence from Spain.

As for your country, the USA, Tom, we like you, we admire you, we watch your movies and can name each an everyone of your movie stars, but we do not want you to interfere in our affairs, so the only thing we ask from you is that to please leave us alone, let us be, let us seek our own destiny.

Thank God, the people of your Country, especially the young and the educated are finally awakening and realizing that they have been feed lies for decades."

And no, we are not communists, however, we will accept help from however is willing to give it to us, including the Cubans and the Russians, and also the USA, not because we like any of them, nor because we agree with them or with their politics, but because we need their weapons.

After all, at the end of the day, a white bullet kills you the same way as a red bullet does.

Any questions Tom?"

"Whoa, Tanya, evidently I had a different version of the historical events of those years, and I respect your faith in the cause you fight for, however, I do not understand how a gorgeous girl, like you got involved in this…were you related to those women that you mentioned were tortured and killed?"

"No, but they were my friends.

My motives are private and perhaps one day you will know them, but for now, thank you for lunch and the conversation, and I hope and trust that you will tell the truth to your people.

Now, I am going to give you something as a reward for being such a good listener, an invitation to an event that would make the evening news around the world.

Just try to be at the Ice Cream Shop "Helados Gloria" in the Avenida La Reforma, for the next few afternoons, go alone and do not mention this to anyone…you will regret it if you do."

Tanya 's voice sounded threatening and as she got up, she retrieved a Glock 9mm that had been hidden all along under their table as she said to a flabbergasted Tom:

"Told you, I do not trust anyone, so please do not violate my trust.

Now, would you, please walk me to the parking lot Tom?"

He again felt, small and confused in her presence and the only thing he could say was…" yes, of course, by all means; And no, I would never violate your trust."

Tanya was smiling again, and both walked to the door of the hotel, she shook his hand, thanked him again for lunch, walked down the few steps, and boarded a red sports Mustang convertible, with the top down, that the Valet of the hotel had ready waiting for her.

She got behind the wheel and blew Tom a kiss as she drove away.

Tom was left asking himself "Who the hell is this gorgeous woman and why is she involved in this shit?"

# THREE
## August 28, 1968
## "Avenida La Reforma"
## Time: about 4 pm

One car, one small delivery truck, — both stolen-, three men on each vehicle, or rather, two men and one woman in each one.

A long translucent nylon piece of rope, and an old RPG-7 was all they were supposed to be needing.

Of course, they also would have firearms, but only 9mm pistols tucked under their belts and covered by the T-shirts.

It was a beautiful late August afternoon; the rainy season was still on, and there had been light rain earlier that morning, but the sun appeared shortly thereafter, and the weather now was cool and crispy.

The boulevard, *"Avenida La Reforma"* aka *"El paseo de la Reforma"* was peaceful and pretty, as well. It was one of the best cared for and best manicured streets in the City of Guatemala, it extended for over five miles, beginning in front of the *"Cine Reforma"* (the most modern movie theater in the city at the time), the botanical gardens and the military school *"Escuela Politecnica"* and ending at the obelisk, just short of the now partially destroyed arches of the old, Roman stile aqueduct.

*Avenida Reforma* had two traffic lanes on each side, divided by a wide medium which flaunted many big trees, and bronze statues of old generals on horseback who mostly were holding their swords pointing towards the sky in a forever act of defiance.

Among the warriors and other famous people long gone now there were statues of animals, distinguishing among them two enormous bulls which had been donated by Spain to the Capital of Guatemala old bullfighting arena, and which were transferred

29

to the current place from the site of the old bullfighting ring, all were artistically distributed, along the *Paseo La Reforma*.

There were also old trees on the sidewalks flanking both sides of the street.

At the end of the boulevard, raised the Obelisk, a small replica of the Washington monument, including a small pool in the front of it, which supposedly commemorated the independence of Central America from Spain. A flower clock that had been a recent addition to the area further decorated the end of the paseo *"La Reforma"*.

Behind the obelisk, above the aqueduct, the sun was beginning to set and further behind, far in the distance, the four enormous volcanoes, *"Agua"*, *"Fuego"*, *"Acatenango"* and *"Pacaya"* rested in their majesty.

The view from the Ice cream parlor where Tom Hopeland was sitting was nothing but majestic, almost unreal.

*"Agua"* ("Water"), the tallest and largest of the four volcanoes, stood alone, defiant, strong, and magnificent, its slopes looking blue from the distance its color appearing to be melting with the color of the heavens.

*"Agua"* was dead now, no fire, gas, or lava, burned any longer on its insides but being the largest and most important of the four, still commanded respect and awe. In no small degree because, even after having been dead for Centuries still managed to destroy the first Colonial Capital of Guatemala built by the Conquistador Don Pedro de Alvarado.

On September 11, 1541, the volcano managed to do that by filling its crater with rainwater, a portion of which collapsed, right on the side of the city thus dumping thousands of gallons of water, rocks, trees, and mud, over the city burning the place and everyone in it. Including one Doña Beatriz de La Cueva the widow of the Conquistador, Don Pedro de Alvarado, who had been killed July 4th, 1541, in what is now the state of Zacatecas, Mexico, during the battle of El Mixton, while attempting to put down a rebellion of Tlaxcaltecan natives.

This tragic natural event led to the survivors to change the name of the volcano from its original Indian name "*Hunapuh*" to the current *Agua* (Water).

Tom did not paid attention to the van from the electric Company parked about fifty feet away, on the right side of the North bound lane of the boulevard, almost across from the ice cream store, neither he thought much about the old, beaten Chevy, which was parked on the dirt road, few meters behind the van, also in the north bound side.

That was up until he saw the motorcade approaching.

Two policemen in motorcycles, one on each side, rode about 5 yards ahead of a big car, a black limousine, that was followed, also about five yards behind by a black Chevy Blazer, with the windows darkened.

As the motorcade approached, a man, wearing a hard hat, crossed the two northbound lanes of traffic and tied something to a tree, after which he got on his knees and pulled something out of a duffle bag. Too late Tom realized that it was an RPG-7.

An RPG -7 is a handheld rocket launcher, sort of like a bazooka but lighter, easier to maneuver and more effective, it was sort of the precursor of the modern Javelin and the stinger.

And Tom also noticed that the limousine had two small United States flags on the front sides.

Too late Tom realized what was about to happen.

And then all hell broke loose:

The cops on the motorcycles did not see the nylon rope tended across the road but they did feel it when they hit it with their chests and were sent flying off the motorcycles, hitting the pavement hard and probably breaking a bone or two.

The guy with the RPG stood in front of the limousine ready to fire a rocket but, as he evidently expected, the driver of the limousine, a Guatemalan fellow, stopped the car, opened the door, and fell on his knees with the hands behind his neck and pleading for his life.

The two bodyguards, likely Americans, who rode in the next vehicle opened the doors of their car and jumped out with guns blazing, they did not even see the guys coming out from the old

Chevy, who, with sniper rifles shoot one of them in the shoulder of the hand holding his gun, and the other agent was hit on the knee, falling on the ground, also losing his weapon.

Then, another man came out from the van and went to try to open the doors of the limousine, at that point, several shots were fired at him from inside the limo, and only a miracle and the fact that he dropped to the floor, saved him from being killed.

A Man came out of the Limo pointing an Uzi at the person on the floor, and pulling the trigger, but missing the guy who was on the ground and who did have no choice but returning fire putting two bullets in the body of the man holding the Uzi.

The wounded man firing the Uzi was John Gordon Mein, Ambassador of the United States of America in Guatemala

The guy who shot him was up now and shouting. "I am sorry commander, I did not mean to do this, but he left me no choice."

A person who was on the driver seat of the van came out and said "do not. worry Carlos, I saw it all and I know that you had no other choice."

After kneeling to check the pulse of the Ambassador the individual, who appeared to be a woman yelled with a loud voice, as if she wanted everybody near them to hear it.

"He is alive, we are going to take care of him, and so, we will be taking him with us."

As she said that, two men carried the wounded man into the back of the van witch immediately drove off.

Tom Hopeland was running to the scene but stopped cold on his tracks as he recognized the commander of the group.

The Commander of the group was Tanya.

# FOUR

**Hospital General San Juan de Dios**
**August 28, 1968**
**4:30 PM**

I was tired, just finishing my day's duty, as I had been on call at the Emergency Room the night before, and it had been indeed a very busy night, with more than the usual share of acute appendicitis, Gallbladder attacks, stabbings, shootings, panic attacks, car accidents and even two poison snake bites.

I was supposed to go home at 4 pm, but, as usual, I hung out for a bit longer at the ER to chat with the pretty nurse I been trying to convince to go out with me...

Suddenly...She was there.

The one and only, Lily Marie Kruger- Beltran.

The one I had prayed to God to never see again.

She was standing at my side, looking terribly upset and shocked, but still very pretty, she was wearing jeans, what looked like combat boots, a baseball cap with her ponytail sticking at the back and a multicolored T-shirt that appeared to be blood stained.

She grabbed me by the arm and simply said with a trembling voice: "You are a doctor, I have seen you taken care of Carlos, I need a doctor right away, grab your things and whatever you need to treat a seriously wounded person and come with me."

It was more like an order than a request, I noticed that she had a pistol tucked to the back of her belt; but at that time, she would not have to beg or threaten me, I would have followed that gorgeous and obviously scared woman, to the end of the earth.

After seeing the blood on her, I asked if she had been hurt.

She answered negatively, just pressuring me to hurry.

So, I did what she requested; grabbed three IV bags one with Normal Saline, another with Ringer's Lactate and a third one with saline and glucose, all with the corresponding IV tubbing; in addition, I collected a suture kit, a tracheotomy kit, needles, syringes, Lidocaine local anesthesia, some, gloves, and surgical masks.

Of course, we did not have the luxury at the General Hospital to use disposable syringes, needles, or gloves, they were all used and re-used, after sterilizing and yet, our rate of infection was only slightly higher than it was in the private hospitals…

I always thought that the Guatemalan poor were very resilient, very tough, very resistant to infection and very hard to kill.

Tanya was driving an old Chevy that somehow, she had managed to drive into the patio of the hospital, facing the emergency room; Carlos was at the wheel and had the motor running.

As soon as we drove out of the gate or the hospital and were about a block away, she produced a black hood, handled it to me and ordered to and covered my head with it, uttering the first words since she had said "come with me" few minutes earlier.

"You are going to wear this for your own protection doctor"-she said,

"Do not attempt to remove it."

I was scared and asked, "Where are we going?". Immediately realizing the stupidity of my question, as if they wanted me to know that they would not have hooded me.

At least the question was stupid enough for her to have a short laugh.

"Doctor, I am beginning to question the wisdom of choosing you to come with us."

Despite my fear, I muster to answer, "you did not choose me, I was the only doctor there that you knew, and I will be very happy if you change your mind and take me back to the hospital or drop me at any corner."

"Sorry Doc, we really need a doctor badly, hopefully and sadly for you; you will have to do."

"That was not very flattering, Ms. Kruger," I said.

"Flattering is not one of my qualities, Doctor. We have an emergency, this is not time for niceness, I may apologize later, and please do not call me that, I do not know who that is.

"Then how I can call you…Miss?"

"You can call me Tanya that is what my men call me, but enough of conversation, I am not in the mood for silly chatting, let's play silence for a while ok?"

"OK," I said and kept quiet.

The trip was noticeably short, less than five minutes, in my estimate, and then I heard a metal door, a large and heavy gate, open and close, after the Chevy went in.

They opened the door of the car, and someone put a hand over my head to protect me from hitting the roof, then I was taken by the hand by probably the same person, and guided for about ten yards, into a place I assumed was a house.

Once inside, someone removed the hood from my head, and after a few seconds my eyes got used to the light and I saw the patient, lying on a dining room table which had been converted into a stretcher.

There was another woman and four men, one of whom I recognized as Carlos, my old patient, the other three, learned later were called Camilo, Ricardo, and Efrain; neither of which were, very likely their real names.

The patient I was forced by Tanya and her men to treat was resting on his back, barely breathing and already had an IV running in to his arm. He was a man in his mid-sixties, lean and fit, with a head full of hair graying at his sides, he was wearing a white shirt, which was totally soaked in blood, his tie and his jacket had been removed and had been placed on the back of a nearby chair. He had a blood pressure cuff in the arm opposite to the one with the IV, but I could not get a reading on it; in fact, I could barely get a carotid pulse.

I immediately realized that the man was dying.

After removing the dressings that someone had put over his wound, I checked his abdomen, it was becoming distended and there were no bowels sounds. As I listened to his chest, I detected no breath sounds on the right, whereas on the left I could hear faint ones.

I realized that his right lung had collapsed, and his right chest was filling with blood and air. Also realized that the pressure that those two elements were exerting on the man's lungs and heart had to be relieved immediately and also realized that he had lost an enormous amount of blood.

He was going to die any minute, but I am a doctor, so I had to try to save his life.

"This man is dying Tanya, He need to go to a hospital, and even then, I do not think he will make it."

"No way we can do that Doc, just do what you can" responded Tanya and added, trying to hold a sob, so not to look weak in front of her men.

"It was not supposed to go this way; we just wanted to kidnap him, ransom him to obtain the freedom of our comrades and let him go. But the dammed gringos always want to play John Wayne, and this is what they get."

"Is he a Gringo? Who, what kind of Gringo?" I asked

"He is the Ambassador of the United States," answered a woman from the back. "I am Maria, I used to be a nurse, I did as much as possible for him," she said, with a sob.

"The Ambassador of the United States? Holy shit! Now I am in the deepest shit that I have ever been."

"Yes, we all are in deep shit, doctor," said Maria. "Tell me what to do. I will try to help."

"OK, I need to open a hole in his right chest to let him breath better and we need to give him blood. Do we know his blood type?"

They all look at each other as if I had asked the question in Chinese, so, I knew that nobody know what the Ambassador blood type was.

So, I said, "Look in his wallet, maybe it is there, if he had ever donated blood."

"Even if he never did, in the US most states require the driver's license to have the blood type," suggested Tanya.

Between three of them lifted the Ambassador carefully and retrieved his wallet from the back pocket.

"It is A positive." Tanya said.

"Shit," I said again.

"Even in fucking blood type, the dammed Gringos want to be different from us. Most Guatemalans are O positive, I do not expect any one of us here to have A+, blood, right?"

"Wrong "...Said Tanya bitterly, "I am A positive. I guess because I have a fucking Aryan Nazi blood. Let us hope that that my dammed blood can this time save a life instead of taking one, please tell me what to do, Doctor!"

"Great! So much better to give him his own type of blood, than using O positive, the universal donor. We can try to do a direct, side by side transfusion. Maria, get a table that it is higher than this one and have Tanya lie there, you stick a line on the vein of her arm, and I do same on the vein of the Ambassador."

They did as instructed and within a few minutes Tanya's blood was flowing into the Ambassador's arm.

Thereafter I injected some Lidocaine for local anesthesia at a spot on the right, posterior side of the ambassador's chest. Using a scalpel, I made a small incision all the way into his thoracic cavity and was very pleased to hear an air hiss as it came out. I was not so pleased to see the blood, lots of blood, coming out of the man's chest.

I put a piece of IV tube in the hole and let the air and liquid drain into a bottle with a seal.

These procedures brought some improvement to the condition of my patient, but then, I was terrified to see that the amount of blood coming out of his chest was too much to be compensated for by the blood and the liquids being infused into him.

I knew that the patient was going to expire within the next ten or fifteen minutes, although I comforted myself by thinking that he would have died half hour earlier without our efforts.

A classic case of prolonging death, while trying to prolong life.

Thirty-five minutes later the US Ambassador John Gordon Mein expired.

Tanya cried and, banging her fists against the table, after pulling the IV off her arm she kept repeating, "Shit, shit, shit, dammed gringos; why do they all want to play John Wayne even when they know they should know better. We were not supposed to kill him, we were supposed to just kidnap him. Why did you shoot at us? Damned Gringo, you had yourself killed and for what reason, stupid, stupid guy?"

"I am sorry, comrade commandant. I was the one who shot him, and I assume full responsibility for the failed mission," said Carlos.

"You had no choice, Carlos. He was shooting at you, and I much rather see him lying on that bed, instead of you. But still, this messes up everything that we had planned, and our comrades who are in the hands of the secret police are going to be tortured more and then murdered."

At that time, I dared to open my mouth and say, "What if we keep this a secret? What if we pretend that he is still alive?"

All the six pairs of eyes in the room were looking at me, as if I were crazy but then Tanya said:

"That is brilliant, doctor, brilliant, but you are not Jesus, and he is not Lazarus. How are we somehow proving that he is alive and find a way to preserve the body for at least two-three days."

"Do they teach you in medical school how to embalm a corpse Doctor K, or do you personally know a mortuary that can be trusted to do that for us?"

I was really surprised and delighted to be called Doctor K by her, which meant that she remembered me. But then I remembered that Carlos had been my patient at the hospital several months earlier. So, maybe it was because of that she remembers my name.

"No, sorry, I do not know how to embalm a body, neither am I acquainted with any undertaker. However, I believe that I know of someone who may be willing to help."

"And who would be that person?"

"Don Rafa."

"Don Rafa.? That, Don Rafa, the guy who prepares the cadavers for dissection at the at the Medical School amphitheater?"

"Same guy."

"You are going totally nuts, doctor? Do you think Don Rafa would like to be mixed in this mess?"

"Listen Tanya, this may sound crazy to you, and most likely it is but what do you have to lose? You cannot ask for the release of your friends, or for ransom money, or whichever you were going to ask for in exchange of this guy. He is dead and our government, his government, the army and even the FBI and perhaps the CIA, will hunt all of you, perhaps even me, if we return them a corpse."

"Yes, doc, but no matter what we do, the man is not going to do a Lazarus number and come back to life, how do you propose that we pretend he is alive?"

I was no longer scared; in fact, the adrenaline was flowing into my veins and all kinds of ideas were coming to my mind.

I closed my eyes trying to concentrate, but, at first, only popped in my head a picture of me and Tanya kissing good bye for the last time, as an army firing squad was getting ready to shoot us. Fortunately that picture disappeared of my mind after only few seconds.

Then, I remembered that I was a recently married man and that my wife was expecting a baby and the realization that if the authorities raided the place at that particular moment, I would be dead, my wife would be a widow and my child to be born, an orphan.

Hopefully, I would be killed on the spot rather than in the dungeons of "La Judicial" – the secret police. Therefore, my most urgent priority was to get out of there alive and to never see or hear of any of those people ever again.

I felt sad and guilty but since I had suggested it, I had no choice but to continue explaining my idea. Even though I was not even sure if Tanya or my captors were going to let me leave that blasted place alive either. Unless perhaps if they accepted the crazy idea that was forming on my head. Perhaps, and if that plan worked, they let me live. So, I figured that I was not really helping them, I was merely trying to survive, to live for my wife and kid.

Therefore, I continue explaining it:

"Let us divide the mission, as you may call it, in three separate acts:

"Act one: Tanya you go talk to Don Rafa, I am sure you can make a good story to convince him to help us ... putting few Quetzales in his pocked, I am sure will help. I do not think the guy makes more than 150 Quetzales, per month, if that. So he may take the money; if not, you can always put a gun to his head; that is usually very convincing."

"Act two: We need a coffin to transport the body to the amphitheater where Don Rafa works, and also a death certificate, you could get both of those at any funeral home, or at the morgue at the hospital."

"Act three, and of all the most difficult, making the Ambassador look alive and breathing. For that we need one of three things: an inflatable cushion connected to an oscillating pump; or an inflatable leg pump, the kind it's used in hospitals around the legs of patients, in order to prevent blood clots from developing, those have the same effect that the inflatable blanket. Or, better yet, a respirator, a ventilator, so I can have him intubated and make his chest rise up and down.

"Problem is, none of those are available at the General Hospital where I work. Those pieces of equipment are expensive and perhaps only available at the private hospitals, and I have no idea how to get them from there."

"I know a place where they have ventilators and I know also where they keep them, I used to work at the Hospital Herrera Llerandi and I am very familiar with the place. They only have one security guard, but we may have to show guns to get to the storage place." That was Maria talking.

"No guns, unless strictly necessary. We have enough corpses for one day. I will go with you while Don Rafa works on the Ambassador," said Tanya.

"Fine, I suppose that I am not allowed to go?" I said.

"You are darn right, doc. You are not leaving this place, until all this is done and over. Is it there an Act Four Doc"?

"Indeed, there is an act four, because you need to show the government and the world, that the man is alive and breathing. You need to bring the press or the TV media to be witnesses, better with film than with photos, so they can see the action; the patient chest rising, breathing. From a distance, of course, so the deception could not be easily detected. Do you people know a media person you can trust?"

"I know someone who would fit the bill perfectly," said Tanya and continued. "Let us start working on these four acts comrades. You, doc, stay here till your job is done. We will let you go after, and you will receive a compensation for your services. And of course you have never been here or seen anything and none of us have ever seen you."

"Maria and I will take the Chevy and talk with Don Rafa. Carlos takes the white pickup and goes to buy a cheap coffin and get a blank dead certificate. Take a blanket or a tarpaulin to cover the coffin. The van would have been better for this, but I do not want to take the risk of using the van, as it can be identified as the vehicle we used for the kidnapping of the Gringo earlier this afternoon.

"We meet back here in two hours; the ones staying here keep an eye on the doctor and be very vigilant for any signs of police in the area.

"Be prepared for anything, place wire trap bombs on windows and doors. I do not like surprises. Have the 50 Cal ready to be mounted on the back of the pickup and the RPG clean, loaded, and ready for any contingency."

Tanya left the room and went in to the next one, open a closet and chose an old, faded and thorn at one of the knees, pair of jeans, an old, faded, white T-shirt barely showing the logo of one of her favorite local soccer teams, "the Municipal" and completed the attire with a pair of sneakers and a baseball cap also showing heavy use. she pulled her hair on a ponytail and treaded it to the back of the cap. She looked like a girl from a poor neighborhood, which was exactly the look she desired to

41

present. She told Maria to dress likewise, but perhaps best to wear a dress rather than jeans.

Then both boarded the old Chevy and left, Maria at the driver's seat with Tanya riding shotgun.

# FIVE
## University of San Carlos Medical School Amphitheater

Being well after 6.30 in the afternoon, they did not expect to find Don Rafa at work, so they got his address from the night watchman at the Medical School who told then that he lived in the neighborhood known as "El Gallito", somewhere near the Cemetery but he did not have his exact home address, so he gave them some general idea of the location of the home.

Then he mentioned that he knew how to get there and for five Quetzales offered to ride with them and take them to Don Rafa's home.

How appropriate, the two women thought that Don Rafa lived near the Cemetery, considering the work he performed at the Med school.

Don Rafa's house was about two blocks from the Cemetery, it was a small, humble home, painted white, with the paint peeling at several sites, the door of the dwelling also was begging for a new coat of paint.

There was no bell to ring, so Tanya just knocked on the door; after several attempts someone yelled from inside that he was coming.

A woman, who seemed to have been way past her sixth decade of life, a lady, with long, but well-kept gray hair, dressed in black but wearing a white, surprisingly clean apron, opened the door and greeted the women.

As they suspected the woman was Don Rafa's wife, and she, very politely, apologized for the delay in coming to open the door, explaining that they were just finishing dinner when heard the knocks on the door.

Then Tanya and Maria inquired for Don Rafa, and he, still wearing the white outfit that he wore every day while performing his duties at the amphitheater, came to the door.

Don Rafa was taller and less dark than most Guatemalans, had abundant gray, almost white hair, dark eyes, and bushy, also grey, eyebrows he wore a big mustache of the same color of his hair and eyebrows. He appeared to be on his mid-sixties but still strong and muscular.

Tanya started talking with a muffled voice and teary eyes: "Don Rafa, you probably do not remember me, but I was a medical student few years ago, I was forced to drop out because I had to go to work full time in order to support my mum, who was very sick at the time. She was a single mother, as dad left us years earlier, when I was just a little kid.

"Mom, bless her heart, died and I was raised by my Godparents; my Godmother also died, a while ago, so I was left alone with my Godfather who was great and very loving to me, and who, although he was not healthy, he still worked part time, so between the two of us made enough money to survive.

"Unfortunately, this morning, my Godfather went to cash his paycheck, and, as he was coming out of the bank was robed, shot, and killed.

"He has family in "Xela" (nickname for the City of Quetzaltenango) and a plot in the Cemetery there. It is there where my God mom, his wife of many years is buried, and he always wished to be buried alongside her.

"The problem is that the funeral homes want a lot of money to transport my dear Godfather's body there and we have no money to pay for a funeral home to transport him to Quetzaltenango.

"A friend offered us to lend his pickup truck to take Granpa's body to Xela, but he works every day and will not be able to drive us there until Saturday afternoon, and, as you know Well, Don Rafa, the law requires that a person be buried within 48 hours of their demise, unless the body is embalmed.

"Embalming also costs thousands of Quetzales, money that we do not have. However, our friends and neighbors are right now making a collection and hoping to raise 5 or 6 hundred Quetzales.

"So, we thought that you could help us with the embalming of our Godfather, and we would pay you, hopefully less money instead. Here is what we have so, far being able to collect."

As Tanya was saying this, she was sobbing so hard that Maria and Don Rafa's wife were crying as well.

She put 250 Quetzales on Don Rafa's hand, told him that at least twice as much would be coming to him, as they expected their friends and neighbors to raise at least another two hundred and fifty additional Quetzales.

Tanya waited for Don Rafa's reaction, which, at first was one of refusal, but under the three women pressure, (his wife joined the girls) he agreed to do it.

He would meet them in one hour at the amphitheater of the Medical School, and make sure to bring the deceased in a coffin, along with a death certificate.

They embraced, the couple, kissed them on the cheeks, and left, sure that they had not suspected anything fishy about their story, and hoping that Carlos had gotten the coffin and the dead certificate.

"What now?" asked Maria, while handling a Kleenex tissue to the guy who had guided them to Don Rafa's home, because he was crying as well.

"First we take this good man back to his job at the Medical School and then we go to prepare for the wake of my Godfather."

So, after they dropped the watchman back at the Medical School and gave him the promised five Quetzales, (which he declined to receive and wanted to donate it to the girl's grandma's funeral fund), but he ended up taken it, as the girls insisted.

Thereafter, Tanya told Maria to head back to the hideout and get ready for acts two and three.

Maria finally said to Tanya what she wanted to say from the moment they left "Don Rafa's" home: "Whoa Commandant! That was really some good acting, what you did there. I didn't know you could do that,"

"Thank you, Maria, I did not know I could do that either, it just came out of the blue, unexpectedly, and spontaneously. I did take some acting classes at school, but I was never particularly good at it."

"Nevertheless, that was some serious acting, really deserving an Oscar from Hollywood."

"Maybe I should have stayed at Berkeley. My life was much more secure then. Yet we cannot change the decisions we make, good or bad, we must live with their consequences. And let's pray that his good action will not bring bad things upon Don Rafa and his wife."

"Amen to that", said Maria.

"Now let us get ready for act two. We need the pickup truck, the coffin, the body, the death certificate, and transport all to the amphitheater, all while hoping that no one will see us, or suspect anything unusual. We need a lot of good luck, and so far, this day, lady Luck had not been on our side."

Maria was praying for good luck and for the soul of the Ambassador, but Tanya questioned whether the Lord would be willing to help people who kill people.

After all, it was against the Sixth Commandment.

Even though, none of the two women had actually and directly killed anyone. Up to that point.

At the bank heist it had been Carlos who killed two men, and both in self-defense as they were about to shot him, and Carlos was also the one who shot the ambassador, in self-defense as well.

Never occurred to her that if they had not robed the bank, or try to kidnap the US Ambassador, all three of those deaths would not have happened.

God knew that she tried to minimize the casualties, but this was war, and in war people die, quite often even innocent bystanders.

It was plain, old fashion collateral damage.

Besides, it was also a sort of self-defense. Were not the soldiers, the police and the paramilitaries hunting and killing the

FAR and any suspected sympathizer or collaborator? And, in their hands there were no innocent bystanders, everyone was a target, women, children, elders, entire villages, with no exceptions.

So again, Tanya felt good and justified, honestly believing in what she was doing, she was putting her own life on the line as well.

When they arrived at the hideout, the massive steel doors opened, and they drove into the patio. The patio where the van used to kidnap the ambassador and the white pickup truck were. Maria parked alongside the van, and they went into the house.

Carlos, the other men, one who had introduced himself as Camilo, with the help of Ricardo and Efrain, had already changed the Ambassador to more humble clothes and placed him inside the coffin that Carlos had purchased.

They had the death certificate that doctor K had filled and signed with a false name and signature.

They all hoisted the coffin on the back of the pickup truck, without Doctor K's assistance, as he was not allowed to step out of the house.

This time, Carlos's drove, Maria, and Tanya sitting next to him.

"Maria, do you have the uniforms?". Inquired Tanya

"They are here commandant" Maria responded.

"Drive us then to the medical school, Carlos, please."

When they arrived, there was light in the amphitheater, indicating that "Don Rafa" was already there, so they drove the truck as close to the door, as possible, without driving on the lawn, and Tanya got out of the vehicle.

They did not need to knock on the door as "Don Rafa" came out to greet them and help carry the coffin. At which time he requested the death certificate, carefully reviewing it and then, satisfied, returning it to Tanya.

Tanya introduced Carlos, as the good neighbor who was willing to drive them to Quetzaltenango the next coming Saturday.

Then they explained that, although she hated to leave her deceased and very dear godfather's body alone with a stranger, they had to leave to prepare the house for the "Velorio" (wake); which according to the local customs, would last all night.

Maria also said that the two women had sensitive stomachs and could not watch whatever "Don Rafa" was going to do with the corpse, so, it would be ok if they return in three of four hours to retrieve the coffin?

"Don Rafa" explained that since they only wanted to preserve the body for less than five days, the procedure would take less than two hours, so it would be fine if they returned in two hours… and could they; please give him then a ride back home? He could ride in the back of the truck along with the coffin.

Of course, they agreed and left hoping that "Don Rafa" would not become suspicious while doing the embalming, upon seeing the wounds, and call the authorities.

Hoping for the best, the three of them boarded the pickup truck and, after the women changed into nurses' uniforms, they headed for the private hospital where they expected to find a ventilator or something like it, in order to show to the world that the Ambassador was still breathing.

They drove south along First Avenue, and turned right at the 12st Street, driving straight to the 12th Avenue and then south to the Hospital Herrera Llerandi, a very selective and expensive, private hospital, where Maria had worked in the past, and were they expected to find the piece of equipment they needed.

There were two private hospitals south over the 12th avenue, "The Centro Medico" and its spinoff "Hospital Herrera Llerandi". Both build on land and with money donated by a Harvard educated, rich, and brilliant, but arrogant and narcissist, Surgeon Dr. Rodolfo Herrera Llerandi, who having built the Centro Medico, and run it for years, had disagreements with the board of Directors, therefore he resigned, left, and build his own hospital, less than two blocks down the road.

Carlos was the first one to notice and said "Shit…the place is full of soldiers.

What now commander?"

Not only soldiers but police, US embassy cars and other unmarked vehicles obviously belonging to the secret police.

"Shit, I did not think of this; of course, they brought the wounded from this afternoon here. Drive normally past the hospital Carlos, stop if they ask you, then we get the hell out."

"What about the machine?", said Maria.

"We just passed the Centro Medico and there was only one small patrol and away from the entrance, seems they just watching all the hospitals, just in case. Someone brings a wounded person there. I bet they have ventilators. most modern and well-equipped hospitals have at least one or two respirators."

"But you never worked there; you do not know where they are kept."

"True, but we can pull another Oscar winning act, we pretend that we work at the Herrera and that they are so swamped with wounded and sick patients that they need extra ventilators, so perhaps we can borrow one. Or lease one for fifty Quetzales or so"

"That is so crazy, it may work, if it does not, we can always show the barrels of our guns," said Carlos.

"No guns, this time, please. If Maria's plan does not work, we just walk out of there. Let us go, drive around the block Carlos, and stop at the Centro Medico

Seconds later the pickup pulled into the hospital parking lot and the two women, dressed as nurses, walked into the lobby and, without being questioned, passed through the sliding doors and into the nursing station.

Maria asked for the nurse in charge and explained to her that Doctor Herrera Llerandi had sent them from his hospital to see if they could borrow a ventilator. They were so swamped with wounded people from the shootout earlier today that they had used the three ventilators that were in working order, they had seven, but all the others were being repaired or in use.

Some of the patients were critical and the need was great, Dr. Herrera was willing to rent the one ventilator they needed for

49

one hundred quetzales, as she showed a bill for that amount and handed it to the head nurse.

There was some hesitation, at first, but then, she took the one hundred Quetzales. And asking them to follow, she took Maria and Tanya to a utility room where the ventilators were stored and, after making sure they were in good working order, gave one to them.

They rolled the machine out of the hospital and loaded it into the pickup truck and drove away.

The first part of Act three had been accomplished; Act two still had to be concluded.

They had to go back to the Medical School and retrieve the body of the Ambassador from "Don Rafa", hoping that the security forces were not waiting for them.

Luck, however, continued to be on their side, as there was no one other than Don Rafa, at the Medical School amphitheater, he had even put the corpse back in the coffin and assisted them in loading it into the pickup truck.

They drove "Don Rafa" back home, paid him additional 350 Quetzales and insisted that he rode with the women in the cabin, as Carlos, the coffin and the ventilator went into the back. They are explaining their outfits by informing "Don Rafa" that both worked at the General Hospital and had the eleven to seven shifts, so, they had to hurry to return the body, prepare for the wake and go to work before midnight.

It was almost nine o'clock in the evening now and they still had a lot of work to do, besides, they had to control their spending, as they were running out of money fast.

The bank heist had been more than three months earlier and, although they had gotten away with almost ten thousand Quetzales, they had to split the money with the guys in the high command and those fighting in the countryside, therefore the share for Tanya's group had been only about five thousand Quetzales and they had to buy supplies, weapons, ammunitions, food and other items, not counting the moneys paid for bribes.

Therefore, they really needed the ransom money for the release of the Ambassador, except that they never expected to return a corpse instead of a living person. Once again, that feeling of remorse, mixed with a foreboding overwhelmed Tanya.

"You guys, go to the house, make sure that Doctor K, does his part of the job, make sure he tells you how to work the ventilator and then, give him 500 Quetzales and drop him in front of the General hospital, which is exactly where you going to drop me right now."

"Where be you going commandant?". Inquired Carlos

"I will be going to prepare for the final act. I will be calling the house in one hour or so, to check and see if everything is going as planned, please wish me luck and good luck to you as, well. I think I be back with you before morning."

"But you do not have a car here". Said Maria

"I will take a taxi, do not worry."

Tanya got out of the pickup truck in front of the hospital, walked inside, as any of the Nurses getting there for the night shift, and then exited through another door.

Once in the street, she hailed one of the cabs that are normally stationed across from the hospital and asked the driver to take her to an address in "La Reserva".

"La Reserva was, a very exclusive and elegant neighborhood, and what she had given the cabbie was the address, of the home where she had lived for most of her 25 years of life as Lily Marie Kruger Beltran.

The cab driver could not hide his surprise as he asked: "Do you live there. At the Reserve Lady"?

"I wish," she answered. "No, I will be just pulling an overnight special caring for a sick rich, old lady who lives there. I know it is hard to do night work after working all day at the hospital, but it is not every night, only three times a week, the lady is really nice, gives me very little trouble, sleeps most of the night , plus they pay me very well, and usually send their chauffer to pick me up, only when he is busy, or has the day off, they tell me to take a taxi and reimburse me for the fare. Besides, I need the money, my dad is out of work right now, I have three younger brothers and my mom is very sick."

"I am sorry to hear that lady, it is nice that you take care of your family like that. My only daughter got pregnant when she was 16 and moved in with her boyfriend, she does not visit or even speaks to me or her mother."

"Unfortunately, everyone has a tragedy in their family."

"Yes, unfortunately everyone has to have a heavy cross to carry; although never as heavy as the one HE carried."- the cab driver was referring to Jesus.

"Amen to that," Tanya responded hoping to end the conversation, but the cabbie continued a monolog, preaching the Gospel.

Tanya fell asleep the rest of the way and did not wake up until the cab driver told her that they had reached their destination: a mansion, perhaps the most luxurious among the luxurious mansions in the exclusive neighborhood of "La Reserva."

She got out of the cab, paid the taxi fare, adding a generous tip (something that only the tourist usually did in Guatemala); a tip, that the driver at first refused, until she reminded him that the homeowners would reimburse her for her expenses, then, keyed numbers on the buttons of the alarm on the side and opened the Iron Gate, waving goodbye at the cab driver.

There were no guards at the entrance, therefore she assumed that her father was not home at the time, something that had to be expected considering that he was the Minister of Defense of Guatemala and had to be very busy giving orders to the different agencies of the Government trying their best to find the whereabouts of the US Ambassador and his captors.

She laughed, and enjoyed the thought of imaginings the pressure that the US embassy, and the US government was putting on her father and colleagues to locate Mr. Mein

The house was dark and silent, the maids probably either asleep, or in their rooms watching their Telenovelas, so she went first to the kitchen, fixed herself a cup of black coffee and finding two leftover "Chiles rellenos" in the refrigerator, she put one in between two pieces of "Pan Frances" (French Bread) and ate it with delight, realizing that she had not eaten anything the whole day. So, after finishing one, she prepared another cup of coffee and ate the second chile relleno sandwich, thereafter, she went to her room, took a long, hot shower, put on a short black dress, long boots and made a phone call to the Hotel Camino Real lobby bar and asked to speak with Juan, if he was working that night.

She was Informed that yes, Juan was working until eleven pm, but he was busy and could not come to the phone. So, she had to give her real name to the person who answered who, after apologizing to her, called Juan to the phone.

"Juan, you know who this is, so do not mention my name, just answer ok? Do you have a car?"

"Yes, a Volkswagen beetle, 1964"

"Wonderful. How do you like to drive a red 1968 Mustang convertible for the rest of the night and most of tomorrow, and get 50 Quetzales for gas on top? Ok, good, now at what time do you finish your work tonight and at what time do you work tomorrow? Eleven tonight, and four pm tomorrow, great, we swap cars sometimes in the morning then.

"And one more thing Juan, is the Gringo, I was talking with the other day at lunch still staying at the Hotel? He is! Ok, thank you Juan. Can you tell me what room he is in? 233. Great!

"Would it be, if possible, for you to provide me with a key, or some other way to get into his room? You see, we are kind of dating, but I suspect he is married and want to find out if he is or not.

"Are you sure it will not be any problem for you? Thank you, Juan, you are the greatest."

With this, she hung up, sat at her desk, wrote a short note, then opened a small safe hidden inside her closet and produced a small book, which had written on it the word MY DAIRY.

Lily Marie, put both the letter and the book inside a manila folder and went downs stairs, she found one of the maids awake and, in the kitchen.

The maid was very apologetic for not being around when she arrived and for failing to prepare something to eat for her. She explained that her and the other two maids where already on her pajamas, watching TV.

The maid was very sorry that there were no Telenovelas that night, as all the TV stations were transmitting news about the kidnapping of the US ambassador.

Lily reassured the Maid that it was ok, ordered her to go back to bed. thereafter, she went to the garage and got into her red, Ford Mustang convertible 1968, open the garage door and drove away.

# SIX
## Camino Real Hotel
## Guatemala City
## August 28,1968

It was very dark outside but Lily Marie (aka: Tanya) drove her powerful Mustang car with confidence and at high speed, turning the radio on, she listened to the news.

It was clear that the authorities did not have the remotest clue of the whereabouts of the Ambassador, his present condition or who were those who kidnapped him.

In less than 15 minutes she reached the Camino Real Hotel, parked the Mustang herself, but gave the Valet a tip anyway, she kept the car keys and -climbed the steps to the Hotel lobby.

Tanya's First stop was at the Front Desk of the Hotel, where she handled the manila envelope to the clerk, with instructions to keep it in the safe and give it later tonight to Mister Thomas Hopeland, in room 233,

"When He returns from our date, it may be late, so make sure you tell whoever comes to replace you tonight to do it," she added.

Thereafter she went to the lobby bar to find Juan, to swap car keys with him and to find out where he had parked his VW.

She had already told the Valet that she was going to let Juan borrow her Mustang, explained that it needed some repairs and that Juan knew a good mechanic.

Then Lily Marie took the elevator to the second floor and looked for room 233.

She first knocked on the door, couple of times and waited for an answer, after there was none, she used the master key that Juan had given her and walked into Tom's room.

It was actually a small suite, not the fanciest, neither the cheapest; the room was in complete disarray; in addition to clothes on top of the bed, in the bathroom and on the floor, there was a typewriter with a half-written column in it, photo cameras, a camcorder and lots of half written papers in the wastebasket also many discarded papers, on the floor.

She picked some up, read them noticing that the name Tanya did not appear in any of them, there was some vague reference to "at least one of the kidnapers appeared to be a woman."

Tanya smiled, so, the Gringo was not yet willing to rat on her…perfect!

After reading all the papers on the floor and the one on the typewriter, she sat on the bed, turned the TV on and remembered how hungry she was when got home and ate those two "Panes con Chile rellenos" and felt guilty about her fellow fighters waiting in their hideout, so she called the front desk and ordered 6 ham and cheese sandwiches to go, along with 6 cold Cervezas Gallo, also a bottle of Rum Zacapa Centenario, ice and a family size bottle of Pepsi cola, all to be delivered to room 233, all to be charged to Mr. Hopeland.

The food and drinks arrived before Tom did, so by the time the Gringo showed up, she had had two rums chased with Pepsi, yet, between the coffee that she had drank early and the adrenaline from all the events of the day, she did not even feel drunk or drowsy.

Finally, the door opened, and Tom Hopeland entered the room, finding Tanya sitting comfortably, this time on the sofa, watching television and with a glass of rum in her hand.

To say that he was flabbergasted would be an understatement, he almost dropped the newspapers he was carrying and was barely able to muster the word.

"You?! How dare you show your face?"

Tom still thought that she had one of the prettiest faces he had ever seen, he was really upset at her, so he continued in a very irate tone. "You used me! You played me!"

"Hello Tom. Please calm down," she said with her most charming smile. "I know that it does look to you as if I used you but honestly, I didn't. True we needed someone from the press to be a witness of the action and I really wanted to give you an exclusive. Don't ask me why but it's the truth. Things did not go as planned, I know, and I know you know as well as you that it was not our intentions to hurt Mr. Mein, but as we all know also, shit happens.

And then, changing her tone to a less dramatic almost festive one she continued, "Did you miss me? You shouldn't have, because I told you that you would see me again."

"How did you get in my room?" What do you want"? Where you there, at that place this afternoon?"

"Slow down Tom, have a drink with me. then ask one question at a time.

"First it does not matter how I got in, let's say that I have the means to do things.

"What do I want? I thought it was you who wanted my story.

Lastly, where is that place you referring to that I was supposed to be at?"

"You know darn well where I am talking about, you practically invited me to attend the event....I am talking about the part you played and used me in the kidnapping and possible murder, of the United States Ambassador."

"Oh…that, yes, I seen it in the news, it has been practically in every radio station and every TV channel all day long…getting pretty boring, come on Tom, cool down, have a drink" …She said as she handed him a half full glass of rum.

Tom took the glass from her hands and drank the whole thing in one gulp.

"Ok, there, are you happy now?"

"Whoa that was impressive, professor, not even during my days at Berkley could I swallow half a glass of rum that fast…congratulations.

"But enough of this game, yes, I was there this afternoon, and we kidnapped your ambassador, and unfortunately things did not go as planned, there was an accident, and your ambassador was wounded.

"And I know for sure that you recognized me there, as I know for sure that you have not been talking to the police or being able to even publish my *nom de guerre*, in your news reports. which is something I supposed I should be grateful to you for; therefore, I am here to repay you and to make you famous.

"I am here to take you to see your beloved ambassador. So, take your picture camera and your movie camera and come with me. Unless you prefer to call the police and see poor old me involved in a shootout with the authorities and ruin some of the settings of this beautiful hotel."

"You are a psychopath, Tanya. You do not have any remorse? You do not feel any guilt."

"Would it help anything if I admit that I do? but What is done is done and we all must live with the consequences of our actions. I am sure you did not give marshmallows to the kids in Vietnam, did you? Are you coming or not?"

"What if I say not? Are you going to shoot me?"

"I sure would shoot you, but I am sure you are not stupid enough to decline be a witness of what easily could be the story of your lifetime."

She got up, grabbed the bags with the food and beers, opened the door and, with the corner of her eye saw Tom picking up his gear and standing ready to follow.

"Bring the bottle; there is plenty of rum left in it. And you paying for it, I ordered to be charged to your room. But do not worry I will pay you back later, I should have some ransom money coming to us."

Tom could not believe that this beautiful and intelligent woman could be so heartless, cool, and rough inside, but he was flabbergasted by her.

They walked together in silence, got to the parking lot, and boarded the Volkswagen Beetle she had borrowed from Juan, the bartender, her red Mustang was no longer at the parking lot.

They drove for several blocks, without saying a word, and then Tom asked, "Is he alive? I saw him being shot."

"Barely, but he is. We are giving him the medical care he needs. We were planning to kidnap him, but he came out of his car shooting. We had no choice. At that point it was pure self-defense." said Tanya having lost all the humor that she had faked early.

"Now, please Tom, put this over your head; it would be for your own good if you do not know where we are going." She said handling him a hood.

Tanya intentionally, did not drive directly to their hideout, driving around in different directions as she knew that Tom Hopeland was smart, had traveled by car, and on foot, all over the city and that he had military training, so it was not remote to consider that he could locate the location of their hideout after they released him.

They passed several military and police patrols, some of which were randomly stopping and searching vehicles, but she managed to avoid them.

Before leaving the Hotel, she had called the house to let her friends know that she was driving a Volkswagen Beetle and to open the door as soon as they saw the lights of the car blink two times.

They arrived without any problems, except for a minor difficulty in parking the VW among the other cars in the crowded patio.

Upon entering the house Tanya found that Maria had all the comrades kneeling and praying the Rosary around the body of the ambassador.

Tanya signaled then to stop and get on their feet before removing the hood from Tom's head; she did that after distributing the food among his fellow soldiers.

She left Tom standing near the door of the room, at about 10 feet from the corpse of the ambassador; The doctor was no longer there but he had done a good job. The ambassador was intubated, and the respirator working, making his chest move up and down as the machine was blowing air into his lungs. He had an IV on his left arm and the tube to collect the blood from the chest on the right, at the site on which Doctor K had performed a thoracentesis; the tube was still connected to a bottle on the floor.

"Well, here he is Mr. John Gordon Mein, your ambassador, as you can see, he is very, very sick but still breathing. You are welcomed to take pictures and films from the place you are standing now, but please do not try to get closer or touch the Ambassador."

Tom was surprised to be told that, but he was not able to argue or refuse. Besides, the pictures he was taking at that moment would likely be seen all over the world in just a few hours, and that would make him very famous and possibly rich.

Tom noticed the smell of formaldehyde, and he had seen enough corpses in his life to realize that he was filming a dead person who was being made to breathe by connecting him to a respirator. Yet, he kept his mouth shut, said nothing and continued filming and taking pictures. He figured that, dead or alive, the guy lying on that table was still news. Besides, he was not 100% sure that the man was indeed a corpse... so he played along.

After 10 minutes or so, Tanya told him to stop, handed him a half full glass of the rum that she took from the hotel and gave him a card and a piece of paper.

"So, Professor Tom Hopeland, you have seen the man that the whole country is looking for; he is going to die very soon if he is not treated in a hospital, therefore it is of outmost importance that our demands are met as fast as possible. This card was in the ambassador's wallet, and we believe it has his private number. After you leave here and get to your hotel, you are going to call that number, ask for Mrs. Mein and ask her to tell her husband bosses to take the necessary steps to free the men, whose names are on that list and take them to the Mexican Embassy.

"In addition, you are going to tell her to ask your government or mine, to pay a ransom of one million dollars, to be delivered at the place we will later indicate."

"We have already been in contact with the local authorities with the same request, but you know that our patriotic government guys always like to get the blessing of our friends from the North."

"You are crazy, Tanya. My government will never pay ransom to criminals or terrorists. No offense, but that is a well-known policy of the government of the United States."

"Well, maybe, but you will try anyway. Also, tell them to establish their headquarters at the hotel, preferable in your room and I will call you in about one hour to see about the progression of your intervention.

"Otherwise, I believe your business here is finished. Be a good boy. Put the hood on your head and let's go back to your place."

Tanya did not drive Tom all the way to the Hotel, she felt that her duty was to stay with her comrades and keep watch, so she drove him to the city's Parque Central (Central Park) where taxis were stationed, gave 20 Quetzales to the cabby and told him to take the Gringo to the Hotel Camino Real, as fast as reasonably, and safe.

…It was going to be a very long night.

The one called Camilo was the owner of the house at which they were staying, and he was also the owner of the auto repair shop, which operated at that site. Camilo, in addition to being an excellent mechanic, was also a handyman and a guy of all trades.

The shop had three telephone lines, neither of which was Camilo paying for, or had registered to his name, he had somehow connected the phone lines, directly from the telephone poles in the street and ran wires to his shop, none was therefore traceable, so, an hour later when Tanya called the Camino Real Hotel, and asked to be connected to Mr. Hopeland's room, she used line number one for that call.

Tom picked up at the first ring and it was very easy to tell that he was not alone in that room.

"Did you deliver the message, professor?" she inquired.

"I sure did."

"And?"

"As I told you they won't negotiate."

At this someone grabbed the phone from Tom's hand and with a very rude, authoritarian voice almost yelled on the phone: "That is right, the US government will not deal with bandits,

61

criminals or terrorists, you all be hunted down and brought to justice."

"Very well then, may the death of your ambassador be in your conscience," said Tanya.

Then someone in the back of the room yelled, "Fuck the US government; fuck the CIA; fuck the FBI; fuck all of you bureaucrats. It is my husband's life that is at stake here…. Give me the damn phone. I will talk to them and I will negotiate."

Everyone was surprised, even Tanya on the other end of the line, this woman appeared to have guts and character, she immediately felt sorry for her. What if she just knew that her husband had been dead for several hours now?

Tanya was also surprised when she picked the phone and heard a female voice *"Quien es Usted, con quien hablo?"*

She was even more surprised when the voice one the other end of the line answered in perfect English.

"You can call me Tanya, Lady. Believe me, we are sorry for having caused all this trouble to you." Immediately she regretted saying that realizing how ridiculous that assertion had sounded, but she had been taken by surprise.

"You must be making fun of me miserable bitch; I know that you can't be sorry!

"From now on I will oversee the negotiations and fuck my government and fuck yours. First, I am going to call the *Ministro de Gubernation*, who is the one in charge of all the police forces to have your five friends released from prison and taken to the Mexican Embassy.

"Now, as far as the money is concerned, since these bastards here don't think my husband's life and all his years of loyal service are worth shit, I am going to try to raise some money myself. However, neither we, nor our friends or relatives can raise a million dollars in cash overnight. So you must become reasonable and work with me. Would you take $250,000?"

Tanya was feeling sorrier for the woman every second it passed but, she had to do what was best for the cause, so she said: "May take some convincing but my bosses may take $300,000."

"Will try to raise $300,000, but I offer no warranties."

"Fair enough, $300,000 no later than 2 pm tomorrow afternoon. I will call you again to give you instructions as to where to drop the money…and we will be watching the Mexican Embassy for our comrades to arrive safe and sound."

Both women hung up the phones, both feeling some strange sensation of respect and admiration for each other.

Tanya also felt a lot of regret, guilt, and remorse…however, as the guys from the ranch say, "Once you are on top of the horse, you have no choice but ride it."

# SEVEN
## 11.50 PM

Free lance reporter, photographer, columnist, writer, and ex-University professor Tom Hopeland, was dropped in front of the steps of the grand hotel Camino Real at about 11.15 pm. He was all at once very tired, very confused, and very afraid.

Afraid for he knew about the methods that the police, in this God forsaken Country used to obtain information from would be suspects, and he most certainly would be one, as soon as he called the number that Tanya had given him.

Even if the police and the FBI believed him, he had a bad foreboding about the whole affair.

So, it crossed his mind to just forget the whole thing, book the first flight for the early morning and leave the Country once and for all. Yet, he knew that he could not do that, it was not in his blood, besides there were lives at stake.

All he had to do was to give the police a credible story and hope that he was believed.

As soon as Tom walked into the Hotel Lobby, he heard his name called by the receptionist at the front desk.

"Mr. Hopeland, your young lady friend left a package for you, here earlier."

Tanya left a package for me. ...why, what...? Then he remembered that she had promised, towards the end of their first meeting, that she was going to tell him the whole story about her life and her reason for having become Tanya.

He took the manila folder from the hands of the clerk and as he walked towards his room, opened it, he saw that it contained a handwritten note and a small book labeled as "dairy."

The note simply said:

*Hello Professor: as I promised, here you will find the reasons why I became Tanya, which, of course, is not my real name.*

*My real name is Lily Marie Kruger Beltran. I am the daughter of General Guillermo Kruger, the Minister of Defense, who is nothing but a murderer, a thief, a sadist, a cheater, a wife abuser, and the cause of my mother's death.*

*Read the diary and you will learn more!*

*Tanya*

After reading that note and fully aware that he did not have time to read the diary, he totally changed his mind about leaving and decided to go along with the instructions.

But first he had to hide the note and the dairy, because he knew that the cops and even, possibly the FBI were going to search every inch of room, 233, so he looked around the second floor and saw that there was a small room, with an ice maker and a soda vending machine, at the end of the hall.

Tom knew that there would be a similar one on every floor of the hotel, so he climbed the stairs three flights above his own room and placed the envelope on the very top of the vending machine on the fifth floor.

Tom was betting on his size (over 6 feet) and the size of the average Guatemalan, which was no more than five three of five four so nobody would be able to see the top of the vending machine.

Then he came down to his room, made the call and waited.

The police first and shortly thereafter several FBI agents did not take long before showing up at the hotel.

"So, you know the woman?" asked the FBI agent, the one who appeared to be in charge.

Tom spoke decent Spanish, but he did not tell that to the police. He preferred to be interrogated in his own language by one of the several FBI Agents who had been sent from Washington, as soon as the State Department was informed about the kidnapping.

"No, I did not know the woman, I said that I had meet the woman before, which is not the same as knowing the woman."

"So, you had seen the woman before?"

"I told you Agent—is it Frisky or Frisbee?—that I met her about a week or ten days ago, we had lunch at the bar."

"It is Frisky. And how did you happen to meet her at the bar for lunch, ten days ago, Tom?"

"I told you agent Frisky, she simply approached me and started a conversation. We had couple of drinks. It was lunch time, I was hungry, she was hungry, and so we ordered lunch."

"You said that you do not speak Spanish, how did you talk to her?"

"I did not say that I do not speak Spanish, I said that I do not speak Spanish well; especially not well enough to respond to a police officer interrogation. She spoke English well."

"Okay, so she spoke English. Was she American? You said she was very young and beautiful and that she told you her name was Tanya. Did she give you her phone number, full name, or a way to contact her?"

"No, none of the above Agent Frisbee."

"So, Tom, you want us to believe that you had lunch with what you had described as a gorgeous woman, and you did not ask for how to contact her again?"

"Believe it or not I did not. I tried, of course, but she was very mysterious about herself. She did say that she be in touch."

"Mysterious? And you did not suspect that something was wrong, Tom?"

"I was mesmerized, agent Frisbee. she was so beautiful and charming."

"And you did not arrange for this woman to come visit you at your room tonight?" asked another agent, smiling at the fact that Tom had purposely mispronounced the last name of his colleague.

"No, I did not; it was a total surprise when she showed up in my room tonight."

Tom had emphatically stressed the fact that the girl was in his room when he entered it.

Thank God she had charged the food and drinks to his room account.

"Do you, Mr. Copeland, think that she is a call girl? The staff of the Hotel says that she comes often and engages in conversation with the hotel guests, usually the tourists."

"Perhaps, but she never asked me for money or anything and she appeared to be well-grown, elegant and educated."

"There are whores all over the world who can fit that bill, professor."

Despite himself, Tom felt offended by the remarks of the agent, but he knew better than to argue about it.

"So, tell us again, Tom, what happened after you had couple of drinks, did you fuck her?"

Again, Tom felt offended but said nothing to defend Tanya's reputation.

"No, I did not fuck her, agent Frisbee." Tom mispronounce the name of the Agent, again and purposely."

"You are beginning to irritate me Tom, and that is not good for you. If you mispronounce my name once more, you are going to look in the floor for your teeth."

"Sorry agent, Frisky, perhaps we should go on first name basis, after all you been calling me Tom all night."

"Fuck you, Tom. Let's recall what happened after you and her finished the drinks?"

"Well, I was under the impression that she wanted me to go elsewhere with her and that I was going to get laid when we got there."

"Elsewhere? Weren't you in a room with a comfortable bed, food, and drinks?"

"She said something about having great respect for this Hotel and she would never do it here. Then she asked me to bring my equipment, because she wanted our kinky sex to be immortalized in film forever.

"Those were her exact words."

"Yes, sir, those were her exact words. Naturally I was aroused."

"What happened next, Tom?"

"I grabbed my equipment. She grabbed the food and booze, and we walked out of the Hotel."

"Then what"?

"We were walking in the parking lot, supposedly to get to her car; suddenly someone puts a gun in the back of my head, another guy puts a hood on my head, and they shoved me into a vehicle. The next thing I know, we were at the place where they are holding the ambassador, and they make me take film and pictures."

"So, you did not have a chance to see their faces?"

"No sir, agent Frisky, I did not, as I said they came from behind and put a hood on my head."

"Can you tell how many where they?"

"For sure two, maybe three, because someone was at the wheel."

"You are sure it was not the girl, the one at the wheel?"

"No, I am not sure, but I do not think so; because they smell like sweat, men sweat. I am familiar with that smell, I server in Vietnam. And she smelled sweet, clean, and beautiful. In fact, now I am concerned that she may have been hurt by those men."

"You are either stupid, or in love, which in my book is the same thing, the woman was most certainly involved, she lured you to the parking lot, asked you to bring your gear to film the Ambassador and show that he is, or was, still alive."

"I guess you are right agent Frisky," said Tom, acting more subdued and cooperative.

"Now, let us talk about the place they took you; can you identify the place or anyone who was there?"

"I am afraid not, I was hooded all the time, they removed the hood when I was inside the house and put it back before they took me outside. They all were wearing ski masks."

"Now Tom, when they released you, they drove you to Central Park and put you in a taxi, you did not see the face of the people who did this. Can you remember the car they drove?"

"Like I said, I was hooded all the time, then they parked their car, where I guess was about a block from the park, they removed my hood, but they told me to walk ahead of them and not turn my head. They may have been wearing ski masks, but I do not know that for sure. This is the third or fourth time that I tell you the story, how many more time do I have to tell it to you, agent Frisky?"

"The answer to that should be, as often as I fucking want, but I will be nice to you this time, so this will be all for now, professor. But I suggest you do not leave town just yet. In fact, we are keeping your passport, for the time being anyhow.

We have arranged for you to move to room 255, because we are setting this room as our headquarters."

"Whatever will be, will be. Can I leave now?"

"Yes, you may. Have a good night...or morning rather because it is past two o'clock in the morning "

"Yes, Ok, good morning agents"

"Two more questions before you leave Tom; One, do you think the ambassador is alive? And two, you fought in the war, what do you think about the Vietnam war?"

"Number one, I do not know if Mr. Mein is alive. He appeared to be alive when they took me there, but right now...who knows?

"And question two...the war in Vietnam sucks, but I did what I was required of me to do and almost lost my eye in the process.

"So, although I hate the war, I am not one of those flower carrying fanatics who go around breaking thing and hurting cops in the hope of stopping our government involvement in fucking Vietnam.

"Hope you happy are with those answer, agent Frisbee."

With this he left the room and walked into his new room 255

# EIGHT
## August 28
## 11.55 PM

General Guillermo Kruger Larrave, (aka: General Willy), the Minister of Defense of the Country of Guatemala, and father of Lily Marie (aka: Tanya) was awaken of its slumber, almost at as the time that the hands of the grandfather clock, in front of his desk, marked midnight.

He was awakened by the ring of one of his phones. In fact, by the ringing of the most private of his numbers.

He had just dozed off about half hour before, he was no longer a young man, and a life of excesses did not help much to keep his youth, but he was still slim and fit, yet, that night he was very, very tired, having been on the phones and from one place to another since early that afternoon, when news of the kidnapping of the Ambassador hit his office.

The General was resting on the large couch next to his desk. Still in uniform but with his boots off, the necktie undone, and the top of his shirt unbuttoned.

Of course, he was at home, and everyone else, including, he assumed, his daughter would be sleeping.

General Willy picked up the phone and grudgingly answered it. The call was from his friend and colleague in arms, Colonel Ricardo Oliva, the Ministro de Gubernation, which was the office that controlled the different police forces of the Country, while General Kruger controlled the Army, Navy, and Airforce.

The General expected that Oliva had good news for him, perhaps his men had located the Ambassador and captured or killed his captors, instead he heard Oliva saying:

"Hey Willy, sorry to call you this late, but I just received a call from the wife of the Ambassador, it seems that the kidnapers contacted her and demand the liberation of the five guys that your people captured during the failed robbery of the Bank of London and Canada, last week and the woman demands, in not very nice terms, that the request of the kidnapers of her husband be granted asap."

"Is that so? I thought that the Gringos have a strict policy of not accepting the demands of terrorists. Wonder what has changed. But if that is what they want us to do, do it. If those prisoners are still alive. Where do they want us to send them? "

"Mexico, of course, through the Mexican Embassy, so I am calling you, not only because you are my superior officer, and my friend, but because it was Military Intelligence the one which captured those guys almost in the act. So, I figure I check with you first."

All this jargon sounded false and hollow to General Willy, as he was fully aware that "Olivita"—as he liked to call Colonel Oliva—hated his guts, and that all flattering was nothing but pure bullshit, nevertheless he tried to answer with his friendliest voice.

"Have we gotten any information from those guys we caught at the bank?"

"Not much. Apparently, they belong to the FAR…which we already knew. They operate in small cells of five to seven men, and they have no contact with the other cells, neither cell knows much about the other cells. In fact, these prisoners seem to ignore how many other cells operates in the city, or in the other Departments of Guatemala.

"Oh, and they did not know shit about the kidnapping of the ambassador, in fact, we worked on them a bit harder than usually this afternoon, since we learned about the kidnapping, and they were as ignorant of the event as we were."

"Very well 'Olivita' (the General knew that Colonel Oliva hated to be called in the diminutive of his name, but mean as he was, found pleasure on doing it, ever since their days at the military Academy). Patch them up the best you can, or call a doctor to do it, and let them go. But put a bug or something on them in case they try to communicate with the kidnapers "

Oliva was not going to waste time explaining to the General that it was against international agreements to put wires on persons given asylum at a foreign Embassy, so he simply said, "Yes, General, good night," and hung up the phone.

General Kruger remembered with great satisfaction the success he achieved by capturing those five members of the FAR cell, and particularly that by doing so he had prevented the robbery of a foreign owned bank, and all without firing a single shot.

Of course, the fact that he had his men torturing for days, the young wife of one of the members of the guerrilla cell, a poor woman, who had confided to "a very good old friend" that her husband was a FAR member.

The woman's "very good old friend" was involved with a member or military intelligence, so her friend was arrested, tortured, made to contact her husband and under the threat of killing his wife, the man revealed the plans of the group to rob the bank.

So, when the group arrived to commit the robbery, agents of military intelligence dressed as bank costumers and tellers were waiting for them, with orders to kill, if the would-be robbers resisted.

There was no resistance, and all were captured without a shot being fired.

The man who rated on the group, was promised to be set free, along with his wife, and get money and passports to leave the Country.

Instead, he was kept jailed with his comrades.

His wife was released with a broken nose and several broken fingers.

What Colonel Ricardo Oliva did not tell his "good friend and superior" was that the captors also asked for a ransom of one million dollars that neither the Government of the United States of America or the Government of Guatemala was willing to pay.

Oliva, in turn, did not know that the ambassador's wife was going to raise the money on her own.

# NINE
## August 29
## 5.30 AM

Tanya woke up at 5.30 in the morning, it was still dark outside, and her comrades were still sleeping, except for Carlos who had taken the last watch of the night.

She put coffee grind in the coffee machine, added water and let it brew while she went to take a cold shower and get dressed for the day.

She dressed as Lily Marie Kruger, the daughter of the General, being careful to choose a different outfit that the one she had worn the night before at the Camino Real.

When she got out of her room the other fellows were already awaken and had made huevos rancheros and refried frijoles negros for breakfast, which they ate together, in silence.

It was eerie and spooky knowing that the body of the ambassador was still lying in the living room, almost next to the dining room where they were eating.

Tanya boarded the Volkswagen Beetle at ten to seven AM and left the house.

Then she headed south, in the direction of the plush-plush area of the city.

Less than half an hour later she was in front of the office of Doctor Silvia Fuentes DMV, her ex-good friend and the veterinarian of her, now deceased, beloved chihuahua dog, "Nena."

Tanya hoped to catch Silvia, before she entered her office, and as it happened, her timing was perfect. The veterinarian was parking her car, as she pulled into the parking lot herself.

Upon seeing Tanya, Silvia hesitated to get out of her car, but eventually decided to confront her and got out.

"I told you it was not my idea to put 'Nena' to sleep. Your dad tricked me in to doing it."

"And he also paid you very well, I am sure," Tanya said.

"Yes, he did, I am not going to deny that; but I did it because he told me that the poor dog was having a lot of pain with arthritis on his four legs. Besides, who is going to say no to General Kruger? Certainly not me."

"Yes, I know that my dad can be pretty cunning, convincing, and threatening, but you, as an experienced veterinarian doctor, should have known that the only problem that my poor 'Nena' had was a dislocated patella, and she limped a little but was not in severe pain. In fact, I do not think she was in any pain at all.

"'Nena' hated my dad's guts, and he hated her back. Perhaps she bit him that morning, who knows. But I do know one thing: the death of that Chihuahua contributed to the suicide of my mom....Because she loved her so very dearly."

"Oh my God, do not say that, Lily; you are making me feel like I am a horrible person."

"Well Silvia, that is water under the bridge now, but I am glad you feel remorseful because you cannot refuse the favor that I am about to ask you."

"Anything you want Lily; I still remember that we used to be best friends...until 'Nena.'"

"Well...That seems correct. Now, let me ask you a question Silvia. Do you still provide veterinary services to the Zoo?"

"Yes, I still do, Lily."

"Then you must have one of those dart guns that put animals to sleep. Do you?"

"Yes, I do, but...?"

"I need to borrow one, and some darts...there is a *Mapache* (Raccoon) coming to the house, scaring the maids, and spilling the garbage. I would like to catch it, but not kill him."

"Sure, Lily, I certainly can do that for you, but I believe it is best to trap them, we have traps I can let you borrow."

"I prefer the darts, as I like to pet the little rascal before relocating him. He is so very cute."

"Ok, Lily, that is fine. The woman Veterinarian said, as she was pulling her keys out of her purse to open the door of her office.

"If you prefer to do that; just remember raccoons are small animals, you have to remove the dart from him as soon as he falls down, otherwise he may get an overdose and die on you."

"Oh, and how much would be an overdose for a larger animal, or a 180 pounds human for that matter."

"The anesthetic can be use in humans, although it is not recommended, perhaps two darts would do on a 180-pound human."

"Ok Silvia, I really appreciate this. Perhaps we can go back to being best friends soon". Lily said this, after she got the dart pistol and four cartridges.

"In case I miss". She said, kissed the veterinarian on the check and left her office.

From there Tanya drove to *La parroquia*, a poor neighborhood west of the city center, in Zona 6. The area was called *La parroquia* because it was a neighborhood that grew around one of the many Catholic churches existing in Guatemala.

Lily Marie entered a small and humble restaurant, ordered a coffee, and a *champurrada* (a large Guatemalan cookie_ and waited.

Five minutes later Juan showed up driving the Red Mustang

"Here is your car, Miss Kruger," he said loudly. "The Mustang is all fixed, now. There was really nothing seriously wrong with it; just needed some change of sparkplugs. It should work like a charm now."

"Thank Pedro, and thank you for bringing my car here, I am not familiar with this neighborhood, and I was very likely to get lost looking for your shop."

"No problem, Miss K, it was a pleasure to serve you."

"How much it would be for you trouble"?

"Only twenty-five bucks and that is because I had to replace the spark plugs."

"Thank you, sir, here is fifty, and the keys of your Beetle. Which, again, I appreciate you letting me drive while you were fixing the Mustang.... It drives great, and it is awesome in gas. I filled up the tank for you anyway. Thanks again Pedro (she deliberately did not use Juan's real name)."

"Now I will be going to Daddy's home" she said to herself with a smile, as she walked out of the café. But first... I need to make a phone call."

It was almost 9 am when she arrived at her home. After activating the automatic garage opener, she drove the Mustang into the garage, noticing that her father's car was still there and feared that he was still at home.

After closing the garage door, however, she realized that father had left for work because the two soldiers in charge of guarding him were nowhere to be seen. Dad most likely had left on his official ministry limousine.

Thereafter, after saying good morning to the maids, she went to her room, changed into jeans, T-shirt, boots, and a baseball cap, putting her black hair on a ponytail which pulled it through the back hole of the cap.

Then, she walked to her father's office and tried the door, which, as she suspected, was locked. So, she pulled a couple of wire instruments, worked on the lock, and opened it without any problem.

Tanya looked around at the many family pictures in her father's office, there was one, with her mother, brother, grandmother, and father she felt was particularly touching, making her wipe a tear from her eyes.

She took the picture from the frame, tucked it under her shirt and then picked up the phone.

Tanya dialed the American Embassy and requested to talk with Mrs. Mein.

She really felt bad about this, but the plan had been started and she wanted to see it carried out to the end.

"Mrs. Mein, do you have the money?"

"Yes, however, we were able to gather only $250,000.00, would that be enough?"

Tanya pretended to hesitate and then said. "Yes, I believe my people would be satisfied with that amount. Here is where you must deliver it.

"Have someone, not you, take the money directly to the office of General Guillermo Kruger, Minister of Defense, at his office in the National palace. Your husband shall be returned to you two hours after we get the money. I forewarn you that he is very seriously injured."

Tanya insisted that the money be delivered to her father by a person other than Mrs. Mein, because she knew that the American lady would become very emotional, perhaps aggressive and that would totally ruin her plan. So, she insisted several times that it was very important that the money be delivered by someone not a member of the Mein family.

After that she then hung up the telephone.

Then she made a call to her bank

And one more to Carlos, at the hideout house

Tanya closed his father's office and walked back to the garage, only stopping at the kitchen to said goodbye to the maids and eat another *chile relleno* sandwich, which she washed with another cup of coffee, her third that morning, she felt the caffeine and the adrenaline working in her blood.

The three cups of coffee were also too much for her bladder, so she stopped to take a piss before going to her room to take a nap and wait for Carlos' to call her back.

It took about half an hour before Carlos's call came.

"All done commander," said Carlos.

"General Kruger knows that someone from the American Embassy is going to bring something to him, and that he should take the package to his home, without escort and without opening it."

"Excellent. I wait for his arrival."

Tanya sat on her bed, contemplating the picture of her mother, and while doing so was sobbing and saying to the picture of her mother:

"I am doing this for your Mama, that son of a bitch is not getting away with it, this time. He is not getting away with your murder."

Her tears fell on the 9mm Glock and the dart gun resting on her bed, and she thought that perhaps using the former would be better. But then decided, no, that would ruin part of her plan, so she simply waited for her father to arrive.

Half an hour later she heard the garage door open and her father walking into the house and closing the door of his office.

Tanya waited about five minutes, then took the two guns, several clips of ammunition and put them in a duffle bag, walked toward her father's office.

She did not bother to knock, just opened the door of the office, and walked in.

Her father was sitting on his desk, looking intensely at the metal briefcase resting on top of his desk, in front of him. He raised his gaze and said:

"Not now Lily, I am really busy, besides you know that you are supposed to knock before entering my office."

"I know, Dad, but I am here to take that briefcase."

"What? Do you know what is in it?"

"Yes, two hundred and fifty thousand American dollars, the ransom they paid for the Ambassador of the United States, one Mr. Gordon Mein."

"How do you know? Are you involved in this? Are you nuts? I am calling the police."

"We both are involved in this, Dad, and you should not call any police, because I would shoot you before you do that," she said as she produced the dart gun (which looked like a real gun) and pointed it to her father.

"Why are you doing this Lily?" he asked.

"Why, you ask me why, Dad? Simply because you killed mother."

"That is ridiculous. Your mom was a sick woman who suffered from depression and killed herself. I was not even home when that happened."

"Yes, that may be true, but she killed herself because she could not take any more of your cheating, your womanizing, your verbal and physical abuse, and the knowing that she was married to a masochistic killer and thief.

"A man who forced my brother, her son, in to becoming a military man, when you well knew that he wanted to be a musician or a lawyer, and on top of that you sent him to the camp of the Americas in the USA, so he could learn better ways to kill fellow Guatemalans. Heck, you even gave mom a venereal disease. She got Chlamydia from you."

She was sobbing and in tears as she added, "Do you know what her suicidal note said, Dad? It said:

*"Sorry kids. I am not able to take it anymore."*

"Well, she was sick, and your brother is a sissy. She was mentally ill, same as you are, and you are not taking this briefcase anywhere. In fact, I am going to turn you in to the authorities."

After saying this he started to come from behind his desk with the intention of grabbing the gun from her hand.

Tanya fired the dart gun into her father's neck, the preferred place in case he was wearing a bullet proof vest, and as the dart found its target, she reloaded and fired a second dart into his leg.

The general stumbled and then fell, hitting his head against the desk and making a cut that started to bleed immediately.

After making sure that her father was not dead and that the wound was not severe or serious, she opened the briefcase, look for tracers inside, found one, left it in place, transferred the money into the duffle bag, closed the briefcase, put it back on top of the general's desk, then closed the door of the office, and walked to the garage to get her car.

As she drove out of the house, she detected the black van parked at the corner, she knew that Guatemalan and/or American agents, were inside, monitoring the tracer.... So far, so good. She should have at least couple of hours till someone found her father, or he became lucid enough to call the police.

When she parked in front of the Bank of London and Canada, in downtown, she was back at being Lily Marie Kruger Beltran, the wealthy socialite… "the general's daughter."

Tanya walked into the bank with confidence, first stopping to get a key of her safe box, open it and then put the ransom money, minus fifty thousand dollars, in the box and walked into the front of the bank requesting to see the manager, with whom she had an appointment.

She was ushered inside almost immediately, and after shaking hands with the manager, a middle aged, pudgy man, who was all courtesy and attention, she declined the offer or coffee or tea and instead asked for some water and asked the banker if he had her money.

The bank manager reached under his desk and produced two plastic bags, each containing one hundred thousand Quetzales, politely requesting that she signed several papers and after that and not even bothering to count the money, put the two bags containing it into the duffle bag, shook hands again with the manager and walked away.

Tanya did get her own money out of the bank as a precaution, so their comrades would get their money in case something went wrong.

She left the Mustang at the place where she had parked and hailed a cab to return the dart gun at the vet, and then to take her to the hideout house at the corner of Avenida Elena and 13th street.

Of course, she did not give the driver that address; she told him to drop her at the corner of 15th Street, got into a small store, waited for the cab to disappear, and walked the rest of the way.

The whole time the operation took was about two-and-a-half hours.

Everyone was thrilled to see her, and more so to see the wads of money that she spread on top of the dining room table. They were counting it and smelling it.

Even knowing that that money was not for them to keep, they were excited, and more so after Tanya told them that they were entitled to keep two thousand Quetzales a piece.

That excitement lasted until Maria picked up a wad of US dollars and asked, "What is this boss, there is a little box in between the greenbacks."

"Let me see" Tanya said and then exclaimed "Shit, it is a tracker, the sons of a bitch put a second tracker in the money... Smash it and flush it into the toilet. We should get out of here now!"

In 1968 the US dollar and the Guatemalan Quetzal exchanged at the same value, therefore two hundred thousand Dollars were the same as 250,000 Quetzales.

# BOOK TWO

# TEN
**Avenida Elena.**
**Guatemala City**
**August 29**
**3.30 PM**

The hideout house was a very big, very old, combination of a dwelling and a business. An automobile mechanic shop, with an apartment on top of it to be exact.

Camilo, the owner, a widower, and a survivor of jailing and torture by the minions of the Castillo Armas regime, operated the automobile shop in the patio and part of the lower floor. He resided, alone with his two German shepherds, mostly in the upstairs apartment.

The dogs were now gone, being cared for by a friend, ever since his comrades of the FAR were using the home as their headquarters.

The house was located at the very corner of Avenida Elena and 14$^{th}$ street. A very old heavy metal door closed the entrance to the patio of the house.

Avenida Elena was an old and busy throughfare located behind the General hospital and the Mental asylum, and extending for several miles from the south, near the general cemetery, and ending at the area known as *Lo de Bran* in the north.

It was generally a poor but quiet area.

Until now!

At that moment, Carlos busted in, saying, "It seems that we are too late to leave, comrades. Those fellows, the military fellows, they are already here."

A helicopter was flying overhead, like a big bird of prey circling around the body of a dying animal. This time circling above Camilo's shop and home.

It was a midsized bird, carrying only four men, the pilot, copilot and one gunner on each side, manning 50 Caliber machineguns each.

The voice of the commanding officer came from loudspeakers: "This is the Guatemalan army. You are surrounded and outnumbered. Drop whatever weapons you have and come out with your hands in the air. You have two minutes to do so before we start firing."

Evidently either the guys in the helicopter did not get the two-minute warning, or they were trigger happy because almost simultaneously with the message, a burst of fire from the 50-caliber machine gun hit the south side wall of the house.

From the South also, two Stuart M5 tanks were approaching, followed by at least two military trucks each carrying at least ten men each , and followed by several police patrol cars.

The commandant in Tanya's blood came to life as she started to give orders. "Carlos, get up on the roof, take the RPG and try to bring down that helicopter and, at least one of the tanks. ...I know you can do it.

"Maria, you drive the pickup truck. Take the money with you. Ricardo and Efrain, mount our 50 calibers in the back of the pickup and drive away like crazy, while firing in every direction. Do it as soon as you hear or see Carlos taking the tank that is in front of the door.

"Camilo will stay with Carlos and me, since this is his house. We had discussed this possibility before, and he said he would not leave."

"We will stay with you till death, commander," Maria, Ricardo, and Efrain all three said at once.

"I know that, and I thank you for your loyalty, but that was not a kindly request; ….it was a direct order.

"Go now; drive north, and then to the safe house in Zona six."

"Best ditch the pickup somewhere along the way and get something else to drive. If you need to split, do so, take two thousand Quetzales, each from the bag. Then, take the rest of the money to RIO HONDO, when you consider it safe to leave the city.

"Try your best to keep the weapons; although I can see that the 50 Cal may be a problem.

"May God be with you; and hopefully allow all three of us to see you later there…Go now, go!"

Carlos was already on the roof, hidden under some old, corrugated metal sheets, aiming carefully at the helicopter, and waiting for it to circle closer.

As soon as it did, Carlos fired the first rocket with deadly accuracy, hitting it in the middle of the belly, perhaps inside the back cabin. It exploded and almost broke in half.

One of the gunners was killed instantly, the other, possibly badly wounded, dangled dangerously from the part that used to be his post, held only by some kind of belt or rope that he was tied by his waist to some part of the chopper.

Spinning out of control, the chopper started falling to the ground, causing the soldiers who were on the trucks below to scramble for safety.

The pilot was still trying to get some control of the chopper, so not to crash on top of his fellow soldiers, or in the roofs of the homes, and he did succeed to a certain extent, being able to avoid the trucks, but not the electric lights and wires on the side of the street. So, it tangled on them, and finally fell on the side of the road. Miraculously the pilot and co-pilot were able to limp away, wounded but alive. Their fellow gunners were not that lucky.

The first of the two Stuarts 5 tanks, having lost some time avoiding the fallen helicopter, was now positioning itself in front of the metal gate of the car repair shop. It was ready to fire. But before it could do that, the next rocket that Carlos fired was a direct hit, right on the turret,

The tank jolted and started smoking. Those inside the tank were trying to get out as fast as they could before it exploded, which it did, after only one soldier out of a crew of three, got out alive and unharmed.

The metal gate of the shop, also seemed to explode at the same time as the tank blew, because the white pickup truck slammed it open and bolted out, while spilling machinegun fire in every direction, with the 50-caliber machinegun mounted in the back. It was being fired by Efrain. While Ricardo was firing from the car window with an AK 47.

The soldiers scrambled to safety, as the truck drove safely between them.

At that moment, a third rocket struck the second tank.

The soldiers were confused, and it took some time for their commander officer to recuperate and reorganize.

There was no way they could catch up with the white pickup or tell how many fighters remained inside or what other type of weapons they had.

In just seconds, they had lost a helicopter and two light tanks…the young commanding officer realized that these guys were good and deathly.

Yet, the young officer in command of the attacking force did not want to lose face with his superiors by requesting reinforcements. He was young, bold, and indeed not a coward.

He had just been taken by surprise but still had over twenty capable, well-trained, and—hopefully—courageous men under his command and he was not going to back off.

So, he ordered them to fire with everything they had, including grenades, at the roof and inside the patio, and inside the house, to take cover behind the walls of the house, and charge.

He did more than that, he led the charge.

Carlos was pinned down on the roof and could barely fire the fourth and last rocket, which he did, but missed one of the military trucks.

Camilo and Tanya were firing AK-47s from inside the house, but some of the soldiers were already in the yard, taking cover behind the vehicles parked there as the young lieutenant ordered men to advance, throwing explosive grenades through the windows and the doors.

Anticipating this, Tanya and Camilo retreated to the inside of the house.

The windows and doors exploded, and a fire broke out on the first floor.

Tanya started to retreat to the steps leading to the roof, as the soldiers had stopped concentrating their fire on the roof and targeting the first floor. She ordered Camilo to do likewise, but he refused.

"You go, boss. I'll will try to hold them here for a bit longer, I still have four clips.

"If Carlos is still up there, you two can jump from roof to roof and reach the back street. There are no soldiers there. The two of you can make it.

"Go, boss, go now! God bless you and long live the FAR!"

"Long live the FAR!" Tanya responded, all full of adrenaline but knowing well that those may be her last days in this world.

The house was on fire, and the fire was now spreading, and the smoke was thick, and it was becoming harder to breathe.

Tanya thought that perhaps the smoke and fire would slow down the attackers. So, there may still be some hope for Carlos and her.

She reached the roof and saw that Carlos was still there, and unharmed. He had thrown away the RPG -7 and was now holding one semiautomatic 9mm in each hand. There were no bullets hitting the roof, now.

Tanya told Carlos to follow her, as she jumped onto the roof of the next house's roof.

There was no more gunfire coming out of the house, or from the street, but the whole house was on fire, they both knew what that meant…Camilo was dead!

They both also knew that it would take the soldiers several minutes to search the house and conduct a "mopping operation" and maybe they even would wait for the fire department, before climbing onto the roof, so, perhaps they would have few precious minutes to escape.... or perhaps not.

Anyway, they continued jumping from roof to roof until they reached the back street, and low and behold, as Camilo had said, it was free of soldiers and police.

Therefore, holding on to the metal bars of the balconies of the homes and jumping down to the sidewalk appeared to be an easy task. Unfortunately, as Tanya jumped down, she landed wrong and twisted her left ankle, hearing a popping sound and feeling an immediate and excruciating pain.

Tanya was unable to get up and walk, so Carlos retraced his steps to come to her help. At that time, a police patrol car turned the corner.

The cops saw them, two cops jumped out of the car, guns drawn, and ordered them to throw their arms, get on their knees, and raise their hands.

As they refused, one of the officers fired, hitting Tanya on the side of the abdomen.

Carlos fired back hitting the officer in the shoulder, making drop his gun and scream in pain.

The other police officer dropped his weapon and raised his hands.

Carlos returned for Tanya and saw a blood splash that was staining her shirt, as two more patrol cars and some soldiers were coming from the far end of the street on foot.

Tanya said: "Leave me here, take the patrol car.... Live to fight another day. Leave me, I said...It is an order! Carlos, an order, do you understand me?"

Carlos tried to continue protesting but was finally convinced that both were going to be killed soon, so he boarded the police patrol car, spooned it around, and drove in the opposite direction from the direction from where the patrols and soldiers were coming.

Carlos last heard Tanya screaming: "I am General Kruger's daughter. He planned this operation. We were just following General Kruger's orders."

Tom Hopeland, many other foreign and National reporters, as well as the Television reporters and written Media, had arrived in droves as soon as they heard that a battle to rescue the US Ambassador was taking place in "Avenida Elena".

They all heard her shouting, and some did record that statement from Lily Marie Kruger.

Tanya repeated over and over the same statement, initially shouting it as loud as she could, "I am General's Kruger daughter. He planned this operation. We were following General Kruger's orders."

Until she lost consciousness.

# ELEVEN
## U.S Embassy
## August 29
## 5.30 PM

The number of military casualties had been staggering, especially when tallied against those of the rebels.

The military had lost one helicopter, and two Stuart tanks; five men dead and ten more were wounded, versus one dead rebel and one wounded and captured.

The official report stated that the captured woman terrorist claimed to be the daughter of General Guillermo Kruger, The Minister of Defense.

Kruger was the most powerful man in the country; The man who had more power than the President; the man who absolutely was the real runner of the show in Guatemala.

And, he was, at the same time, the man most hated, not only by the population at large but also by most of the military officers under his command.

And now, Kruger was being accused by not other than his own daughter, of being the mastermind behind the kidnapping —and now murder—of the US Ambassador, whose body was found half burned in the house the military stormed.

There was no question in the happy mind of Colonel Oliva…that his hated rival was finished. Not only was the daughter accusing him, but there was the fact that he was found to have the briefcase which contained the $250,000 ransom money in his hands in his own house….

$ 250,000.00 seemed like peanuts for someone like General Kruger, but perhaps that was just the icing on the cake. After all, according to the Gringos, the ransom caller had reduced the amount of the rescue from an initial one million to one-quarter of it....

That was not something that one does lightly, unless the daughter did it in panic, in order to get the ambassador out of her hands and into a hospital as rapidly as possible.

Or unless Kruger had some particular grudge against the ambassador...which was always a possibility.

With General Kruger, you never knew.

His enemies were not known to live happily ever after, or too long for that matter.

True, Kruger had called the authorities after his daughter allegedly shot him with anesthetic darts, and he fell and hit his head on the desk. But the police found no darts at the scene, and yes, he had a big cut on his scalp, which was closed immediately with stapples by the paramedics, as he declined to be taken to a hospital. Yet he claimed that he sustained that injury as he fell down under the effect of the tranquilizing darts and that the head injury made his mind get foggy thereafter.

In Kruger's favor was also the matter of the second tracker, hidden inside the money, which, in the end, had led to the raid on the bandit's compound.

Too bad that they had found the ambassador dead and badly burned, in his opinion, most likely, as collateral damage from the attack.

Maybe he could pin that down on Kruger as well, after all, although indirectly, he had been the one ordering the attack on the compound.

And there was also the matter of General Kruger okaying the release of the rebels and their transfer to the Mexican Embassy.

Oliva had recorded that conversation.

Oliva happily thought that he had plenty of evidence against his hated rival and ordered his detention.

"Arrest General Kruger on the charges of collaborating with the enemy, treason, kidnapping, and causing the murder and wounding of several members of the Guatemalan Armed forces.

"Take him to Fort Matamoros for initial interrogation and call me when you have him there," Colonel Oliva ordered his subaltern.

Then, he left to deal with the US Federal Agents and the widow of the Ambassador.

Also, he did not know what to do with Lily Marie, the general's daughter. Oliva had known her since she was a child and never imagined her as a guerrilla fighter and a very capable one, as the evidence indicated.

Oliva knew her as a fragile, beautiful, spoiled rich girl and could not contemplate the idea of her going to a military hospital or the infirmary of the jail, so he had ordered that she be cared for at a private hospital, under heavy guard, of course.

On the other hand, Mrs. Gordon Mein totally distrusted the reports of the authorities (both from the USA and Guatemala), and firmly believed that the death and subsequent burning of her husband had been due to the irresponsibility of the Guatemalan Army, who, under orders from General Kruger, and the ok of the US government, conducted an armed attack on the rebels at a time when she had already arranged, and paid, to have her husband released.

"Damn you, savages! You killed my husband!" was the last word that Oliva heard from her.

Mrs. Mein even refused to let the Guatemalan doctors perform an autopsy on her husband's body, deciding instead not to allow any autopsy at all, either in Guatemala or the USA.

Within two hours after the end of the "Battle of the Avenida Elena" (as the folklore of the people later called the skirmish), the body of the late US Ambassador Mr. John Gordon Mein was flying back to Washington on board Air Force One,

The plane had been specially sent by the President of the United States to transport the remains of the loyal servant.

He was to be buried with honors at Arlington National Cemetery two days later.

General Wilhelm Kruger (his birth name before he changed it to the Spanish version of Guillermo) was detained and transported, under heavy guard, to the Fort of Matamoros, to be interrogated, like any other prisoner.

However, Kruger was too darn important, and still popular among some politicians and military officers, to just put a bullet on the back of his head or dump him from a helicopter into an active volcano, as it had been the General's style to deal with his prisoners.

So, there would be a trial…after the interrogations, and deposition, all about which Oliva and his cronies had severe reservations and fears.

The Military was not sure what to do with Tanya. Or even where to put her after she was discharged from the hospital.

If she lived, of course.

Tanya was seriously wounded and unconscious, but the doctors believed she would live if she survived the surgery.

The military wanted her alive, to be a witness against the general, her father.

Initially, the official version was that they had taken Tanya to the military hospital, but then they realized that even though it was a military hospital, it lacked the proper security; it had too many entrances and easy-to-open windows. Too easy to reach if her comrades tried to rescue her.

Besides, Colonel Oliva had already decided that she would not go there. Therefore, she was transferred to Hospital Centro Medico, under heavy guard, both inside, outside, around the premises, and even inside her room.

# TWELVE
## Hotel Camino Real
## Guatemala City
## August 29
## 6.00 PM

Reporter Thomas Hopeland had been, along with many of his colleagues, near "the Battle of Avenida Elena", getting as close to the action as it was safe and permitted by the Guatemalan Army.

He had witnessed the capture of Tanya and heard what she had said about her father before being taken by ambulance to the hospital.

He believed it was time to read the documents she had left for him. So, he went back to the hotel and the fifth floor. He searched for the top of the ice-making machine and retrieved the manila envelope.

Carefully looking around to make sure that nobody had seen him doing so, he walked to his room.

Tom set the manila envelope on top of his bed but fearing that the FBI had put cameras in his room, decided to place the documents inside of a folded newspaper and go outside of the hotel to read them.

After walking a couple of blocks he entered a small caffe, ordered coffee and pastries and, after some hesitation, broke the seal of the folder and opened it.

There were two items in it. A letter and a small book whose cover read "MY DAIRY."

He read the letter first.

It said:

*Dear Professor:*

93

*I told you earlier that I do not trust anyone; however, for some strange reason, I trust you.*

*As you read the DAIRY, you will see that there is not a Dairy, but a chronology of the events of my life, especially those who let me choose the role that you had seen me playing.*

*Of course, my name is not Tanya; it is Lily Marie Kruger Beltran.*

*Yes, I am the daughter of that horrible man, General Guillermo Kruger, the minister of Defense of Guatemala.*

*My mom was a saintly woman named Maria Beltran who killed herself because of the behavior of the General, who was abusing her physically and mentally.*

*The General is a killer, a womanizer, a cheater, and a thief, among other things, so you would have to be careful of what you write about him, or else your life may be in jeopardy.*

*I trust, however, that when you are reading this letter, General Kruger will no longer be a menace to anyone…yet you never know when you deal with such a snake.*

*So, please, although I authorize you to publish any or all parts of my dairy, I also trust that you will keep for yourself the most private and embarrassing details.*

*Also, please, please, please, avoid publishing any part of this narrative that may serve to exonerate my father…*

*THIS IS THE MOST IMPORTANT PART OF THIS DEAL TO ME.*

*Please comply with what could be my last wish.*

*Thank you.*

Tanya.

Tom, read and re-read the letter before opening the first page of the Dairy, and as he did so, he became more curious about the story of the mysterious woman whose pseudonym was Tanya, the daughter of the General.

After that Tom opened the first page of the Dairy and started reading,

Of course, it was handwritten in very neat and clear cursive letters. It read:

*Hello:*

*In the strict sense of the word, this is not a dairy, as most dairies go.*

*It is mostly a chronology of events to assist, however reads it to understand me, and the reason why I have become the person I am now...Tanya, the Guerrilla fighter and cell commander.*

*It may be boring to some, but I would like to begin with a brief history of my family.*

*First, I will start with that of my dad's, General Guillermo Kruger, family, not because I love or respect him but because he is the actual reason, I am who I am.*

*His family comes from Germany, his father, Maximillian, was born in Hamburg, in 1897, or so. He enrolled in a Military academy from where he eventually would have graduated as an Architect, but then WWI started and so he was given a military rank as a Lieutenant of the Kaiser's Army and sent to the front.*

*He fought in WWI and was wounded, I believe his face and eyes were burned with mustard gas, and he was left almost blind of one eye; therefore, he was transferred from the front to a military Hospital, in or about 1916. In the hospital he meets a nurse, fell in love, and eventually married her.*

*They had one child, a boy, also named Maximillian, born in 1917.*

*Maximillian Jr. mother died of Influenza in 1919, and my grandfather moved to Vienna, to continue his Architecture carrier.*

*While in Vienna, Maximillian being an opera lover, meets a Jewish/Spanish opera singer, by the name of Dolores Larrave, who was the leading singer of a theatrical group performing there, at the time, and he falls madly in love with her.*

*They married in 1920, living happily ever after, spending most of the summers in a Villa that my grandfather's family owned in the Spanish Costa Brava, at the shores of the Mediterranean Sea.*

*My Father was born there in 1920. So, I do not know if he is Spanish, German, or Guatemalan, although he brags about his German blood.*

*Coincidentally 1920 was the same year that Hitler wrote Mein Kampf from prison.*

*My grandfather continued working for the German Military, as an Architect and as a Capitan in the Army; as such, he witnessed firsthand the changes that were taking place In Germany, since the ascend of Adolph Hitler to power, and the rise of Nazism, and the anti-Jewish sentiment.*

*Although he was a Nazi and a Hitler sympathizer, and, in spite of the fact that my grandmother, Dolores, -the Spanish opera - singer, had converted to Catholicism, he realized that it was not safe for her, or the family, to remain in Germany.*

*The love for his wife prevailed over his political inclinations, therefore he moved with the family to the villa at the Costa Brava in Spain.*

*While they were there, the Spanish Civil war broke out, and with the Germans help, the Realists won, and General Francisco Franco came to power.*

*Francisco Franco was a Nazi at heart and a tyrant who slaughtered thousands of people who either fought for the Republic or sympathized with them.*

*Grandfather did not fell that Spain was any longer safe for his half Jewish family and decided to cross the Atlantic and come to America.*

*As the reader may remember, Grandma, maiden name was Larrave. two of her grand uncles, were of noble origin, Mariano de Larrave, and Jose Antonio de Larrave, both had been among the signers of the Declaration of Independence of Central America, in 1821, so apparently, she had some relatives in Guatemala, therefore, here they came, in or about 1933.*

*My grandfather never regretted, doing that, not only because he may had saved his family from the Holocaust, but also because he did very well here, in Guatemala, establishing a construction Company, who upon his death my father, the general, sold, to an American company, for several million dollars.*

*Another reason why my grandfather never regrated having left Germany was because he was ashamed and had guilty feelings about the atrocities that Hitler and the Nazis committed across Europe.*

*My paternal grandmother died some years later; I am not sure from what, but I suspect she had cancer.*

*Grandpa used to say that he had a family because he had made the right decision at the right time, and that the worse crime that the Nazis had committed was to place a permanent stain on the good name of Germany and its people.*

*My half-brother, Maximillian, choose to stay in Germany, with his biological mother's family. We never heard from him, granddad tried to find him to no avail, and we think he died in the war.*

*He remained an ardent believer in Hitler and the Nazis.*

*However, I believe that my dad, who at the age of fifteen decided to join the Guatemalan Military, enrolling at the Escuela Politecnica, had somehow embraced the Nazi philosophy.*

*Anyhow, my father did graduate from the military school with honors and first of his class, and shortly thereafter he married my mother.*

*I never knew if he really loved my mother or if he married her for her money and social status. I know for sure that she loved him very much…, at least she did, at first.*

*The Beltran's, my mother's family, came from wealthy, and according to them, blue blooded Spaniard Family*

*My maternal great grandfather came to Cuba from Badajoz, Spain, right after the Conquistadores, he learned there how to make rum, but decided that Cuba had already her share of rum makers.*

*Therefore, Great grandfather Beltran sailed to Central America and eventually settled in Guatemala where, to this very day, the Beltran family owns the largest, rum, and other spirits producing company in whole Central America, and at time it was only rivaled, by the Cuban Bacardi company.*

*Great grandad was single, and good looking, when came here from Cuba.*

*In Guatemala, either he pretended to be, or really was of aristocratic Spanish blood. Therefore he was well received and somewhat hunted by the Guatemalan families with daughters at the age of marriage.*

*So, he eventually married rich: a girl from the best and wealthiest families of the times.... Lily Novella, whose family owned the only cement producing company in the Country.*

*As far as I know, they lived happily ever after and had five children, two of which died as a complication of measles and one drowned.*

*The survivors were a girl and a boy.*

*The girl, named Lily also, died giving birth, along with her baby, and the boy Mario, survived to become my maternal grandfather.*

*As it happens everywhere in the world, money attracts money, so Mario Beltran married Lidia Castillo, a member of the family who owned the one and only beer producers in Guatemala.*

*They only had two children.*

*Juan Jose, a boy who his parents sent to Spain to finish his studies, when he was only 14 0r 15. He was there when the Spanish Civil War broke out, so, being young and idealist, Juanjo joined the foreign legion to fight for the Republic and against the Franco troops.*

*They never heard from him again, so it was assumed that he had been killed by the Franco loyalists.*

*Then it was my dearly missed grandmother, Doña Luisa, who lived into her seventies and died some months before my mother's passing.*

*Grandfather died young. I believe it was from the flu, so, Doña Luisa only had one child..., mom.*

*I am not totally certain of how mum and the general meet but for the bits and pieces that I heard from my mother, apparently, they meet at a ball, or perhaps at a friend's wedding party, and after a courtship of about one year, they become married.*

*I was born on April 9, 1944, and my brother Mario, two years earlier.*

*Apparently, everything was nice and sweet amongst them...or so, my brother and I imagined.*

*There was money, there was luxury, there was glamour, expensive cars, best schools for us. Mother seemed to be happy, although, in retrospect, I remember her coming out of her room with red, blotched eyes, and sometimes with bruises, that she explained to us as having had minor accidents.*

*We never dreamed that our beloved and tender father was the cause of those...till much later.*

*Meanwhile, my brother and I were growing up as most rich and spoiled kids do, however, despite that, we both turned out to be good kids, with dreams for the future. I wanted to be a doctor, my brother wanted to be a lawyer and a musician, he was talented and able to play most musical instruments, well, at least piano, guitar, drums, and cello.*

*I entered medical school at the University of San Carlos and loved every minute of it. Even though I only stayed two years, I volunteered at the General Hospital, before I officially qualified for hospital rotation.*

*My brother was less fortunate, as my dad forced him to enter the military school and to become an officer. Right now, he is receiving special training at The School of the Americas, somewhere in South or North Carolina.*

*Then, our world fell apart, as one day I found mother dead, from a self-inflicted gunshot wound to her chest and a note that simply said, "SORRY KIDS, I CAN NOT TAKE IT ANYMORE".*

*At her autopsy Doctors also found barbiturates and alcohol in her system*

*It came as a shock but not as a total surprise, as mum had been depressed since the death of her mother several months earlier. They had been very close, and Grandma was the support and counselor of my mother.*

99

*After grandmother Luisa passed, Mum was devastated and then came the death of our little Chihuahua dog, Nena, who was very close to us, especially mother, but who hated my father.*

*So, one day the General took her to the veterinarian, who was a friend of the family, and lied to her about the health of the poor dog.*

*He told my friend that Nena was in constant and horrible pain, which of course was not true. She had a dislocated patella and limped some but was not in pain—nevertheless he convinced and paid the veterinarian to kill our beloved little dog."*

*I believe Grandma knew about my father's abusive behavior but advised my mother to stay in the marriage for her children's sake and because, according to her, that was the will of God, and the role of a good wife.*

*She was, of course a staunch Catholic as we all in the family were.*

*Mum's death hit me much harder than I could ever imagined, I dropped out of Medical School and became a 24/7 party girl, drinking, doing drugs, sleeping around, to the point that I became an embarrassment to my father, who decided to send me to school in the United States.*

*I went to Berkley, in California, where I continued the party life, attending classes only a few times, a few days a week.*

*Then, one time that I came Home for Spring break, I went into mum's room, who had been left closed and untouched, sat on her bed, and cried my eyes out.*

*As I opened the drawer of her night table, looking for a Kleenex, I noticed that the back part of the drawer had a double panel, and it was slightly open. Curious that I am, removed the panel and found behind it my mother's diary.*

*It revealed the cruelty of my father towards her, and towards anybody who was below him, his cheating and womanizing with every possible woman, including some of our young maids; apparently, he felt that he never had enough sex.*

*It was bad, even to the point of giving mother r a venereal disease (Chlamydia).*

*Mother put up with him because of the advice of her mother, also because she was also a devout Catholic, but, mostly, because she was terrified of my father.*

*She described the beatings when she refused her body to him, or simply when he was angry at someone else, and she described her efforts to conceal the abuse from my brother and me.*

*But that was not it, Mom was aware of my father's business and the ruthless ways he used to treat his enemies, and anyone he perceived as his enemy, or potential enemy.*

*In fact he used to describe to her vividly the horrible tortures he had submitted his prisoners to that day, and hinted that she would suffer the same fate if she was not nice to him or if she told anyone about his abuses.*

*We had the money that he got from selling my grandfather's company to the Gringos, and my mum's family was multimillionaire, but it was never enough.*

*He became part of the group of Officers that betrayed President Jacobo Arbenz and one of the ones, demanding his resignation, easily forgetting that he was his President, his commanding officer, his friend, and a comrade in arms.*

*After Castillo Armas came to power, he became one of his close collaborators and somehow managed to "purchase", at a very low price, the ranch that used to belong to Arbenz. A ranch which was purchased with President Arbenz's wife money, as she belonged to one of the richest families from El Salvador.*

*Nevertheless, the Ranch was confiscated by the so called "liberationists." Claiming that it was obtained with money stolen from the people.*

*All of which was a blatant bunch of bullshit.*

*Thereafter, he rapidly ascended in the military ranks, becoming eventually a General; a rank that had been eliminated by President Arevalo and reinstituted by President Miguel Ydigoras Fuentes later.*

*Mon said in her diary that we probably have numerous siblings, all over the Country, although she knew for sure, only about three.*

*I was never aware of that until that day, and to this day, I do not know who those siblings are.*

*They were probably the kids of some poor girls from the ranch that father stole.*

*Mom closed her dairy with the Lord's Prayer and the same words that she wrote on her suicidal note:* **I Can't Take It Anymore**

*I was so enraged, and full of hate, after reading Mum's book, that I looked for the gun she kept on her night table, to go shoot my father there and then.*

*I forgot that that it was the same gun that Mom used to kill herself, and the police had probably returned it to him, so, I did not find it.*

*It hit me that Mom, even in her hour of deepest desperation, conserved a drop of vanity, as she had chosen not to shoot herself in her beautiful face, but in the chest, right through her loving heart.*

*Then, I took a shotgun from my father's many guns and walked into his bedroom. He was sound sleep and snoring, however, as much as I hated him, being at the foot of my father's bed, and seeing him sleeping so peacefully, I could not bring myself to shoot him.*

*Therefore, I thought it would be best to destroy my father in some other way, attack his ego, his status, his reputation, his fortune.*

*Perhaps destroy someone he really loved. Me.*

*So, I decided to join the FAR, and become Tanya.*

*It was not easy, because I did not know anyone involved with the movement, but then, I recalled some guys from Medical School that I overheard one time or another talking politics and the FAR among themselves.*

*So, I re-enrolled in Medical School and patiently sought those who could be involved with the FAR, gained their confidence and eventually was introduced to a cell leader.*

*First, I was used only as a spy, carrier, and observer.*

*It was very difficult to gain their trust, as it was for me to forget that I was there just to avenge my mother.*

*However, little by little, I became convinced that their struggle was a patriotic one and that their way, the armed struggle, was the only way to improve the living conditions of the Guatemalan people.*

*I went to Cuba for three months, for training and after my return; I was assigned to drive the getaway car of an almost failed bank heist, during which one of our comrades was wounded and I had the honor of saving his life.*

*Finally, officially I would say, as loud and as often as I am able to, that my father and I planned and executed the kidnapping of Mr. Gordon Mein, the US Ambassador in Guatemala.*

*To this I would swear to the end of my days in front of anyone and in front of any court.*

*And, if there is a part of this narrative that you may think excuses my father from being found guilty, I beg you to omit publishing it, because it is my wish and my right to take him down and drag him into the mud.*

*If I am not dead when you read this, I would be soon, and if I survived and my father is acquitted, he will most likely have me killed, therefore, I beg you again. Do not publish anything that he can use for his defense.*

*Please, please, please.*
*THIS IS MOST IMPORTANT TO ME*
*Thank you.*
*Tanya.*

Tom read and re-read the letter and the diary again, and again, and each time he did it, he became more confused.

He knew that the correct way to proceed was to turn the documents to the authorities, but then, he knew the consequences would be terrible for Tanya, and her hated father will be set free to continue being…well…to continue being what he always was…General Kruger, the psychopath.

But what if all that story was not true?

He could not sleep for the rest of the night and by morning; he had not yet made up his mind.

After showering and having a light breakfast, he decided that the best was to wait. Speak to people, to local reporters, dig deeper into the life and carrier of the general, try to find out if really was the psychopath that his daughter described and, hopefully, talk again with Tanya…if she was still alive.

Then he caught the latest news on TV…the General had been arrested accused of treason, kidnapping, collaboration with the enemy, conspiracy to commit murder and many other charges.

Apparently, he was being held at a military facility.

The news did not describe exactly where that was.

Apparently, Tanya's wish started to convert in reality.

# THIRTEEN
## The new hideout

Maria, Ricardo, and Efrain drove the pickup truck north, over Avenida Elena, making a left turn on 5th street and heading west towards 6th avenue, then taking 6th North towards Morazán Park, and then take La Calle Nueva, to Zona 6.

Efrain had ceased firing the 50-cal machine gun as soon as he realized that the only police patrol car that had dared to follow them was hit by his bullets in the front and smoke was coming from the engine, then, it sputtered and came to a stop.

They ditched the pickup near park Morazán; put the heavy weapons inside the bag containing the ransom money; hotwired a black pickup that was parked nearby, it was a double cabin Ram, so all three fit inside comfortably.

Then, after circling one time around the park, drove over the Calle Nueva towards the exit leading to the route to the Atlantic. But before reaching it, she took a left turn and drove along small and narrow streets, till they got to their destination.

Before that, they had heard, on the car radio, that all of them were dead and that one female was captured. Since the two men and the woman in the truck were alive and Tanya was captured, they knew that one or two of theirs were dead.

Not sure if Camilo or Carlos, or both.

Tanya had been wounded and captured.

Efrain got out and opened the old Iron Gate, allowing the truck to be parked inside, totally out of sight of anyone on the street. Then, all three went inside the house, confused, afraid and tearful, not at all certain of what to do next.

Final consensus was they would wait there, overnight, and, if nothing else happened, and if they received no news about Tanya, Carlos, or Camilo they all would drive out of the city, to Zacapa and Rio Hondo, as Tanya had ordered.

There was a small television set in the house, and they frantically searched for the very few channels available for the latest news.

They did not have to search much, as all of the Guatemalan networks were broadcasting the same news, with video of the downed helicopter, the burned tanks, and the evacuation of the wounded.

They were presenting the point of view of the young officer in charge of the operation who justified himself by claiming that they were taken by surprise, they did not know about the high-power weapons that the rebels had and the rapidity of their attack.

He justified himself in front of the cameras by saying that the main objective of the operation, aka the liberation of the US Ambassador, John Gordon Mein, had been achieved and several of the rebels, probably all, had been killed or captured.

The young officer was saying this although it was evident that the Ambassador was deceased, his body badly burned, and they had seen the body of only one dead rebel.

When asked if it was true that the captured rebel was the daughter of General Guillermo Kruger, as they all had heard her screaming, the young officer said that he had no further comment and stop the interview, instructing his men to seize the reporter's photo and TV, cameras, although by then it was too late, the whole world had seen the broadcast.

Maria, Ricardo, and Efrain, were elated to hear that their beloved comandante, was alive, but at the same time, sad about the death of their comrade and very concerned that their commandant had been taken prisoner.

And then, who was killed? Was it Camilo, Carlos, or both?

The answer came about two hours later when there was a knock on the door and Carlos showed up, sweaty, bloody, and smoke-stained, but otherwise unharmed.

He related their escape from the burning repair shop, by jumping from roof to roof, how Tanya had twisted or broken her ankle when jumping off the roof, Carlos described how she was wounded by a police patrol officer and how he tried to carry her, but she gave him strict orders to get away.

Carlos explained how he did escape by using the same police cruiser, from the cops who shoot Tanya, a police patrol car that he ditched about five street blocks from this house walking the rest of the way.

And yes, he was very sorry to say that Camilo had been killed, but he added that he did die fighting like a hero.

After that Carlos asked for some water and responded to the many more questions they had.

Then, it was his turn to speak.

The number one priority, their main mission from now on, would be to rescue comandante Tanya. But he did not have the authority to order them to help. Besides, they probably would need more manpower and more intelligence, as none of them knew the whereabouts or the condition of their boss.

Therefore, he suggested that the four of them drive, or ride a bus, the following morning to the town of Rio Hondo, deliver the money, tell the story, and request help.

Also, Carlos asked if anyone of them knew that the woman they knew as Tanya was the daughter of the feared and hated General Guillermo Kruger, who they nicknamed among themselves *La Bestia* (The Beast)

Nobody, admitted to having had knowledge of that, except for Maria, who said that she suspected she was the daughter of someone important because, when they shared the same sleeping quarters, she would mumble sometimes something on her sleep, which at the time did not make any sense to her but now…it did.

Couple of hours later, came the news report that the General had been arrested and charged with planning the kidnapping of the US Ambassador.

And, come morning, Maria, Carlos and Efrain took a bus to Rio Hondo, in the state of Zacapa to seek help in rescuing their beloved commander.

# BOOK THREE

## FOURTEEN
**Florida, USA**
**November 2022**

Even now, after more than sixty years, if someone asked me why I studied medicine, why did I become a medical doctor, the most honest answer I can give is …I don't know.

There were no physicians in my family, on either side, I do not recall playing doctor as a kid; I do not think that I "had the call", or the vocation; in fact, because my mother—bless her heart—was so protective, she had not even allow me to ever attend a funeral, or seen a death person, before entering medical school.

Besides, Mum always wanted me to follow in the footsteps of my good-looking, wealthy, and very successful cousin Rene, who was a well-known architect.

I could say that perhaps it was an act of rebellion, or, perhaps because I always suck at mathematics, but most likely, was due to the reputation of the Medical School as being the most radical, rowdy, fun seeking, and party going school of all the schools in the San Carlos university system.

I recall my initiation, the cutting of the hair, the long line of freshmen parading all the way to Central Park, to be thrown into the fountain at the center of it. This humiliation and abuse were supposed to be fun and a reason to be proud. The following year we would do the same to the freshmen.

My first exposure to a dead corpse was after those initiations. It took place at the Medical School amphitheater, where cadavers were dissected after being properly preserved and prepared by "Don Rafa", the boss and expert handler of the place.

Funny, I do not recall being scared, shocked, nauseated, or disgusted…the smell was weird and stuck to you but that was it.

Looking back, I can say without a doubt that the years I spent in medical school and hospital practice were the best, happiest, more exiting years of my life.

Also, some of the most complicated

I was neither the best nor the worse student.

I have no doubt that I could have done better had I applied more, but between my partying, my political activism, and the girls, I had very little time to study.

Besides, I suspect that I always had a touch of HADD (Hyperactivity, Attention Deficit Disorder).

Although in high school I was shy among women, when I started hospital practice, soon learned that the hospitals were like a smorgasbord of women, nurses, nurse's aide, therapists, a whole menu to choose from.

There is also a danger that you could make someone pregnant.

But dating, and potential parenthood, required money, and to get money one had to work, or steal.

I chose the first of the two options.

Therefore, and perhaps thanks to the influence of one of my Mentors, Doctor Gerardo Alvarado-Rubio, on whose hospital ward I had worked as a student and later as an intern, and who happened also to be married to one of my half-sisters, I got a job at *Centro Medico* (Medical Center) a reputed private hospital, on which Dr. Alvarado was an important member of the Board of Directors.

If he put a good word for me, I never knew for sure, the fact is that I got a moonlighting job at the *Centro Medico de Guatemala*, as a resident.

After graduating in 1964 and approving an admission exam I became a surgical resident, at the Hospital General San Juan de Dios, where I did all my pre and post graduate training, and I continued working at *The Centro Medico* because by then I was married with a baby on the way.

Even though my wife continued working and She probably made more than the Q 140 that I was being paid as Surgical Resident at the Hospital General money was very tight.

Yet, things got better after a nationwide hospital strike, on which I took a prominent role, and ended up obtaining from the government, a general increase in Salaries (mine climbing to whooping 250 Quetzales).

Never mind that the Hospital's walkout almost cost me my life and freedom, as my home was searched and the police were looking for me to throw me in jail. I was marked by the death squads for elimination, and my job at the Centro Medico was in jeopardy because all the Head Honchos there were right-wing, extremists who believed the government propaganda against the leaders of the strike.

Those days were dangerous and stressful... full of testosterone and adrenaline, but, at the same time, they were very helpful in learning who your real friends were and who are those who supported you.

Yet, I was able to handle the stress and the danger, but the effort to work at two hospitals, with almost no off time, was too much, therefore I decided to quit Centro Medico, at the end of that month.

It was after the middle or end of September.

Then, as I presented to work my shift at the: Centro Medico, I was surprised to see a Jeep, loaded with soldiers in front of the Hospital and upon inquiring, I was informed that Lily Marie Krueger Beltran, aka Tanya, had been admitted in critical condition, after having been seriously wounded at "The Battle of Avenida Elena."

I remember those days very well. And I got a chill going through my spine.

She was not my patient; I was not even on duty the day she arrived, I learned about it through the vineyard, as I was informed that no one of us was allowed to enter her room.

There was no ICU in our hospital, in those years, but we had special rooms for critically ill patients.

After Tanya returned from a complex surgical procedure, to patch her liver, suture holes in her small bowel, and removal of a piece of it, a procedure which lasted several hours; she was admitted to one of those special rooms, under heavy guard.

Two MPs were standing at her door, a military nurse, who looked more like a cow because she was very heavy and wearing camouflage fatigues, was always with her inside the room.

A Jeep with about six or eight soldiers, all fully armed, was parked in the parking lot outside the Hospital 24/7.

Everyone in the Hospital was curious about her and wanted to see her.

But not me, I was the exception, I was very afraid that she would recognize and identify me, so I stayed as far away as I could, now more determined than ever to quit working at that place, as soon as possible, if not sooner.

Perhaps now I am a coward, but I was not a coward back then, yet I had a wife and a baby close to being born, so I really was not looking forward to making my wife a widow and the baby an orphan.

Ever since that afternoon when I was called to revive Mr. John Gordon Mein, the kidnapped USA Ambassador in Guatemala, (most likely at the house where the battle of Avenida Elena took place), I had been paranoid, thinking that every person who walked by me was a member of the Secret Police, or the Army Intelligence coming to arrest me.

In fact, I had been working more shifts at the Hospitals, to be surrounded by people I knew and trusted, feeling somewhat protected by their presence…as if that would really help in those days.

I had even considered leaving the Country, because I had not touched a cent of the money Tanya gave me for my medical services, but I could not bear leaving my pregnant wife, and son, behind.

I thought that, if I was arrested, I could say that I was kidnapped and forced to attend the Ambassador – which was actually true-, and that my head was covered -also true- and that, once there, I could not refuse to treat a dying patient –partially true-, but deep inside I knew that none of those arguments would have any weight with the government hoodlums.

If I was arrested, I'll be tortured and eventually killed. That is what they did in those days.

That was a fact of life, or rather, a fact of death.

It was not until later that I learned that Tanya had accused her father of having been the brains of the operation to get the Ambassador and that he had been arrested, and charged with kidnapping and murder, as well as high treason.

If a prominent fellow like him was arrested… what a, nobody like me, could expect?

So, I stayed away, lay low, talked the least possible, not make any comments about politics or about the patient, and especially never say that I knew her.

Not even mention her name

And above all, I solemnly promise myself that I would not, now, or ever, get mixed up with Tanya and her group.

That was going to be easier to say than to do.

# FIFTEEN
## Langley, Virginia
## CIA headquarters
## September 6, 1968

There was a knock at the door; a door that had a plaque with the name Richard M. Helms Director. The Chief of The CIA was on the phone, seating behind his large Mahogany desk, and simply moved his index finger to tell the agent to come in.

He did so and stood in front of his boss's desk until he finished his conversation, then asked.

"What is the problem, Smith"?

"No problems, sir, just thought that you may be interested in knowing the results of the autopsy of Mr. John Gordon Mein."

"Autopsy? I thought that Mrs. Mein did not want the body of her husband to have such a thing done."

"You are correct Sir, but apparently the mortician detected a strong formaldehyde odor on the corpse that nobody could explain, so the mortician did call the coroner and, without the Widows' knowledge they did a limited examination of the corpse."

"And what did he find?"

"Well, sir that is the interesting part. The ambassador did not die of smoke inhalation, and although there were serious burns on his body, he did not die from those either...he was long dead when the fire broke out, perhaps a day or more."

"Interesting; and the coroner was able to determine that without doing a complete autopsy, as you said?"

"Yes Sir. Dr. Williams, the Coroner, is very good at what he does and was able to determine all that just by probing the Ambassador wounds, suctioning some material from his airways, and testing small pieces of skin and other organs."

"And why do you consider what he found so interesting?"

"It is all in this report, sir," Smith said putting a folder on the director's desk

"I have no time to read those lengthy reports, Agent Smith, and you know that I get confused with all that Medical jargon, so, if you are kind enough, please give a summation resume of what those reports says."

"Yes Sir. Dr. Williams basically found that what killed the ambassador was a single bullet wound, probably fired from the ground, which perforated the abdomen, probably made several holes in his intestines, traveled across his liver, went into his chest, perforating the lungs; with the bullet finally being stop by the right scapula. That is the shoulder blade Sir."

"I am not that ignorant of anatomical terms Smith; I know what and where the scapula is."

"Sorry, sir, I apologize, the fact is that nobody could possibly survive such a wound. Infection in the abdominal cavity would have developed, sooner or later due to the perforated gut, but what really killed him was the wound in the lungs. The chest cavity would have filled up with blood and air leaking from the lungs and he would die either from asphyxia, hemorrhage, or both."

"So, he died immediately?"

"Not quite, Sir, according to Dr. Williams, a person with a wound like that would probably live one hour, two at the most. However, Mr. Mein was given some sort of medical care, as proven by a stab wound in his chest to which plastic tubing was probably connected to drain the blood and air from there.

"Also, there are needle tracks on his arms indicating that some type of IV solution was administered.

"However, after he died his body was preserved with formaldehyde, surely because the kidnappers wanted to give the impression that he was still alive while negotiating the ransom."

"Didn't the Guatemalans who stormed that house see that? And take pictures?"

"Apparently not, sir, they were in such a hurry to get the ambassador out of the burning house that did not bother to do any of that. And whatever was used to treat him with was lost in the fire."

"Is that it then?"

"Only another small detail, sir; the coroner found blood on his excellency's skin and clothes that, although it was the same blood type as his, belonged to someone else."

"That suggests that someone gave him a direct transfusion, right? The sons of a bitch, really tried to save the poor bastard's life."

"Yes, sir, and that goes along with your original theory that their intention was not to kill Mr. Mein, but only kidnap him for ransom."

"But poor John would not let that happen, came out of his car shooting and was shot in the exchange."

"According to witness, sir, it seems that he hit someone, they saw a guy falling down to the ground."

"That must have been the same person who shoots him, because according to the trajectory of the bullet, that Dr. Williams gave you, that bulled was fired from below."

"They found no other blood in the pavement, sir."

"Maybe he was wearing a bulletproof jacket, or his wound, if any, was superficial "

"Maybe, sir. Perhaps we will never know. The Guatemalan Army killed one guy at the house, and another was wounded, and is apparently unconscious. A few others escaped."

"I hope the Guatemalan government is hunting them down and will kill them all. Oh, Smith, one more thing, not a word about these findings to Mrs. Mein. She should continue believing that her husband was alive as she was collecting the money to pay the ransom."

"Yes sir, I know you are aware that she blames us, the US government and the Guatemalan Army for the death of her husband."

"I am aware of that Smith, and do not give a rotten piece of shit about it. Let the poor woman blame us if that helps her grieve. And make sure that she gets back the $250,000 that she paid from her savings and those of her friends."

"Yes Sir, but I doubt she will take that money from us."

"Smith, use your brains, I know that she would not take the money if she knew it is coming from us, but she can be told that the Guatemalan authorities, being unusually honest, recovered the ransom money and they are returning it to her."

"Ok, sir, anything else?"

"I know the Guatemalans think they have solved the case and arrested a prominent general, a member of the President's cabinet, as the ringleader of the kidnapping, because the woman who negotiated with Mrs. Mein, requested that the ransom money be delivered directly to the General's office, because that woman was very likely his daughter, the same person who was wounded during the fire exchange with the army, and who accused his father of being the Mastermind of the operation. However, to me that is absolute bullshit."

"How so, Sir?"

"First, motive… they claim that the General hated the ambassador's guts because he disagreed with the General's drastic methods he uses to control the FAR. I doubt, very much that was enough motive for a man in his position to risk name and fortune, over a simple disagreement."

"How about the ransom money, Sir?

"250,000 dollars is peanuts money for a guy like General Kruger, he has at least two hundred times that amount, if not more.

"Also, General Kruger is not stupid. Even if he needed the money, he would not have been dumb enough to have it delivered to his own office."

"What about the accusation from the general's very own daughter, sir?"

"What about that? I believe Kruger was set up by his own daughter. I believe that she is FAR, and I believe that she hates her father for whatever reason. Now tell me Smith, what do we know about the girl?"

"Well, her name is Lily Marie Kruger, she is an extremely beautiful, now twenty-five years old woman, who was a straight "A" student during grammar and high school, she enrolled in medical school, after graduating. She was also an 'A' student at the University of San Carlos School of Medicine, in Guatemala, but that only lasted about two years.

After Her mother killed herself by overdose and a bullet to her heart everything went downhill from there for her. She became a party girl, did drugs, alcohol, slept with anyone around her, getting to the point that she overdosed and had to be admitted to a hospital. After her discharge, the general sent her to California, enrolled at Berkley for about two more years, where she continued the partying and drinking. Then, she went back to Guatemala for summer vacation and then, she disappeared."

"Disappeared; what do you mean, Smith?"

"I meant that, sir, she disappeared, left home one day, took a plane to Mexico City and from there…she vanished. For several months her family did not hear anything from her or about her, then, as suddenly as she had disappeared, she reappeared, apparently having become a good girl again.

"She returned to live with her father and brother, enrolled again at the university, had few friends and spent a lot of time at the public library. It's possible that she enrolled at some rehab clinic in Mexico."

"Or it's possible that she went to be trained in Mexico or Cuba to become a guerrilla fighter."

"Yes, sir, that is very possible, especially considering the information we have about the fight that she put up during the rescue of his Excellency Ambassador Mein."

"Has she been identified as the woman who lured and kidnapped that reporter, what is his name, Copeland out of the Hotel in Guatemala?

"Yes, sir, it is Hopeland, Thomas Hopeland, but yes she has, and, in fact it seems that she was quite a regular at that hotel, waiters, waitresses, bar tenders and valet parking personal remember her well."

"Ok, Smith, let me tell you what case scenario I see developing in Guatemala."

There is no question that General Kruger is a son of a bitch and a psychopath. He has made his fortune by kissing the asses of some, including ours, and cheating or murdering others, including his own fellow officers, therefore they hate his guts, and although they are probably arriving to the same conclusion that I have. They will be very happy to arrest him.

The general has been set up by his own daughter, and his enemies are not going to miss this opportunity to screw him. They have him already in custody, and they can't let him go because they fear his retaliation, so, most likely the general will be found dead in his cell or killed during a fake escape attempt. In a few words, they have the general by the balls.

They, however, probably do not know what to do about the girl, if she survives. Most likely they will keep her alive, making public statements about her father's involvement in the mess and keep the charade for a month or two. But then what? Set her free, put her in prison, or kill her?"

"Sir, we can bribe easily the Guatemalan military to do whatever you want them to do with her."

"I know that Smith, but I do not trust those sons of a bitch and I do not want to start a direct intervention, as the Dulles brothers did during the McCarty communist paranoia. I am convinced that the FAR and other guerrilla groups all over Latin America are the direct consequence of our intervention in Guatemala in 1954."

"So, what would you suggest we should do? Let the Guatemalan Military solve this problem themselves?"

"I would not take that risk either, but always remember that one prominent and loyal representative of our government in Guatemala was kidnapped and murdered, that crime cannot and will not go unpunished, certainly not on my watch."

"Then what do you suggest we do, sir"?

"Smith, do we have any fields agents now in Guatemala? You know someone who would not hesitate to kill a pretty woman?"

"I believe Tony Benedetti is now either in El Salvador or Honduras, just finished a mission there."

"Good, tell him to move to Guatemala City and wait for a person to contact him with his orders."

# SIXTEEN
## Casino Militar
## 11 calle y 5a. Avenida
## Guatemala City
## September 10, 1968

It was called *El Casino Militar* (The Military Casino) but, it was nothing like a casino: no slot machines, no baccarat tables, no blackjack tables—although from time to time, some Officers got together for a game of poker, in one of the smaller, more private rooms.

*El Casino Militar*, was a fancy officers Club, located in the heart of the Zona 1, the oldest and busiest, area of the City of Guatemala, were most of the expensive stores, movie theaters, the restaurants, and the cafes were located at that time.

The 6$^{th}$ and 5$^{th}$ Avenues were the places to be especially the 6$^{th}$ avenue. It was the place for the young teenagers to hangout, the commercial and entertainment areas of the city.

At least it was so in 1968 when Guatemala City's population was only 854,000 vs. 3,036,000 or 7 million, in 2022, if one includes the surrounding towns which have today become part of the Capital city.

That was before the rich moved to the suburbs and the shopping malls popped all around the city.

And it was before the street vendors moved in and converted the area into a cheap open market, bringing with them dirt and crime and effectively killing the brick-and-mortar stores, which could not compete with their lower prices, contrabanded merchandise, and zero overhead.

So, the area gradually declined, and the stores eventually died, so did the restaurants and movie theaters that closed or moved elsewhere, generally to the malls.

119

The city governments unable, afraid, or unwilling to remove the vendors, let them remain there for several years watching passively as they killed the downtown life.

Several Attempts to remove the street vendors led to confrontations with the police and harsh critics from the press.

That was until a few years ago when a gutsy city mayor sent bulldozers in the middle of the night to tear the pavement and sidewalks of 6th avenue from Central Park to 18th street.

Working all night, the bulldozers removed the pavement and sidewalks, surprising the vendors who did not realize what had happened until the next morning; so, they no longer had a place to set their wares, and although very angry, the vendors had no choice but to move elsewhere.

Of course, that happened many years after 1968, when the story of Tanya takes place, and when Sexta Avenida was still a busy and popular place.

Sixth avenue is now closed to vehicular traffic, a street with trees and flowerpots planted in the middle of it and on sidewalks. Restaurants and commerce are gradually returning, dilapidated business facades have been repaired and painted. Now the place, although less vibrant than once was, has become a promenade for people to walk and shop.

But I digress; therefore, I am taking you back to September 10, 1968, and to the *Casino Militar*.

Four military officers, two generals Ramiro Zelaya and Mario Camacho and two colonels Ricardo Oliva and Benito Benitez, all high ranking members of the government had just finished dinner and moved in to a smaller private room, close to the bar, to smoke cigars, drink cognac and, more than anything, plan their next move regarding what to do with General Kruger, and his daughter, a problem which had become a thorn in the side for all of them.

After taking a long puff of his cigar, which made him cough, Colonel Oliva took a sip of his brandy and said to the others:

"Gentleman, although this situation comes at a wrong time, as we are all busy preparing for the fifteenth of September to commemorate Guatemala's Independence Day, with the customary parades and parties, it is not a secret to anyone of you, that we have a very serious and delicate problem, as well as a unique opportunity.

"It is not a secret either that all of us hate the guts of Willy Kruger, or that we all want to see him gone, if possible, forever. And, as it happens, fate has presented us with the perfect opportunity to do so.

"However, we must be careful, the man is very cunning and sneaky, and also still has some power. He controls the paramilitary and has many sympathizers among the clergy and many of the landowners."

General Zelaya intervened: "Whatever it is you have in mind, Oliva, I hope it does not include setting him free. That will be yours and ours death sentence. The Man, Kruger, is a Nazi and a snake. After all, we arrested him, and we all know that he knows who was involved in doing it, even if we let him go free, he will seek revenge on all of us."

"Indeed," said the third man, Colonel Benito Benitez. "Not only does he hold grudges, but he is also a traitor and a thief. Remember, he was Jacobo Arbenz's best friend, and as soon as the gringos and the *Curas* staged the *Liberacion* hoax, they paid him to become a turncoat while also promising to make him a big man in the next government, so, he turned against Jacobo."

"Not only that," said General Mario Camacho, "he also stole Jacobo's ranch, *El Cajon* under the excuse that he had been bought with money he and his family had stolen from the government. This was a blatant lie, of course."

"I thought he bought it, after the Government of Castillo Armas confiscated it and thereafter auctioned it," Colonel Oliva said.

"Yes, but he bought it for a small fraction of its value, by threatening and scaring other potential buyers," continued Camacho.

"So, we all agreed that there is no way we can set Willy Kruger free. So, what we shall do with him?" asked Zelaya.

"No way can we send him to prison, because he eventually will come out and find a way to seek revenge," said Oliva.

"I say best put a bullet on the back of his head."

"I believe we all want to do that but that may not be the wisest way to dispose of him."

"Then how. What do you all suggest? General Zelaya, I am told you have a plan?"

"Indeed, I do. First, we continue making public the accusations of the daughter against him. Next, we avoid the water boarding and use a silk gloves to treat him.

"At the same time, we present our excuses and keep telling him that we believe that his daughter is lying, that she framed him, and that we think he is innocent. I believe this is the truth, but the truth never has been synonymous with justice or retribution.

"However, he has to understand that, since so much publicity has been made about the daughter's accusations, it is impossible for us to set him free right now.

"We tell him that it is going to be a trial, for which he will be provided with the best lawyers of his own choice and his name will be cleared at that time.

"Meanwhile, we moved him from a cell to a private room and provided him with all the comfort possible, including gourmet meals, wine, and fine scotch. We do that for a week or two, and then we add poison to the wine or the scotch, or both."

"That is bright, Ramiro. No wonder you have become a general and we are below you. But what about the girl? What shall we do with her?" said Benitez?

"Hum, the girl. That is right. What about her. Any ideas?"

"She must go as well, she is with the FAR, as we all know. And although we are not sure why she wants to frame her father, her effort is more than welcome, up to this point. Yet the gringos also know that she is lying and want her punished for her role in the kidnapping. In fact, the guy that is substituting for the deceased Ambassador will be here soon. His name is Richard Morton.

"As usual, the Gringos believe that we are morons and he will be here to tell us what to do about her and her father, so, not a word about our plans to this Morton guy.

122

"As far as I am concerned, the girl is now extremely useful to us and, as long as she continues to voice her accusations against her father, we need her alive. Besides, both the freaking press and the people had made the girl some sort of a superhero. They are even selling T-shirts with a picture of her dressed as the Wonder Woman."

"Agreed, now we have to see what the gringo has to say."

At that moment, the waiter came to announce that Mr. Richard Morton was at the Casino and looking for them.

Mr. Richard Morton was a fat, short, balding blond guy with a greasy, sweaty forehead, rosy cheeks, and itsy bitsy, little eyes which kept behind thick eyeglasses. He was wearing a rumpled grey suit and clearly did not feel comfortable being there or playing that role.

Morton sat without being invited and without shaking hands; asked for double bourbon, even though it was obvious that he already had had few of those.

"So, gentlemen, what is the plan? That is if you have any," Morton said with an air of superiority, as if he was talking to kindergarten kids

"Yes, we have a plan, Mr. Morton, but we would like to know what your government has in mind, what your government suggests," said Oliva, playing the role of a humble inferior.

"Well, we know that the girl, Tanya or Marie, whichever her name is, is lying, she is FAR, and either she or her bosses planned this whole thing.

"We are not sure why she is trying to frame her father. Perhaps he abused her or perhaps she blames him for the suicide of her mother. Who knows, but we are sure that the father is innocent. At least innocent of this caper. And since he has been a good friend and collaborator of our government, we would be delighted to see him exonerated of all the charges, while we want the girl punished for her crime with the full extent of the law. Or even outside of the law."

The military officers remained silent, knowing well what Norton had meant by the words "outside of the law," while

Morton drank his bourbon in one single gulp and getting up simply said:

"That is the message I have from the government of the United States, but you do what you think it is best. Good night gentlemen."

And he walked out.

All four officers said at once after he was gone: "Fuck you, fucking asshole Gringo."

"He does not seem to be aware of the popularity that the Kruger girl has among the people."

"She is popular now even internationally, some Magazines are calling her, besides Wonder Woman, Joan of Arc and other names of heroines."

# SEVENTEEN
## September , 1968
## "La Aurora Airport"

Antonio, Giovanni, Francesco Benedetti was born in Brooklyn, New York, the son of poor Italian immigrants, and the third of five siblings, three of whom were girls.

The parents came to Ellis Island, with the three older sisters. The mother got pregnant during the boat trip, so Antonio (Tony) was born a few months after they arrived in America, and younger brother Gino was born four years later.

The Benedetti family had a challenging and difficult beginning, they lived in the basement of a rundown building, and there was where Tony was born.

The Benedetti family survived, with the father doing small, menial jobs and the mother doing laundry and cleaning houses but nevertheless they managed to send their kids to catholic school, paying for it with their work, dad as a Janitor, mum as a housekeeper and seamstress of the uniforms for the children.

Tony, as his family and friends came to call him, was a very smart but unruly and overly ambitious kid.

He had a unique ability to learn languages, so in addition to English and Italian, he soon learned Spanish only by listening to the Puerto Rican kids of the neighborhood and to their parents.

Tony was an avid reader and spent most of his early adolescent years reading books that he borrowed from the library.

However, Tony was not happy or conformed with being poor, so he decided that if society put something out of his reach, he would have to find a way to take it from society, by force, if necessary.

So, it started with petty theft, candy, or fruit from the local vendors, and then gradually escalated to more profitable things, like burglary and robbery.

By his good, or bad luck, one time, Tony and two of his friends mugged and robbed a guy who happened to be collecting money for the Gambino family.

The Gambinos were obviously not amused.

So, it was only a brief time after that, that the three kids were captured and taken to Carlo Gambino, the boss.

Usually, anyone who dared to interfere with the Gambino's family business, would have ended with a bullet in the back of the head and visiting the fish, at the bottom of the Hudson River. Luckily somehow Carlo took the kids' liking, and they got away with returning the money and being beaten by Carlo's henchmen.

It was not, however, a light beaten, as the three boys ended up in the hospital, two of them with broken bones, one with a ruptured spleen.

But then, after a week, Carlo himself visited them at the hospital, paid their hospital bills and offered them a job with his organization.

One could say that out of fear, but it was mostly for ambition and the idea of becoming part of the largest criminal organization in the country, which motivated them to eagerly accept Gambino's offer.

At first, the jobs assigned to Tony and his friends were mainly to run errands and collect extortion monies from business owners. Still, gradually, as the cash kept increasing and the business expanded, Tony found himself being favored by the boss and the jobs assigned to him became more complex and riskier.

So, it was just a matter of time before he was ordered to make his first hit.

One associate was charging the business owners larger amounts of money that those established by The Gambino and also making the prostitutes under his control, up-charge fees beyond those set by the family.

Tony had been sent twice to warn him to stop doing that, and he just told him to go fuck himself. It was his business, and he could do as he pleased, as long as the Gambino got their piece of the action.

Carlo did not like that and ordered the guy killed.

Tony was the one to do it.

And Tony did it, brazenly and openly just walked into a restaurant where the guy was eating and put two bullets into his head.

Did Tony feel remorse, did he feel bad?

None of the above, he was proud that he had done exactly as he was told.

Except for the eyes.

Tony could not get the eyes of the man he had killed out of his mind. Those eyes who showed panic when he saw the gun pointing at him, those eyes who, without saying, were asking for mercy, those eyes which remained open even after he was death.

Tony did not promise himself that he would not kill again; he just promised himself that he would never look at his targets right in the eyes.

There were two more kills, after that first one, but all were shot in the back.

Usually in the back of the head, with a small caliber gun

It was the last kill, the one who got him in trouble, it happened, in Manhattan, outside Brooklyn, where the Gambino had less influence with the law, and there were too many witnesses, many able and willing, to identify him.

Luckily, Toni's draft card came just in time, and he happily enrolled in the Army, hoping to disappear from there later.

But he liked the Army.

He passed boot camp with some difficulty due to his failure to adjust to military discipline, but that was overlooked when they found him to be an exceptional sharpshooter.

So, Tony went to Vietnam as a sniper and in only eight months in the jungles, he scored seventeen kills, thus earning him the nickname among his platoon buddies of "Long Shot Tony."

127

Of course, he never saw the eyes of any of them, nor was he sure they were VC or just innocent bystanders, but, of course, it was Vietnam, and he was credited with every single one of the killings.

That was until he ran out of luck and got a dose of his own medicine.

Tony and his platoon were searching through a village when, suddenly, out of nowhere gunfire came from the jungle. Two of his buddies were hit, right in the middle of the foreheads, one right after the other, one on each side of Tony.

Tony never knew if there were one or two snipers, but instinct and training made him hit the ground just as a third shot came out of the jungle.

He never knew how it happened and neither he nor the men on his platoon were able to kill the snipers, but as he fell to the ground, a punji stick pierced his leg and went deep enough to hit the bone, barely missing the femoral artery.

That marked the end of Tony Benedetti military career although not the end of his killing career.

He spent several weeks in the hospital, fighting infection and remarkably close to having his leg amputated, but he recovered and was returned to the United States, where he received the Bronze Star and an honorable discharge.

His roommate at the hospital was a fellow GI named Thomas Hopeland, who was recovering from a face wound; they became good friends.

However, it had been only two years since he murdered the man in Manhattan and there was a real risk of being arrested and charged, if he returned to New York.

Carlo Gambino sent him some money but made clear that his presence near him was not comfortable or safe, for the family, so, he told him to go to work in Las Vegas, work at the family casinos, at least for the time being.

Tony was unhappy with that decision; he loved New York and wanted to be close to his blood family and friends, but he had no choice.

Then, just as he was getting ready to go to Vegas, two men in dark suits approached him and offered a job, he gladly accepted.

The men were recruiters for the CIA.

They explained that the agency was impressed with his Vietnam shooting record, and they were willing to overlook "the other problems from New York," if he agreed to work for them.

Tony was not sure if one could refuse an offer from the CIA, especially when they knew about his past, and he knew, as well, that the Gambino family would not object to him taking the job.

Especially since, apparently, both the CIA and the Gambino had agreed not to cut Tony's connection with the family completely, as long as the Gambino continued giving them information about any threat to National Security, while the CIA allowed Tony to do an occasional sniper job for the Italian family.

So, still with a bit of a limp, Tony Benedetti went to Langley for further training and to sharpen his knowledge of languages, as he now spoke some Vietnamese, in addition to English, Italian, French, and Spanish.

Because of his latest ability, most of the CIA-related jobs assigned to him were in Central and South American Countries. He had just completed a job in Honduras when he was called to go to Guatemala.

Tony was a good-looking, well-dressed and all together gentlemanly appearing man. He was five feet eight inches tal, shorter than most Americans but taller than most Guatemalans. Yet, he was not tall enough to attract attention.

His black hair was well combed and flattened with grease, as it was the fashion of his youth in the Brooklyn neighborhood where he grew up.

Tony's eyes were dark green, and his face pleasant and handsome; he sported a thin mustache, a muscular body, and in general, appeared to be younger than his actual age of over forty.

Needless to say, that he had a great deal of appeal to women and that he took advantage of such appeal.

Yet, although Tony had had many women, he considered himself "A serial Monogamer," that is, he had only one love interest at a time. Whether it lasted days, months, or even years, while that relationship was active, he did not cheat on his women.

In fact, Tony Benedetti was a very considerate, loving, tender and generous lover, who showered his women with expensive gifts, jewelry, and trips to exotic places. Never mind that sometimes bringing the women along on trips was part of his cover. But then, it was just matter of time before he got tired of them, the flames extinguished and he flew, like a bee to the next flower.

His way of severing a relationship was most peculiar and, you may even say cowardly because there was one thing he could never do: look them in the eye or see them cry.

So, when he felt that he had enough of one woman, he would leave quietly, in the middle of the night, early in the morning, or any time before she came home or wake up. And his farewell was always the same: three dozen or red roses arriving shortly after his departure, with a card, with the same words, written in whichever language the lady in turn spoke.

So, it was either: "Goodbye, love, forgive me"; *"Arrivederci, amore, perdoname"; "Adios, amor, perdoname"; "Auf wiedersehen lieves, es tut mir leid", "au revoir mon amour, pardonne-moi"*; etcetera.

Tony had not left a card nor three dozen roses in Honduras, he had been there, found his target, and then, before he could stay to enjoy the beauty of the country or get involved with a Honduran beauty, he was called to Guatemala.

His plane landed at the "La Aurora" airport in Guatemala City. He had only a small carryon suitcase, so, after clearing customs, he went outside, hired a cab, and asked the driver to take him to the Hotel Camino Real, where a room had been reserved for him and where he was ordered to wait for further instructions.

The instructions, of course, were to kill Tanya.

# EIGHTEEN
## Fort Matamoros
## Guatemala City
## September 17, 1968

The Fort of Matamoros, *Castillo De Matamoros*, or simply known as Matamoros was located between Zona 1 and Zona 5 of the City of Guatemala. It was the largest of three old forts in the City, the other two being *Castillo San Jose* and *La Guardia de Honor*.

Fort San Jose had been destroyed during the revolution of 1944 and never rebuilt (eventually, the National Theater was built at that site).

The other was *La Guardia de Honor* (The Honor Guard Fort) a smaller garrison located behind the Military School, and in front of the *Campo de Marte*.

*Campo de Marte* (Mars field) was a treeless area, about ten acres long, with an elegant tribune at the end. It was dedicated to hosting military parades; some military exercises, and it was the place where the grand parade of Independence Day ended.

Fort of Matamoros, on the other hand, had been rebuilt and refurbished, not only as a garrison but also as a prison for important political prisoners and rich crooks.

That was where General Kruger was being held.

General Guillermo Kruger- Larrave was not in a particularly good mood.

This although he had been transferred from a cell to an officer's room and, in spite of the fact that Coronel Oliva had assured him that his days as a prisoner were going to end soon and that he be treated according to his rank, more like a guest than a prisoner.

Moreover, he was informed that he be allowed to order his meals "a la carte" either from the kitchen of the Fort or from the restaurant of his choice, and that included wine and any alcoholic beverages.

The general accepted that, not with grace, but as something that he considered himself more than entitled to due to his rank and the rude ways in which he had been previously treated,

He still wanted to be set free and re-instated to his previous job immediately; it did not matter that Oliva had reassured him that this detention was temporary, that nobody believed his daughter's accusations, that, although likely false, nevertheless were serious and severe.

And unfortunately, the people, the press and the President wanted the matter totally clarified before setting him free.

The officers informed the General that perhaps would be a trial; not sure if at the military or a civilian criminal courts, unfortunately everyone had been off their jobs those days, due to the coming celebration of the Independence of Central America, on the fifteen of September, and he should remember that usually that is a three day holiday, including the fourteen and the sixteen of September, and then there was a weekend before those days therefore nothing could be done until after.

General Kruger was aware that Oliva and his fellow officers hated him and that this current situation presented them with a unique opportunity to get rid of him, yet he did not think that they would have the guts to have him killed while in prison.

But you never know, he knew that he would have already done that , under the same circumstances.

Once he would become a free man, he will have to find a way to deal with each and every one of those fucking four traitors. And whoever else had been involved in this plot against him.

Of course, he would have his food and drinks tasted by an enlistee, before consuming any of them. Of course, He did not want to be poisoned.

This was something that Oliva, Zelaya, Camacho, and Benitez had anticipated so, did not object to the General's wishes in this regard.

They just had to be patient, the general would get tired of that game and eventually become confident enough to eat or drink without hesitation, and there was always the possibility of just getting him drunk and then giving him the poison.

Or, if push came to shove, they were willing to use a slow poison, sacrifice the life of whichever enlisted poor soul was to taste the general's food at that time.

General Kruger had been puzzled about the accusations his daughter had brought against him; his mind needed to be clearer about the issue with the briefcase, her attack on him at their house, and then her verbal accusations.

He could not understand her motives or her reasoning, he realized that he had done terrible things during his life, something he justified as having been done for the good of the Country, but he had never done anything but give love and support to both of his children.

General Kruger was even more than surprised not only to learn that his own daughter was none other s than the infamous guerrilla woman nicknamed Tanya. The ghostly woman, that he, and his men have been looking so diligently to capture, for long time. But Kruger mostly was flabbergasted that his daughter had been the one who set him up.

Perhaps the Communists had brainwashed her. Yes, that was the most logical and plausible explanation and the one he would have his lawyers use to defend him in court in case things get to that point.

But, more than anything, he wanted to have a face-to-face talk with Lily Marie.

Oliva had informed him that she had been seriously wounded at "the battle of Avenida Elena" and that she was still in the hospital, unconscious and doctors predicted that it would be some time before she became able to be moved. Oliva also ordered that the local newspapers be delivered daily to the general, so he be up to date on the news.

However, Oliva did not budge on his requests to be taken to the hospital to see his daughter. Kruger was not allowed to visit his daughter, and his daughter was unable to be moved from the hospital, so he had no other choice but to wait.

However, the General could receive visits from his lawyers and from his son, Captain Mario Guillermo Kruger Beltran, who, upon being informed of the tragedies involving his family, took a leave from his training in the "School of the Americas" at Fort Bragg and flew back to Guatemala.

Unfortunately, Captain Kruger did not have an explanation for the behavior of his sister and, like his father could not find a reason for his sister behavior, he loved her very much and was overly concerned about her medical condition.

He regretted reporting to his father that he had not been allowed to visit her either.

The general made a mental list of the requests he would have the next time Oliva, or one of the others showed up to demand that his son be allowed to visit his sister and for him to see his daughter as soon as she was fully conscious and out of danger.

Eventually, and unanimously, the fellow officers promised to grant him these two wishes.

They were also curious to know why the daughter had turned against the father.

Everyone in the military and most in the government, and the police were surprised and certainly annoyed that the press and a most citizens of the country were regarding Tanya as a national hero.

She was compared with Joan of Arc, the Valkyries, Wonder Woman, and other female hero fighters, as Tanya, with only a handful of friends had been able to destroy almost a whole army brigade,

# NINETEEN
## Rio Hondo
## Zacapa, Guatemala
## September 15<sup>th</sup>, 1968

Carlos, Maria, and Efrain had left the safe house in the city and separately traveled by bus to the area of the Country where they had come from: the small town of Rio Hondo, in the state of Zacapa, near the Honduras border.

The guerrilla headquarters and camp were in the mountains surrounding the town, but the town itself was practically their territory, so, most of them moved almost freely in the streets. The army had been expelled from there months before, yet all the fighters and the townspeople were painfully aware that a counteroffensive would be coming sooner than later and it would be brutal and bloody.

Carlos brought the ransom money to the guerrilla chieftain and, after relating the events that had taken place in the City Capital, he requested assistance, and a plan, to rescue their comrade, Tanya, who now lay seriously wounded in a hospital and surely, if survived, she would be submitted to torture and death.

The bosses, as well as Carlos, Maria, and Efrain, were, at that point, ignorant of Tanya's accusations towards her father, but as they learned about them, although they doubted his involvement, were rightfully concerned that the girl had used her position in the FAR, to exact revenge, for whatever sin her father had committed against her.

They were reluctant to provide help to Carlos and the others. Also considering the serious risk involved and the manpower that was likely required to rescue her.

However, the commandant understood and praised the group's loyalty towards Tanya and allowed them to go themselves to obtain enough intelligence about what place she was in, the security surrounding her, etc., but forbade them to attempt to rescue her by themselves.

Only if they could come up with a logical, safe, and feasible plan to conduct the rescue, they would be willing to spare a few men to assist them.

Carlos, Maria, and Efrain returned to the city disappointed moved back to the City Capital, again, traveling separately and it did not take them long to find Tanya's whereabouts, as it had been made public by the press.

They worked day and night, for over a week trying to produce a plan, but other than storming the hospital, in which case they be killed long before they could reach Tanya, no feasible plan occurred to them. All inconspicuously and carefully surveyed the hospital and surrounding areas looking for an opportunity, or a weakness among the people guarding her, before moving in.

Yet, after several days, the best they could do was to locate the hospital Tanya was in, which was not hard to do, as it was in the news almost daily.

Otherwise, they had not even been able to find in what room of the hospital Tanya was kept. That was until Efrain recognized a Physician who worked there.

I was that physician.

So, it was just a matter of time before I was contacted.

I told them that I was not allowed to enter her room, that I had never seen her and much less examined her.

Yet all the information I could provide them with was that she had had a couple of surgeries, was still unconscious, or under heavy sedation and was in room 261.

I memorized her room number, 261, and the number of guards assigned to her door, how many were in the corridors, and how many were outside the hospital.

Also, how often the guard was changed and that, in addition to the guards, there was a military nurse inside her room, all 24/7.

"Other than the doctors and nurses in charge of her care, most of them not even doctors from the regular staff of the hospital, but military physicians, no one else was allowed to visit or enter her room.

Oh, except for her brother who was now allowed to visit but only for half an hour every other day. However, the girl's brother, even when he was not allowed to enter his sister's room, stayed around the hospital grounds most of the time."

"There are rumors that a judge will come to take her Deposition but, her condition is certainly not yet ready for that. She has not even been able to really talk to her brother because she is not yet fully alert. I know it is frustrating but that is all the information that I can give you guys.

"And, please, leave me alone, I do sympathize with your cause, but I do not want to get involved anymore."

# TWENTY
## Centro Medico
## Guatemala City
## September 16, 1968

Tony Benedetti walked into the Hospital without being questioned or stopped, by anyone.

He was wearing a lab coat with Captain Jaime Garcia, MD, embroidered on the lapel.

A stethoscope hung from his neck, and he walked in full of confidence and without hesitancy around the hospital.

He carried no weapons. The tools for conducting his mission were a simple vial of insulin, a needle, and a syringe. The Vial of Insulin contained five thousand units of regular insulin, more than enough to kill an elephant.

He gave a military salute to the guards at the door and walked into room 261, totally unmolested.

The military nurse was snoring while slumped on a chair next to the patient.

And lying on the bed was one of the most beautiful creatures that Tony Benedetti had ever seen. She was also sleeping.

Tony stood there for a couple of seconds contemplating the sleeping beauty, and for another second, he hesitated, but then, he thought, orders are orders, this is going to be painless, and she will just go from one sleep to a permanent sleep.

And for him, it would be another mission accomplished.

He approached the bed, drew the insulin into the syringe, and as he was about to inject it into her IV.

She opened her eyes.

Not only did she open her eyes, but she looked at him and spoke.

"Hello Doctor, would you please give me some water."

That was all she said, but he had looked into her eyes, and after that he was not able to execute his mission.

In fact, he realized that he would never be able to kill this woman. Instead, he was going to do his best to rescue her from their captors and get her out of that place.

But this time he could not do it alone,

He decided it in his head and immediately developed a plan, however, he would need help to carry it out.

Fuck the CIA and fuck the Guatemalan Military

He gently held the head of the woman he came to kill, and gave her couple of sips of water, then after looking again at her eyes, Tony left the room.

He would come back tomorrow, as her doctor and visitor.

He would later call the CIA office and tell them that the target was extremely well guarded, and it would be very difficult, if not impossible, for him to be able to approach her. So, he had to wait for an opportunity,

The Nurse was still snoring.

She woke up when Tanya's brother walked into the room, for his thirty minutes, every other day visit with his sister.

Captain Mario Kruger entered his sister's room Less than five minutes after Tony Benedetti had left her.

He did not see Tony, but Tony saw him.

After kissing his sister's forehead, Captain Kruger asked the nurse about his sister's medical condition, and she said that she was getting better and stronger every day. Tanya opened her eyes and said: "Hello brother, the doctor was just here, he did give me some water. I was so thirsty."

"Shush, do not talk, do not exhaust yourself, sis'.

Mario Kruger did not know what else to say. He had so many questions to ask that he did not know where to start, but those must wait. He was not sure if his sister was up to it and certainly, he did not want the nurse to hear whatever Lily had to say.

But it was her, the nurse, the one who gave him the green flag. Likely because she was afraid that the captain, who was obviously her superior, had seen her sleeping while on duty.

"She can talk sir, not too long yet, but soon because they are fixing to take her deposition any of these days."

Captain Kruger held gently his sister's hand, and kissed it, while a tear rolled from his eyes, and getting close to her face whispered to her ear: "Why, Lily, why?"

She simply whispered back "Talk to Tom Hopeland, a reporter, at the Camino Real Hotel. He knows why."

Then she kissed her brother's hand and went back into her slumber

The thirty minutes allowed were over, but he knew that the nurse was not going to kick him out, so he stayed half an hour longer, while pondering his sister's words.

He knew about this guy Hopeland. He had been at the Avenida Elena house where they had the ambassador, took pictures, and filmed his last minutes of his life.

Hopeland was under police and FBI surveillance. he had been authoring articles about her sister in the most popular a well-read international Magazines, such are Time, Newsweek, National Geographic, and others.

Hopeland had made his sister an international celebrity and a National Hero.

But what did he know about the reasons for her transformation from a spoiled, smart, socialite girl, into a ferocious guerrilla fighter, an outlaw.

He was certainly going to find out.

# TWENTYONE
## City Bus number one
## Guatemala City
## September 17, 1968

I do not have a car now.

I did have one, my first car ever, an old Opel that I bought from the dealership only two months ago and, of course, I am still making payments for it, even though I no longer have the car.

What happened was that I went to have a few drinks with four of my buddies and on the way back, a huge, and I mean huge, light post placed itself right in front of me, and I hit it.

The darn thing did not even have a dent, but my dear old car was seriously damaged, and all four of us ended up in the ER at the hospital. Thank God nobody was seriously hurt, other than my pride and my reputation as a driver, but, myself and the guy on the passenger side were admitted to the hospital overnight for observation.

So, while my car is being repaired, which likely will take weeks, if not months, I do have to take the bus to get home, because the Hospital Centro Medico is in Zone 10 of the city, and I was living in Zona 1.

Coincidentally I have to take bus number 1 to get there.

Being worried about these things, and many more, I did not pay any attention to the man with the Atlanta Braves baseball hat, who got on the bus right behind me.

Neither did I notice him when he got off the bus at the same bus stop.

Not until the man approached me from behind, and softly, as if afraid of startling, or scare me he said: "Doctor K, do you remember me? I am Carlos, and we need your help again.

Commandant Tanya needs your help."

I stopped right on my tracks, turned around, and faced Carlos saying—louder than I should have—although fortunately, the street was deserted and there was no one around to hear us, "Yes, unfortunately I remember you very well, Carlos. You folks got me in big shit last time and, after that, I made very clear that I had enough of you and with your organization. I know what you are going to ask me to do. I feel bad and sorry for her, but there is nothing I can do to help.

"I have already told you that your commander is very sick, she is under heavy guard: two sentries at her door, four more in the corridor, I do not know how many more in the yard and I am not counting the ones in the Jeeps outside the hospital; trying to get her out of the place would be suicidal."

"Whoa, Doc, take it easy. You must understand that if we do not get the commandant out of that hospital soon, she is as good as dead.

"All we want now from you is information, like what room is she in, a sketch of the outlining of the hospital, times of guard changes, when is she is going to be moved and transferred and where are they going to move her."

"She is in room 261, and that is all I know, and all I can help you with. They do not let us regular interns or residents near her room. Only the surgeons, who operated on her, and her brother, who is military, are allowed to visit. Other doctors and nurses come from the military hospital, end of story."

"Ok, fair enough, how about a sketch of the outlining of the hospital?"

"That I can do if you have pen and paper. Good, here.

"This is the entrance of the hospital, right in the middle, reception desk, admitting, emergency room. Seven patient rooms on each side of the corridor operating rooms at the end, of the north side. Ten patient rooms on each side going south; cafeteria, kitchen, laundry at the south end. Room 261 is in the middle of the south side. Are you happy now?"

"Yes, that is good for now Doc. Thanks, we will stay in touch, if you know something else, just place a small flag in your window and one of us will contact you."

And with this Carlos disappeared.

Shit, I want so bad to have my car back.!!

# TWENTY-TWO
## September 18, 1968
## Hotel Camino Real
## Guatemala City

Captain Mario Guillermo Kruger Beltran was having some trouble finding a parking space for his military Jeep, as the parking lot of the Hotel Camino Real was full of vehicles. So, after circling around a couple of times, he decided to let the hotel valet do the parking.

It was obvious that the valet in charge of parking the cars did feel minimized by having to park the old military Jeep of the captain, but he felt much better after Kruger put five Quetzales in the man's hand.

Then, Captain Kruger walked into the lobby and went directly to the reception desk to ask for Thomas Hopeland, hoping that he was still lodging there.

He was informed that he was, but was not in the premises at the present time, although he was due to return any minute, because he had programed a telephone conference with the United States, at 5.30 pm.

It was 4.50, according to the clock on the wall behind the reception desk.

So, after identifying himself, Captain Kruger told the clerk that he would wait for Hopeland at the bar, and to please let him know that he was waiting to talk with him.

Yes, he could wait up until after Hopeland's teleconference with the USA was finished.

Exactly while Captain Kruger drove into the hotel parking lot, Professor Hopeland was attempting to park his rental Toyota Corolla at a tight parking spot in the same parking lot. The spot was so narrow that he realized that even if did not hit any of the

144

cars on the sides, it was going to be hard for him to get out of the Toyota. Unfortunately, it was the only space available, and he was expecting a phone call from his editor.

He was running out of money and his editors had not sent him any in two weeks. The hotel was awfully expensive, and although the newspapers paid for his room and meals, he had other expenses and many hands to grease...

Yes, this was Guatemala, a banana Republic, everyone was for sell and certainly for much cheaper than in Europe or the USA; but still, the money ran out fast.

Damn it, that such a luxurious hotel did not have an underground garage.

He accomplished the parking successfully thanks to the assistance; of a young woman, who was selling lottery tickets in front of the hotel. The woman even used her apron to protect the next car from the door of the Toyota scratching it.

Hopeland, reached into his wallet to get couple of Quetzales to give to the woman, when she said:

"I see you do not remember me, professor. I am Tanya's best friend."

Hopeland felt like a jolt of electricity hit him and he looked at the woman more closely. Now he remembered her. She was at the house the day Tanya took him there to take pictures of the dying ambassador.

The pictures that had circulated the entire globe. The pictures that had made him famous, but not yet rich.

This woman was Maria, the nurse attempting to save the ambassador of the United States from dying.

"Oh, now I remember you. You are Maria. You were at the house, and you must have taken part in the battle. But I thought that everyone was..."

"Dead? No.., only Camilo—rest in peace—died there, all the others got away...except Tanya, who, you know was wounded and captured.

"The government, to save face, told the media that the Army had killed every one of us, but, as you see, I am alive and well...

Shit. They do not even know that there were two women in the group."

"Ok Maria, I am incredibly happy you are alive, but what are you doing here now?"

"I need your help, professor. We need your help and Tanya needs your help."

"And how do you think I can help? Are we talking about rescuing Tanya from the hospital? That would be impossible, she is surrounded twenty-four-seven by a fucking army.

"They do not allow reporters inside the hospital, much less in her room. They do not even use the hospital own doctors; they brought military doctors to treat her."

"But can you at least get some information, or send a note to her?"

"Listen, Maria, I sympathize with your cause, and I admire your guts. As an ex-military and a man who has been in action, I was in awe when I saw what a small group of you, a group that I am learning now, including two women, could have taken on a whole military unit. Tanks and helicopters included.

"But then you had the element of surprise on your side, and a pompous, stupid, and overconfident young officer on the other side. This will not happen again; they are now ready and waiting for you.

"Sorry, I want to help, but I do not want to commit suicide or rot in a Guatemalan dungeon for the rest of my life. Good luck and goodbye."

Hopeland saw the tears in Maria's eyes and turning around said, "She is in room 261. If I can find something more, I will let you know. How do I contact you again?"

"Just tell Juan, at the hotel bar that you want to buy lottery tickets. He will find a way to deliver a message to us."

"Of course, I will do that and best of luck to you, Maria," he said as he walked towards the hotel, feeling bad and guilty.

Kruger was in the middle of his second beer when Hopeland walked into the lobby.

The clerk at the reception desk had informed him, upon arrival, that once he finished his conference call to the USA, one

Captain Kruger was waiting to see him, and he pointed in the direction of the bar.

Hopeland walked towards him, shook hands, and asked him to wait ten or fifteen minutes till he took his international call.

The call took less than ten minutes, and Hopeland was quite happy, as his editor had informed him that they wanted him to remain in the country until the whole Tanya Kruger affair ended. And that they had opened an account at one of the local banks, in his name with an initial deposit of fifty thousand dollars, plus he would get a bank credit card paid for by Time Magazine. And they wanted him to write a book about his experiences, for which they offered to pay five times that money.

Hopeland hung up the phone and returned to the bar to meet Tanya's brother.

They shook hands again. Hopeland noticed that Captain Kruger had ordered two other *Gallo* beers.

After a few formalities and a couple of sips of beer, Hopeland went straight to the point "And to what exactly do I have the honor of your visit Captain Kruger?"

"I understand that you were a military man, Professor Copeland. Therefore, I hope you understand that I have loyalty to my country and to the military and that I have the duty to protect both.

"But I also love my family, my sister, and my father and now I am torn apart because I must choose between one and the other."

"As ex-military and as a decorated veteran and with all due respect, I would respond that the first part of your speech is bullshit.

"However, everyone is entitled to believe what he pleases and to express it freely. So, I respect your right to do so, as I have dedicated most of my life, both as a soldier and as a reporter, to fight to defend the right of people to have and express an opinion.

"However, in your case, I believe you should give priority to the family part."

"Fair enough. That is why I am here. I want to know what is going on with my family. Why is my sister accusing my dad. Why was she involved with FAR? Why did she tell me to come to you, a perfect stranger, for answers?"

"She told you that? So, she can talk now? Praise the Lord!"

"Yes, she can talk and told me to see you for explanations. That is why I am here this afternoon."

"Yes, captain, I have the whole story right from the pretty hands of your sister, but I also have documentation to confirm and prove the story, which, I warn you, is not a pretty one.

"Moreover, I have your mother's diary, which I have not read yet, as your sister summarized it pretty well for me. I also believe that you should know the entire truth.

"However, I am being watched. I have a tail on me all the time. My room phone is bugged and, probably, they put hidden cameras in my room as well.

"The documents are well hidden and safe, I made copies of them that I mailed to myself in the USA. But the originals are here, in the hotel. I just do not think it is safe to get them out now. I promise I will get them tonight and give them to you tomorrow."

"Ok, but can you at least give me a hint why? I think I would sleep better if I knew."

"Let me just say that your dad is not the nice guy you think he is and that your sister had strong reasons—at least in her mind—to do what she did".

"Somehow I am not totally surprised to hear that, Mr. Hopeland. But you are right, if it is not safe to meet here, let's meet tomorrow, for lunch at a bar somewhere out of here."

"I am sure you are familiar with the bar *El Portal*, across from the presidential palace. Tomorrow is Monday and they serve this delicious *caldo de cagrejos* (crab soup) with all the drinks."

"Been there, soup is good. So is the beer on tap they serve. Let's meet there. Till tomorrow then professor Hopeland"

"Till tomorrow, Captain Kruger"

Tom needed time to sneak out of his room and unscrew the aluminum plate that he had bolted at the top of the vending machine under which he had stored the diary, the letters and all the documents that Tanya had given him.

But he had to make absolute sure that nobody was watching him. And for that he had to wait till everyone in the hotel was asleep

# TWENTY-THREE
## Hospital Centro Medico
## Guatemala City
## September 22, 1968

I do not remember anyone in the hospital who did not like Doctor Jaime Garcia. Even when considering that he was not a member of the medical staff of *Centro Medico*.

Or, maybe, it was precisely because everyone knew that he was not part of the medical staff of the hospital. Although most doctors in the staff were either respected, admired, or despised, all were feared and considered an arrogant bunch of bastards.

Not Garcia, he was charming, nice, funny, friendly, very down-to-earth, and of course incredibly good looking. He was a very likable person, the kind of guy that men would like to have a beer with, watch football with and be friends with. the kind of guy that girls like to go to bed with and hope to marry.

Never mind that he had a slight limp, and a foreign accent that nobody could tell if it was Gringo or Italian, or both. He told us that he was Italian American, that he had failed the grades to qualify him to get into medical school in the USA, so he had studied medicine at a Caribbean University, and he had completed his residency at the Gorgas hospital in Panama and thereafter was hired to work at the *Hospital Militar* in Guatemala.

And now he was assigned to follow the progress of the recovery of Ms. Lily Marie Kruger. So, he dutifully visited her every day, spending about ten to fifteen minutes in her room.

He told us that he was promoted to captain whereas he had been fighting in Vietnam and was wounded there, and for this he got a medal, so, apparently because of those credentials it was that his rank was legally accepted by the Guatemalan military.

150

Nobody ever bothered to confirm if this story was factual.

All members of the Hospital staff were fascinated with his war stories, his charm and also the doughnuts and other pastries that he brought for the staff and for the soldiers on duty, especially to those guarding the door of room 261.

Therefore, nobody paid attention to the fact that he never accompanied the other military doctors on their rounds to visit the patient in room 261; or that he never talked to any of the physicians, members of our hospital staff. Or that he always did his rounds with the patient in 261, in the early afternoon, after the surgeons had finished their surgeries and gone and after the doctors in other specialties had finished their morning rounds and gone as well to see patients at their private offices.

Neither did they pay particular attention to the fact that Dr. Garcia was gone before the doctors from the staff returned for the evening rounds.

He sometimes had lunch with us at the cafeteria, and there he would share war stories, travel stories, or local politics. He loved to discuss local politics as he said he found the politics of our country really fascinating.

He was mostly obsessed with the stories about his patient Tanya Kruger. Especially those stories written by Thomas Hopeland, whom he claimed to have met personally as he was his roommate at a hospital in Washington DC, where both were recovering from wounds sustained in the battlefield.

And he seemed extremely interested in learning about the political orientation of every medical resident working at the hospital. So, Doctor Garcia and I became close friends, in a very short time.

The only other person that Captain Jaime Garcia, MD, seemed to favor and had long conversations with, was Captain Guillermo Kruger, the brother of his patient in room 261.

Everything seemed to be normal, among the abnormal, in our hospital and about Dr. Garcia, till one afternoon when he showed up for supper at the cafeteria and told me, in secret, that he had relievable information that the following day would be the day when representatives of the judicial and the military were coming to the hospital to take a deposition from Ms. Kruger.

What he did not tell me was that he was planning to record it.

And so, he did. Doctor Garcia placed a small cassette recorder under the pillow of Ms. Kruger's, told her to activate it at the beginning of the deposition, turn it off at the end, and to make sure that it was not discovered.

It was not.

# TWENTY-FOUR
## Kruger Mansion
## *La Cañada*
## Guatemala City
## September 25, 1968

The three of us met in the wine cellar of the Kruger family mansion. It was the first time I was formally introduced to the brother of Tanya.

I wasn't sure why I had been invited to the luxurious Kruger family mansion. But I soon I found out.

It was a day after the lawyers took the deposition from Lily Marie. And it was the day when Dr. Garcia displayed the whole deck of cards that he had been holding on his sleeve, in front of me and Captain Kruger.

Doctor Garcia played the tape of the interview for all three of us.

There were nine people involved in the taking of the deposition. Three from the Military courts, three from the civilian courts and three defense attorneys, hired and paid by Captain Kruger, who, of course, was not allowed to attend.

The recording started with the polite introductions, followed by the usual and customary questions.

"Please state your name, age, and date of birth."

"Lily Marie Kruger Beltran, age 25, born April 9, 1943."

"Thank you, Miss Kruger," was the unanimous answer. It was followed by other routine questions such address, occupation etc. And then it moved to more relevant questions such:

"Are you related to General Guillermo Kruger-Larrave?"

"Yes, he is my father."

Unfortunately, the recording did not identify who was asking the questions at any given time. But it went as follows:

"Are you, Ms. Kruger the same person known as Tanya, a member of the FAR?"

"No, I am not."

"Are you familiar or acquainted with that person?"

"No, I am not."

"We have a picture of said person, taken during a bank robbery and it certainly looks like you".

Apparently, someone showed the picture to Lily Marie.

"It is blurred, and the woman; if it is a woman, is wearing a baseball hat and dark sunglasses. Both are cheap brands. No, it is not me."

"Can you tell us where you were on the day of that robbery?"

"On what date that would be sir?"

"February the 20th, 1968."

"My dear sir, I am not sure I remember what I had for breakfast this morning, you pretend me to remember where I was more than six months ago?"

Her statement caused most of the audience to laugh and one of her lawyers to intervene:

"Let us not forget that Ms. Kruger was in a coma for several days after her recent injuries. Doctors can attest that it could affect her memory."

"Indeed, we will ignore that. Let us move to the next question."

A different voice, likely a military judge or lawyer, asked the next question.

"Were you present at the so-called Battle of Avenida Elena, Ms. Kruger?"

"Yes, I was"

"And may I ask you why you were there?"

"I was guarding the Ambassador of the USA, whom we had kidnapped on orders from my father, General Guillermo Kruger-Larrave."

"Therefore, are you stating that your father ordered the kidnapping of the ambassador? And did he order the ambassador's assassination as well?"

"He did not order us to kill the ambassador, just to kidnap him. But I believe he would have ended up killing him, probably after making him suffer. My dad enjoys that sort of thing. Inflicting pain to people that is."

"Those are profoundly serious accusations, Ms. Kruger, and only your opinion, not a matter of fact. I request that that statement be erased."

"Sorry, the statement will stay on the records."

"What would have been your father's motive to order the kidnapping of the ambassador?"

"He did not tell me, and I do not usually question my father, but I believe that he had two reasons. The first was because he had had several disagreements with the ambassador regarding the way my father was managing the control of the rebels, the FAR, as you call them.

"His excellency thought that my father's methods were far too brutal and that those methods were counterproductive and created more discontent among the people, and therefore produced more rebels."

She paused, evidently tired, and then continued.

"Also, he, my father, believed that Mr. Mein was reporting him to Washington."

"And the second reason?".

"The second reason was that my father hated the FAR so much that he wanted to put the blame of the kidnapping and murder of Mr. Mein on the FAR, to obtain more economic help from the United States, to combat the guerrillas."

"So, he did not tell you all that. That is only a supposition on your part. Correct?"

"Yes sir"

"And how did General Kruger participate in the events leading to the kidnapping and death of Mr. John Gordon Mein?"

"He provided the information, the coordination, organization, the time, the place, and the route. And of course, he provided the weapons we used."

"What about the ransom money? It seemed too small amount for a man in his position?"

"He was not really interested in the money. He wanted it to pay the other men he used."

"How many men were involved? Who are those men, and where are they?"

"The government says that they killed them all, so, you should have five dead bodies. I should have been the sixth."

"You mean to let us believe that only six persons caused all that damage and casualties, Ms. Kruger? How?"

"You can believe whatever you want, sir. As to my response to how? Well, With a bit of luck, the element of surprise, and overall, a lot of determination and big cojones, sir"

"What about the names of those men? Do you know their names?"

"No, I do not know them by their names, and the names I knew them by probably are not real names; I did also ignore their addresses. Father hired them, and according to the news, they all died in the confrontation with the Army."

"What about the weapons? It has been reported that you used an RPG, a portable rocket launcher. How did you get that weapon?"

"Father provided it, of course. And it surprised us that whoever commanded the troops who assaulted the house did not know we had such a weapon.

"We used it to stop the limousine, and there were many witnesses, mostly the driver, who rapidly realized what it was and stepped out of the vehicle and knelt at the side of it."

"Is that so? What about the money? What happens to it?"

"I do not know that either. I gave it to my father, and he gave it back to me to pay the men. Dad wanted a million dollars, but I reduced it to a quarter of that because I panicked when I saw that the ambassador was seriously wounded and needed urgent medical care. I been told that the place burned down, maybe the money burned in it."

"Did you try to provide some medical attention to his excellency?"

"Yes, we did. I have two years of medical school and one of the men in the group; I believe was a nurse or a medic. We did what we could under the circumstances."

"You killed the ambassador and several members of the armed forces, are you remorseful about that?"

"The loss of any life is regrettable sir, but I did not kill anyone. The ambassador fired at us and one of the men returned the fire. As for the casualties among the soldiers, we simply defended ourselves, knowing very well what happens to those that are caught alive by the military."

"But you said that you believe that General Kruger was going to kill Mr. Mein anyhow. Would you have cooperated with such action?"

"No, I believe that I would have tried to talk my father out of doing such a thing."

"Sorry Ms. Kruger but that is hard to believe. After you said you and your men kidnapped Mr. Mein and had the purpose of keeping him captive, even while you suspected that he was going to be eventually killed."

"You do not know my father, sir. He is a cruel and imposing man. Either you do what he tells you to do, or you face grave consequences. But yes, I was planning to let Mr. Mein escape from us. I was going to let him wound me so I could tell Dad that he had overpowered me and fled."

"Miss Kruger, did your father, General Guillermo Kruger, ever sexually abused you?"

"I object to that question," said one of her lawyers.

"It is okay, I was expecting that question to come up some time or another. And the answer is, no, never."

"What about your brother, Captain Mario Guillermo Kruger? Did your father ever abuse him?"

"Not sexually, no. But physically and psychologically, yes. Father ran the household as he did the troops, very sternly and with very strong discipline, and there was punishment for disobedience. Father still has the German-Nazi discipline on his blood."

"And yet, there was a time in your life when you lived your life in a dissipated and scandalous way. Didn't your father object to that?"

"He did, and because of that, he sent me to California, against my will. Same as he forced my brother to join the military against his will."

"Do you love your father, Miss Kruger?"

"In a way I do. But it is difficult to love a monster, and my father is a monster, a psychopath."

"Why do you think so Miss Kruger?"

"I told you that he loves inflicting pain, watching people suffer. And he believes, like the Nazis, that all other human beings are inferior to him and deserving of punishment, even death. Even those he is supposed to love, like my mother, he drove her to kill herself."

At this, Lily Marie started crying.

And that was the end of the deposition.

# BOOK FOUR

## TWENTY-FIVE
**Kruger Mansion**
*La CAÑADA*
**Guatemala City**
**September 25, 1968**

As we all listened to the tape, we were utterly flabbergasted. No one more than Captain Kruger who was the first one to react.

"My sister is lying. Some of the things she said are true, but the rest are simple lies. She is just trying to punish Father for the suicide of our mother."

"How so?". I inquired.

"My father may be a cruel man, a psychopath, even a monster, as my sister says, but one thing he is not is stupid. He is a very smart and cunning man.

"This whole thing of setting up the kidnapping and wanting to kill the ambassador, all for such small ransom and because of petty disagreements, is totally unreliable and complete bullshit."

"You think so, Captain Kruger? I totally agree," said Dr. Garcia

"I know so, guys, I know so!" said Kruger. "Just think for a moment about how small was the ransom money? Nothing could be more bullshit than that. If anything, father would have asked for a couple of million, at least, and never had settled for—how much it was? A quarter of a million.

"I believe that Lily thinks that our father was, or is, responsible for our mother's suicide; and maybe she is right

159

about that. Therefore, she set up a trap to punish him and get revenge for our mom's death."

"If you are correct in thinking so, there is no question that she did an excellent job. Don't you think, Captain?" said Doctor Garcia.

"It seems like she did. Father is in jail; his career is ruined, even if he can beat the rap. His daughter is in the hospital and at risk of going to prison for the rest of her life—or put before a firing squad. And we are here in his home, at his cellar, and drinking my father's wine."

All I could say was, "Life can be funny sometimes and there is nothing we can do about it."

"That is when you are wrong, my dear Doctor K. There is something we can do about it, and we are going to do it," Doctor Garcia said.

"We, as in all of us? Like what?"

"Yes, Doctor K and Captain Kruger. We are going to do a lot more than sitting, drinking wine, whining, and complaining. Although I admit that this is an excellent wine. Captain Kruger, we are going to free your sister.

"For that I need the cooperation of both of you, and few more men, plus a few other items." said Dr. Garcia

The Captain and I looked at him as if he was totally crazy. Soon we realized that he was totally serious.

Especially after Garcia pulled a typed piece of paper and gave a copy to each one of us in the room.

"This, gentlemen, is a list of the items we are going to need in order to rescue Ms. Lily Marie Kruger, aka Tanya, the feared FAR guerrilla leader from the hospital."

After each one of us read the paper, Garcia said, "Memorize that list and destroy it, but be aware that each one of the things on that list is essential for our success."

Captain Kruger read the numbered list out loud:

"1. A double-bottom flask, of the kind we use to sneak alcohol at ballgames

2. Fresh blood, 30 cc. minimum, no more than sixty

3. A 9mm handgun

4. Four trusted men who can ride motorcycles and are good at driving cars

5. At least one of them should be an excellent car driver

6. A Winchester M70 rifle with a scope

7. At least two motorcycles

8. A utility van (with a logo for an electrician, plumbing, or phone repair man)

9. Two large trucks or buses

10. A recently deceased female or a living female that can be considered expendable of about the same age as Ms. Kruger

11. A small airplane

12. A trustful man or a woman, able to pilot the plane all the way to Mexico,

13. A place to store and hide it, ideally near an airport or a landing strip

14. A two-way radio with long-range reach

15. The exact date when Ms. Kruger is going to be taken out of the hospital to visit your father

"What? Is she going to be taken out of the hospital to visit our dad? How do you know that?"

"Well, let's say that I took the liberty to have someone sneak up into the office of Colonel, or General—it's hard to keep up with these fast changes of ranks in your military—Ricardo Oliva and into the home of his associate General/Colonel Ramiro Zelaya and bug their telephones, so I heard that General Oliva and his clique are planning to take her to the Fort of Matamoros, where they are keeping your father. Probably soon, but not likely tomorrow. Before doing that, they are letting General Kruger listen to the tape of his daughter's deposition. The same one that we just heard."

All of us wondered how Garcia been able to do such a thing and, for the first time, we suspected that he was not who he pretended to be.

We both held the paper with the list in our hands, not knowing what to do with it until Garcia detailed his plan, after which both of us further questioned his sanity. As he proceeded to explain it:

161

"There are a couple of three-story buildings, with roof access, about a block north of the hospital. Two men—at least one of them a sniper—are to position themselves on the roof. The other man could help the shooter or be there just to keep civilians from reaching the roof of the building at an importune time. The two men get up there disguised as electricians or plumbers or safety inspectors, whatever you prefer, and wait."

Garcia paused to see the effect of his words on the two men with him, then proceeded to explain the rest of his plan.

"The day of the trip to visit her dad, Miss Kruger demands to ride with her brother to the interview with their father. Of course, he is not allowed to carry any weapons; therefore, he has none with him.

"His only weapon is the double-bottom flask. One tier, the top, contains rum, whiskey, or whichever liquor you fancy; the other, the bottom, has blood in it."

He paused again.

"And that is the part where Doctor K comes in. He must procure the blood, which I am assumed be easy as he works in two hospitals."

"Blood, what do you need blood? What is the blood for?"

"The blood is for you, Captain Kruger, to spill on your sister's face after she gets shot."

"My sister is going to get shot. How? why? By whom?"

"She will be shot by the sniper, of course."

"The sniper, and where are we going to find a sniper?"

"I am. I am going to be the sniper. But do not worry; I will just nick one of her pretty ears, or perhaps the side of her head. Then, she drops to the ground, and you pour the blood on her face Captain Kruger. Doctor K. checks her pulse, and shouts, very loudly that she is dead.

"You, Captain, carry her in your arms back to the vehicle she came in, and we all take off."

There was a question that both Captain Kruger and I had been pondering:

"What if you miss?"

Garcia's answer: "I never miss. At least I have never missed up to this point."

Garcia paused, then continued:

"Just tell your sister to stand up facing north from the time she gets out of whichever vehicle she is transported in, till she hears my shot."

He told us that he had been sniper in Vietnam and had seventeen kills over only few months.

"Vietnam was long ago for you Doctor Garcia; you may be out of practice. Also, you seem to forget that she will be handcuffed to a soldier or nurse. How do you propose to solve that?"

"Let's just say that I have been practicing my shots regularly all these years since Nam.

"As for your second question. My second shot will hit whichever person is handcuffed to Ms. Lily Marie, right in the arm that is connected to her. Therefore, I expect that someone is bound to release the handcuffs after that, person is shot."

"Ok, but supposing I could pick up my sister from the ground and carry her in my arms to the vehicle, don't you think that, by then all those soldiers will be all over me?"

"Maybe yes, maybe not, by then you will have an automatic gun in your hand. A gun that would have been previously hidden by Doctor K, under the mattress of the stretcher, or in the wheelchair. The very same stretcher or wheelchair which will be used to transport the person with the wounded arm to the Hospital Emergency room."

"So, if I am carrying my sister and holding a gun in my hand, how am I going to get into the vehicle and drive away?"

"We hope to have a man waiting in the restaurant across the street from the hospital; he would take care of the driver and do the driving."

"Supposing that my wounded sister, with a cast on her ankle can be placed on the vehicle, and suppose that your man, from the restaurant across the street, is able to get in the driver seat, we will be followed by those military Jeeps, within seconds, those are equipped with heavy machineguns. We will be riddled with 50 caliber bullets and death before reaching the next block."

"My third shot, or a shot from the guy with me, if he is a good shooter, will disable the machine gunner, and thereafter, two other guys will block the streets leading to and from the hospital. That is why we need a couple of trucks or buses.

"As soon as her transport passes the street intersection, our men will drive them to completely block their paths. We placed one truck on the south corner, another truck on the north corner. This in case someone decides to drive around the block to chase you, it be also useful to protect my getaway."

"What will happen to the drivers of those trucks?"

"They will leave the trucks right there and take off riding motorcycles or cars. Motorcycles are best because they can wave into traffic. I will do the same, along with the guy helping me on the roof."

"Obviously, that would be only in case we are unable to return to the utility van, otherwise we would just drive away on that.

"Then, you, captain, and your pretty sister will drive to a shopping mall or any place with a covered parking, where you will abandon the ambulance, and transfer to a vehicle that has been previously left at the site. And from there you ride happily into the sunset."

"And where you say the sunset is?"

"First your ranch in Escuintla, and then Mexico, Captain Kruger"

He told us that he had an apartment in a place in Mexico called Puerto Vallarta. Puerto Vallarta was a place being developed as a fancy resort, but he had bought his flat before that was started, and got it relatively cheap, at pre-construction prices.

Captain Kruger informed us that there was a small airplane and a landing strip at Kruger's ranch. He could have that fueled and ready in no time at all.

The ranch would also be a good place to lay low for a few days.

Kruger said that he could fly the plane. Garcia said that he could do it too, but it was better that the captain stayed at the ranch taking care of the wake and funeral of his sister. And he, for personal and work-related reasons, would be unable to leave the city, as he had to report that Miss Kruger had been mortally shot.

Then Captain Kruger said that they both knew a man who probably be willing to fly the plane. That man's name was Professor Thomas Hopeland.

Kruger had taken a liking to the man, during their conversation, over several beers, at *El Portal* bar when he provided him with the copy of his mother's dairy, and of his sister letter and dairy.

Kruger had noticed that Hopeland was infatuated with his sister, and he did not mind that a bit. Specially after Hopeland had elevated her to the category of a superhero in the many articles he had written about her.

He was also a Vietnam veteran and perhaps had known Doctor Garcia there.

Garcia said that he, himself, would provide the Winchester M70 with a scope.

The issue of the cadaver of a woman was motive for strong arguments, and I knew that we could not use Don Rafa, from the medical school again. Although I did not mention to these guys my previous involvement with him.

But Garcia insisted that finding a fresh cadaver was a crucial part of the plan, simply because if Lily Marie was known to be alive, by the authorities of either Guatemala or the USA, after the rescue, they would not rest until she was captured and extradited, or simply send an assassin to take care of her.

After all they had done that before this time sending him to do it. But of course he did not tell Doctor K or Captain Kruger that part.

Luckily, Tanya had opened her eyes in a nick of time before he murdered her. And by doing so had turned her would be assassin into her would be rescuer.

Unfortunately, someone was needed to take her place at the grave.

Hopefully, someone who was already dead.

That plan was so crazy, and far-fetched that it may work.

So far, the conversation had been mostly between Captain Kruger and Doctor Garcia, but when the later asked if we had any questions, I raised my hand and asked a simple one:

"I am assuming, Doctor Garcia, that you have all the men you needed for this operation, well trained, trustworthy and ready to go. Am I correct?"

"No, doctor, you are not correct. I do not have any men that I could trust with this at my disposal, but I was hoping that you, who may have had a previous contact with FAR, could find someone.

"And you, Captain, could ask your sister how to contact some of her trusted comrades in arms who could assist us on this matter."

That observation shocked me, as I had not told Garcia of my involvement in treating some wounded FAR operatives at the General Hospital and certainly not about my role in trying to save the life of the Ambassador.

Who the hell was this guy who apparently knew so much about us? That made me even less enthusiast about participating in the rescue mission. I really did not want to be involved. Yet it seemed that I had no choice.

Perhaps this guy was working for the police, and this master plan of his was nothing but a ruse to draw as many members of the FAR as possible into the open.

I would discuss this later in private with Tania's brother.

Meanwhile, I consoled myself by thinking that the role that I was supposed to play seemed to be a minor one.

At least, I hoped so.

# TWENTY-SIX
## Anywhere in Guatemala
## Years before 1968

Claudia Gonzalez was an average fourteen-year-old girl, the youngest of seven daughters of a very conservative Protestant Baptist Pastor. Her parents enrolled her at Belem, a private, but modestly-priced school since second grade.

When Claudia was in 10$^{th}$ grade, she fell in love with one of her teachers, a handsome married man, but about ten years her senior. This fact did not become known to her parents until she could no longer hide her pregnancy.

Her father, "fearing the wrath of God upon his family," kicked her out of his house, and the girl found herself homeless and without any working skills. She was expelled from the school as well.

The teacher, the father of her child, was willing to rent a room for her and gave her a small monthly pension for food and clothing. That was until the child was born.

After the child was born—a baby boy, the father took the baby with him and never returned it to her, disappearing shortly thereafter.

It was not until much later that Claudia learned that the man's wife was not able to have children and that they, most likely, had just used her womb to have a child.

Claudia never saw them, or her baby, again, and at the end of the month, when the rent was no longer paid, she was evicted from the room. Claudia found herself homeless again. Her family, once again, refused to take her in.

The landlord of the house where she rented the room was an old alcoholic, solitary and grouchy guy, who, nevertheless, had had his eyes on Claudia, and taking advantage of her situation, offered her to move in with him.

Claudia was disgusted and, at first, refused, but after a few nights sleeping in the streets and with no food in her stomach, she returned to the home and submitted to the desires of the old alcoholic.

That was when Claudia had her first drink. Before her drinking became a habit, she would have two or three drinks before letting the old man touch her, in order to be able to tolerate having sex with him. Soon they were drinking together to the point of passing out.

And drinking daily, and not necessarily before sex, which was an endeavor that became less and less frequent, and less and less important in their lives.

After about three years of Claudia living this life, the old man died. One day the old goat got drunk, passed out, and never woke up again.

Once again Claudia found herself homeless because, as soon after the old man died, his two daughters who had not seen, nor visited him for years, suddenly appeared, claiming to be their father's right heirs, and taking possession of the house.

At first, Claudia tried to work as a maid but, since by then she had become an alcoholic, her employment did not last long, and soon her reputation became widely known, and it was so bad, that nobody would employ her.

Claudia found herself homeless once more, now she was not only an alcoholic, but also unemployable. Yet she was also in her early twenties and had a sensuous body. Therefore, she used those attributes to survive and became an independent sex worker.

Her independence however did not last long, because, although prostitution was legal in Guatemala, it was regulated by the health authorities. Most women sex workers preferred to work at whore houses where at least food and shelter was available to them.

According to the law, All the sex working women had to be licensed and undergo physical, gynecological, and blood testing periodically. Those women who tried to practice independently were usually arrested and fined, after being sexually abused by the cops.

Claudia was arrested several times and rejected at the whore houses due to her increasing alcohol dependency and because she had been found to have a plethora of sexually transmitted diseases, such are syphilis, gonorrhea, and chlamydia, either together or at different times.

She had lost everything, her family, her child, her pride, her dignity, her health, her decency, even her name, because after a while, the people in the streets, starting with the homeless, forgot her name, stopping from calling her Claudia and called her instead "stinky." That was the name that stuck, and everyone knew her as.

Stinky had several miscarriages, or abortions, which even herself was not able to tell which was which.

Some of these abortions were self-induced and led to hemorrhage, and she also had several episodes of PID, most requiring hospitalizations and eventually a hysterectomy, all done at the Hospital San Juan de Dios, aka the General Hospital.

"Stinky" became a rather known and frequent customer at the General Hospital emergency room and wards. When her condition required to be admitted, she was treated, bathed, given fresh clothes, and eventually released with the hope that she would stop drinking.

She would stop for a few days and then relapse.

It was during one or more of those hospitalizations that Claudia met Maria, who worked as an emergency room nurse at the time.

While Claudia's alcohol dependency became worse by the day, and she slipped further and further down a darker slope, Maria fell in love with a man who, later she found out, belonged to the FAR. One day, this man was wounded, arrived at the ER, had surgery, and was hospitalized.

However, just when the man was on his way to recovery, the secret police discovered his whereabouts, came for him, and beat him to death, right then and there, in front of patients, doctors, and nurses.

After that Maria joined the FAR

Meanwhile, Claudia got worse and worse, she was only about thirty years old and looked like seventy. She would give herself to anybody for just a quart of booze.

Of course, she became a petty thief, but as her addiction got worse and she developed tremors and weakness, she eventually became unable to steal.

Stinky contracted tuberculosis, in addition to her recurrent sexual diseases, becoming gradually just skin and bones. Stinky tried to kill herself several times and even failed at that.

She was now a dirty, humble, stinky beggar asking for a handout at the door of the hospital or at the entrance of any church in town. Stinky was usually present at the atrium of those churches that had patron saint celebrations or other religious festivities.

Oddly she became very knowledgeable about the events' dates and places which attracted the most worshipers.

Stinky had not been inside any church since her father kicked her out.

# TWENTY-SEVEN
## Hotel Camino Real
## September 26, 1968

Thomas Hopeland had been idle, most of the day, sitting by the pool of the hotel and drinking Margaritas while working very little and sporadically, on a new article for Times magazine. All the time without being able to erase the image of Tanya from his mind.

Once the sun started to go down and the day started to get dark, and the Margaritas started clouding his head a bit, he decided to go for a walk and then return and have a late dinner at the Hotel main dining room.

The walk took him farther than he had anticipated, the evening was warm, and he was sweating, yet it was getting too cool to take a dip in the pool, so he went up to his room to change and shower. He chose a white shirt, beige trousers, a dark blue jacket, and brown shoes, then he put on a necktie in his pocket, in case the etiquette of the place required wearing one.

Tom did not like to dine in the hotel's main dining room. It was too elegant and sophisticated for his taste. This was only the second time since his arrival to Guatemala, almost a month earlier now, that he had dined there, as he preferred to either eat out of the hotel, at the hotel bar, or at the small gazebo by the pool.

However, he had received, earlier in the afternoon, a written invitation to diner at the main dining room, at 9.30 pm, which was a bit late, even for Guatemalan standards, and at that hour, the place would have few customers. So, he figured that whoever had sent the invitation wanted privacy.

Therefore, Tom was curious.

Although he was in general a very punctual person, knowing that when the Guatemalans invited you at one hour, you are expected to show up much later, Tom choose to show up at 9.45, also hoping to see beforehand, who was his mysterious host.

He was wrong. The hostess walked him to a table that had been previously reserved by the mysterious host who happened not be yet present. The waitress informed him that the gentleman who had reserved the table had called, offering apologies, and stating that he had been detained but that he be there shortly.

The waiter came to take an order for a beverage and, since it was free and the person who sent the invitation was late, which was rude, in his opinion, regardless of reason, Tom ordered a bottle of the most expensive wine he could find on the menu.

He was not requested to put on a tie and the wine was rather good.

Tom was on his second glass of wine when someone came from behind, taped him on the shoulder, and said, "It has been quite a long time Tom Hopeland. I am delighted to see you still alive after all these years, lucky son of a gun. How is your eye?"

The man's voice sounded familiar, but Tom could not yet see his face, so he turned around and faced the person.

"Tony, Tony Benedetti, son of a bitch! Where have you been all these years?"

The men embraced and sat down.

"I see you got good taste in wines. That is an excellent choice, even though it is not Italian."

After, one more bottle of wine (Italian this time) and a meal of fettuccini alfredo with shrimp for Tony, and steak and baked potato for Tom, they ordered brandy and cigars. Both men had been drinking most of the afternoon, so both were a little tipsy. The dining room was nearly deserted by then.

Tony said, "Ok, buddy, I will be honest with you. This invitation was not entirely to get reacquainted but to ask for your help."

"You need my help, Tony? Why? For what?"

"The girl, the Kruger girl. Anyone who has read any of your articles about her realizes that you are more than fond of her. Am I wrong, Thomas?"

Tom's face flushed, and it was not because of the wine. "No, you are not wrong; you are entirely correct, Tony! I think about her every minute of the day and dream of her at night. Those nights when I can sleep, of course.

"And also, I am very, very concerned about her fate. I do not believe she is coming out of this alive, especially not when she threw away any support she could have from her general father through the window."

"You are absolutely right, Tom. But the fact that she is accusing her father of concocting the plot to kill the ambassador for revenge and ransom may actually help her. At least temporarily."

"Why is that, Tony?"

"Because I believe that the other generals—Kruger's enemies—are more interested in getting rid of General Kruger than killing his daughter. A fact which, at least for the time being, is keeping her alive.

"Also helping her, saving, or at least prolonging her life, are all the articles that you have written about her which have transformed her into some sort of national hero.

"Unfortunately, once those factors disappear, she is as good as dead. You and I know how they deal with the rebels and enemies of the regime here."

"So, what is your point, Tony? And why are we having this dinner and this conversation? Obviously, it is not just for old time's sake or to take a walk down memory lane."

"Ok. I'll be honest with you. But first answer two questions: one, would you be willing to help us free the girl? And second, are you able to fly an airplane?"

"The answer to both questions is a definite yes. But how do I know that I can trust you, Tony? I have not seen you since we were in the hospital after Nam, and I have heard rumors about what you did before that and also some rumors about what you have been doing after that."

Tony remained silent.

Tom continued. "You are probably aware that The Guatemalan Secret Police, and also probably the FBI, have a tail on me all the time because they suspect that I know more about the kidnapping and murder of Mr. Mein than what I have told them. And I believe that they would love to set a trap and send me to rot in prison for a few years, after breaking few of my old bones, of course."

"Ok, Tom, fair enough. I will tell you the truth and my side of the story as candidly as I can, which I may add is not my usual style, and then I will let you decide. We do have a plan, for which we need an airplane pilot, someone we can trust".

"Ok let's hear it, Tony. I am all ears".

"This is my story, Tom: I joined the Army and went to Nam to avoid going to prison for having killed a man in New York. Therefore, the Army discovered that I had the unique skill of being able to hit a target from as far as two hundred meters. Thus they made me a sniper. I killed over seventeen men in the few months I was in Vietnam."

Tony paused to see how his words had affected his old Army buddy.

"Then as you may remember, I was wounded, and given the Bronze Star. However, the government was still not happy and had not finished with me yet. They blackmailed me and had me by the balls, threatening to revive my past unless I joined the Agency. In short, they recruited me for the fucking CIA. And since then, I have been all over the world doing their shitty work."

Another pause.

"And now, the CIA sent me to Guatemala, about two weeks ago, to kill your precious girl Tanya, or Lily Marie, whichever name you want to remember her by."

Tony took a big gulp of brandy and a puff of his cigar before continuing.

"So, Tom, whether you believe it or not, and lucky for her, once I was at her bedside and ready to do it, something strange occurred to me. I was paralyzed and unable to kill her. All I had to do was to flush a big dose of insulin in to her IV tubing and she would have gone from one slumber to a permanent one."

Tony took another gulp of his brandy and continued. "That was not the only thing that occurred to me. Also there and then, I decided to help her get out of there and escape her captors. So, I concocted a plan for which I need your help.

"She is going to be free, and we are going to do it. Me by shooting her, you by flying her in a plane to Puerto Vallarta, Mexico".

Tom was totally flabbergasted and could not believe what he had just heard, it was too fantastic to be a lie, however, now he felt more distrust towards his old friend than before. In fact, he was scared of him. Knowing that he was a CIA assassin was not really reassuring.

"So, Tony, are you telling me that you will shoot her? I assume you are talking about using dud bullets or shooting her while wearing a bulletproof vest, or using sleeping darts?"

"None of the above, Thomas. Real bullets, actual shooting, fake death, yes. Just a flesh wound looking severe enough to convince everyone, including my bosses at the CIA, that she was actually killed."

Tony was still talking. "Therefore, she will have to be officially deceased, so her dear brother will need to have a funeral for someone posing as her, while you fly Ms. Tanya to Mexico and into the sunset. Her brother will be interring someone else's body in their ranch cemetery.

"We do this in the hope that the authorities would believe the ruse and be happy that she is dead and buried, and the agency would be happy with me, knowing that their orders have been carried out by their loyal agent, just as expected, just as always."

Tom Hopeland took few minutes to digest all the information that Tony had given him and then responded: "Thank you for leveling with me, Tony. I think I believe your story; it is just too weird not to be accurate."

"I give you my permission to write it and publish it but only after you learn that I have died, OK."

"Ok, it is a deal. Now, tell me how many men, besides you and me, must carry on your plan."

"My dear Thomas, that is a little problem for which I do not have yet the answer. So far, we have only you, me, the brother of the girl, and a doctor who works at the hospital where she is being treated. Only those know about this plan, and we need at least four more men, and we have very little time to recruit them."

"Perhaps I may be able to help with that, just give me a day or so."

"Tom, we may not have a day or so, you have seen how guarded she is?"

Our only hope is to rescue her when she is taken out to visit her father at the Fort of Matamoros, and that could be any day now."

"You just said that I have seen how guarded she is, so you have seen me at the hospital? When how?"

"Not a secret, Tom. You have been there almost every day since she was admitted."

"That was another clue about my feelings, right?"

"I would not deny that Tom, again it was pretty obvious, she is beautiful and a firecracker, a truly amazing woman."

"I have not been able to see her, though."

"I know, I have, and I know she is ok and in good spirits. They took her deposition this morning."

"How do you manage to get to see her then?"

"I am supposed to be one of her doctors. But do not worry, Tom, I have not examined her."

They both laughed, but before departing, Tony said, "By the way, neither the brother nor the doctor knows me as Tony Benedetti. To them I am Doctor Jaime Garcia. I would appreciate it if you kept it that in mind and my real name in secret."

"You got it, buddy; I shall carry all your secrets to my grave unless, of course you die before me."

They laughed again, got up, embraced, and said good night.

Tony never told Tom that he was staying at the same hotel where he was until the very last minute when he said: "You can find me in room 366. Have pleasant dreams."

"You sneaky son of a bitch, when were you planning to tell me that we have both been staying at the same hotel?"

He got no response from Tony; he simply waved his hand at Tom.

Before going to his own room, and just to be sure, Tom stopped at the bar to see if Juan was still there, but it was too late, and the bar was closed.

He expected that Juan would be going to be working the next day. But just in case He left him a note simple saying that he wanted to buy some lottery tickets from his friend.

Tony Benedetti went to his room, taking the stairs rather than the elevators because, for the first time in his life, he was confused.

Tony had no doubt about what he was going to do, because he was determined to do it, but he was confused because he was not sure what his real motives for doing it were.

Why was he doing this? Why would He be risking his life?

He admitted that he was highly attracted to Tanya.

But was he in love with her also?

He tried to justify himself by thinking that he was doing it to screw the CIA, which he hated with all his heart. Or perhaps it was because he had kept inside that old loyalty that soldiers have towards their comrades in arms. Tanya was a soldier, as much as he was; her brother was a soldier, and, last but not least, a soldier was his old buddy, Tom Hopeland, who was in love with the same girl he had warm feelings for.

He certainly had been happy to reacquaint and have dinner with Tom.

But Tony knew that he was not being totally sincere with himself. Was he doing it really and mostly because he had fallen in love with the girl.?

And what about Tom Hopeland and his feelings for her? Would it be possible for two men to share the love of the same girl? He remembered having seen a movie about that a long time before.

And what if that was not possible, what if this was really love? And what if Tom got in his way?

Would he be able to take his old buddy out?

Tony really did not know. Maybe he was getting old and soft with old age.

He was not able to sleep well that night.

Meanwhile, elsewhere in the city, Doctor K had placed a small Guatemalan flag on his window.

# TWENTY-EIGHT
## Fort Matamoros
## Guatemala City
## September 28, 1968

General Guillermo Kruger was furiously pacing the floor.

He was not held prisoner in a cell or a dungeon; he was lodged in the officer's quarters. The room had a regular bed, a night table, a desk, a dining table, a comfortable sofa, reclining chair, and a complete bathroom adjacent to his room. A small television set and a radio were sitting on an additional table.

The most important local Newspapers, *El Imparcial* and *La Hora*, were delivered daily to him, so he was up to date with the current events.

He, however, had no telephone nor access to one. Other than his son, and his lawyers, no visitors were allowed. There were two sentinels, one on each side of the door, but they hardly ever came inside.

The General was allowed to go outside his room for walks in the fort courtyard but always under his sentries' vigilant eyes. He had his meals in his room and always had them tasted by the server before eating them, fearing that he could be poisoned. He was allowed to have wine and booze as much as he wished but he requested that the bottles were closed with the original cork or top.

The General had just finished reading the local papers, and he was furious. Both papers had headlines reporting that a deposition had been taken from his daughter and, according to an anonymous source, the daughter's declarations had been devastating to General Kruger.

He could not believe what he read, so he demanded to see Colonel Oliva, Zelaya, Benitez, Camacho, or all four and get the full story from any of them.

Oliva, who by then, and supposedly due to his exceedingly good services to his Country, had been promoted to General, was the first to respond, sending a message that he would visit General Kruger later that afternoon.

General Kruger took that response as an offense, considering that not long ago, if he had summoned Oliva to his office, he would have come immediately, even if he was taking a shit and had not yet cleaned his butt.

Oh, but he will get out of this place, beat this rap, prove his innocence, and then deal properly with these fucking traitors!

Oliva showed up a couple of hours later and pretended to be very nice and polite. Kruger was loud, rude, demanding, insulting, aggressive and in general continued acting like he was still the boss and in control of the situation. He demanded to see his daughter, or to be set free immediately to go confront her.

Oliva, very aware that he had the upper hand, listened patiently to the General's tirade and trying to maintain his composure spoke softly: "My dear Willy, I am afraid that you do not fully understand your situation.

"Most of the other officers and I, even the Gringos, were at first, finding difficult to believe that you were the mastermind of the mess of the kidnapping of the US Ambassador. I still do not believe it. However, when your own daughter is accusing you of it and, now, she is doing it after giving a deposition under oath, it is very little that I can do for you, Willy."

"You can fix this for me, you traitor son of a bitch. I know you can, so do it damn you!"

"I would like to do it, Willy. You know that I would do it, but it is now out of my hands. Even the President and the Vice-president are afraid to speak in your defense. Your daughter's testimony is just too strong and devastating."

Oliva stopped, took a deep breath, and continued: "If you do not believe me, here it is, listen to it. This is the tape of her deposition. See what you think after you hear it.

"I will leave you alone for now; thereafter you give me your opinion. I will be back in a couple of hours."

Oliva placed a small cassette player on the table, in front of General Kruger, put a cassette tape next to it and left the room.

Once out of the room, he went looking for a telephone and when found one, he called his friends General Ramiro Zelaya, General Mario Camacho, and Colonel Benito Benitez.

It was a brief conversation, as he did not want to talk too long, he simply desired to get their agreement on what to do next.

Yes, General Willy was obviously behaving as General Willy, loud and abusive, but now he is listening to the tape of his daughter's deposition."

He stopped to listen to the person on the other end of the line and then said, "I am willing to bet my rank that not only he be more upset after that, but also that he will demand an interview with her as soon as possible.

"Of course, we cannot risk taking him to the hospital to see the daughter, on the other hand, although she is still weak and has a broken ankle, with a cast in it, she would be able to come here. And, in her condition, I am sure she would not be able to escape. So, unless she is really Wonder Woman, she cannot go anywhere.

"Besides, nobody will know the day, time, or hour on which that meeting will take place as only her doctors, nurses, and her brother are allowed to visit her. And neither would be informed about it until the last moment."

All agreed and General Zelaya added, "We should give Willy that as his last wish before his last supper."

They all laughed and understood and agreed that the time had come to finish the feared and hated General Guillermo Kruger Larrave reign of terror.

After that conversation, General Ricardo Oliva called his liquor store, ordered two bottles of *Neidenberg Helden Riesling's* 1960 white wine to be delivered to his office and went back to see General Kruger.

Just as he expected, Kruger was more furious than before and had smashed the cassette player against the wall, destroying it completely, also breaking the cassette, and unrolling the tape.

"This is total and complete fucking bullshit. It is all lies. I do not know what you gave to her or what you did to her, but that is not my daughter. That was not my beautiful, beautiful little girl.

"You bastards did something to her, brainwashed her, poisoned her, tortured her, something to make her said those lies about me."

"Come on Willy, calm down, I cannot believe her story either, but perhaps you have not paid much attention to her lately.

"Do you know when she joined the FAR? Did you know when she stopped being Lily Marie and became Tanya? Didn't she kill the US Ambassador? Didn't she send the ransom money to your office? Didn't she, as you claim, shoot you with tranquilizing darts and took that money from you?

"Think about all those things, Willy Think about all those things."

"But why, Oliva? Why would my beloved little girl do something like that to the father who had given her everything and anything she wished for?"

"I don't know Willy that is a question that only she and you can respond."

"Precisely, that is exactly what I want to do. Can you take me to see her Oliva?"

Oliva was delighted, that was exactly the request that he expected the General to make, and he much preferred that it came from him, rather than at his suggestion. He had rehearsed several times his answer to that request.

"Of course, Willy, I think that is the best thing for you to do. Confront her. Ask questions. Maybe she has lost her mind.

"However, as you know this is a very delicate and complicated matter because, true or false, those accusations are, or will be of public domain. And both you and your daughter are right now considered dangerous criminals to be keep under lock and heavy guard.

"Thank God that you have friends, like me, otherwise you be locked up in the dungeons and eating the shitty food that prisoners eat. You do realize, of course, that you are receiving VIP treatment? What had you done if I was in your situation, Willy?"

The General did not answer immediately and did not give thanks to Oliva, simply saying, "Do whatever you can, but make it happen."

Oliva left and phoned again to the other generals: "He took the bait. He wants to be taken to see his daughter."

"No way, Jose! That would be way too risky. He is going to take that chance and dash," said Benitez.

"He still has loyal men amongst the enlisted men; they can try to pry him out," said Camacho.

"And let us not forget the paramilitaries, rumor is that he has an army of them, and all are ruthless killers," said Zelaya.

"Then we bring the girl here. She is not much at risk for escaping. She was seriously wounded. Had a hole in her liver and several in her intestines. She had to have several inches of those removed, and, in addition, she has a broken ankle that is still in the cast. There is no way that she can escape in such a pitiful condition."

"Ok then. We will bring the girl here. I believe the day after tomorrow would be a good day."

"Day after tomorrow it is then."

"And, after that, the last supper for General Willy"

# Twenty-nine:
## *Casino Militar*
## Guatemala City
## September 30, 1968

The would-be rescuers of Tanya Kruger met for lunch at the *Casino Militar*, basically to get acquainted with each other and to go over their plans.

This was at the suggestion of Captain Kruger, who thought that the best way to avoid suspiciousness and the secret police was to meet in plain view and at a public, military place.

Doctor K and Tom Hopeland had already informed Carlos and Maria about the meeting.

At first, they were hesitant but, in the end, they figured that there was nothing to lose—except their lives—and if that was the only way to liberate their commandant from the government's grip, they were willing to risk them.

Carlos and Maria had to shop for simple but proper attire to wear at the luncheon. Maria wore a simple pink dress, black high-heeled shoes, and a black necklace with matching black earrings. She carried a large black handbag on which she carried a Smith-Wesson 9mm pistol and several clips of ammunition. She looked very pretty despite wearing very little makeup.

Carlos wore beige trousers, brown laced shoes, and a dark blue blazer. He had a Beretta 9mm tucked on the back of his belt.

They arrived separately, about five minutes apart. A waiter showed them to a table placed in a private room next to the main dining room. There were a couple of guys at the bar, which were already too drunk to pay any attention to them. Otherwise, the place was empty, as expected on a weekday at 2.30 in the afternoon.

Tony, aka Dr. Garcia, was already there, so after the introductions, Captain Kruger ordered a bottle of wine, which Maria declined to drink and asked for a Coke instead. Carlos preferred to drink rum and Coke.

That bottle was consumed by Dr. K, Dr. Garcia, Captain Kruger, and Tom Copeland, followed by another one after the meeting.

Captain Kruger had a lot of questions to ask Maria and Carlos. Questions relating mostly to the Battle of Avenida Elena and her sister's role in such battle, both denied having been there because of fear that he would blame them for his sister's fate and accused them of having abandoned her.

Then they hadve a simple lunch, chicken, beef, vegetables, fruit, and dessert. The bottle of wine was finished by the four guys. Carlos limited himself to one drink and had water only thereafter.

Then a copy of the list of items needed was given to each one and the plot to rescue their beloved leader Tanya was discussed in detail. The role of each one of them was discussed and each of the six was requested to ask questions and make suggestions as they feel necessary.

After explaining the idea of the sniper and hijacking the vehicle carrying Tanya. They discussed the blocking of the streets with trucks or buses and finally the getaway car and the need for a woman's body, dead or alive, to be buried at the ranch instead of Tanya.

Maria would oversee that, and she would drive the person, or corpse, to the ranch a day or so ahead of the day of the rescue.

Tom Hopeland would also drive early to the ranch to make sure that the airplane was in good condition and ready to fly to Mexico.

Captain Kruger would ride with his sister, after rescuing her from the Hospital.

They then discussed the need for several additional men, one to be with Tony on the roof of the building, another to be a lookout at the Fort of Matamoros and report by radio the moment that Tanya left from the fort to be taken back to the hospital.

Two more men would be needed to steal and drive the trucks to block the path of any would-be pursuer, one more to drive the getaway car, and one more to drive a car to the parking lot where they were going to leave the ambulance and change vehicles.

"That is a total of six men or five more besides Carlos," Explained Tony B.

Carlos spoke for the first time and said: "We can certainly provide that many men, and more if needed, but I believe that the more persons involved, the more likely that someone's tongue slips. The less they know the better it be; especially important is the fact that we need to make everyone think that the commander is dead and keep secret after the fact that she is alive. Of course, that is if Doctor Garcia does not miss"

Garcia interrupted, "I never miss my friend, I never miss."

"At least not yet," interrupted Tom Hopeland

Carlos said: "I hope, for your own sake, that you will not miss this time either, doctor."

That sounded like a threat, but it only made Garcia smile.

Carlos continued, "I believe that the person doing the lookout at the fort, the person driving the ambulance or whatever vehicle she be on, and the person driving the final getaway car to the ranch can be the same person. And I want to be that person, I can do it and I want to do it, I want to see the commandant, and tell her that we did it for her."

"And how did you propose to do that Carlos?" asked Tony aka Dr Garcia.

"Simply. Captain Kruger will drive the getaway car to the Oakland Mall parking garage early in the morning, leave it there, then take a cab to the hospital, or one of our men can drive him".

"Good idea, that eliminates the need for one man," said Kruger. "I can take the family wagon and leave it at the mall then take a cab. The cab idea is better, I think."

Carlos continued explaining: "OK then, Captain Kruger. I will ride a motorcycle to the front of the Fort and hide in the bushes across from the fort or in a house nearby. I have the radio with me, and I radio Doctor Garcia, informing him when the ambulance with the Kruger siblings is leaving Matamoros and heading back to the hospital.

"Then, I ride my bike again, get to the hospital, way ahead of the motorcade, as motorcycles can wave through traffic, and I believe the motorcade would not exceed the speed limits. Thereafter, I park the bike in one of the side streets, near the hospital, go to the restaurant across from the hospital main entrance for coffee and a sandwich and wait.

"When I see that Captain Kruger has freed his sister, I jump on the driver of the ambulance, wait for the captain to load his sister into it, and drive away.

"As soon as we pass the intersection our men in the trucks will block the front and the back street intersections. One of them can use my motorcycle to get away, so we may only need one other motorcycle, unless they want to ride piggyback.

"However, I do not recommend, piggyback, as I prefer them to ride alone and in different directions."

"How do we know that nobody is going to steal the getaway car from the parking lot at the mall?"

"We don't, so we can either put one of my guys to watch it or we could easily steal another one. I prefer option one, the man will not need to know why he was watching that car"?

"Seems like a good idea. It puts two less men in danger of their lives," said Captain Kruger."

"Ok, that makes sense to me also, Let's do it that way then. Are you all in agreement?" said Tony Benedetti.

All raised their hands.

"Now the biggest problem, will be that of procuring a female body, and a relatively young one," said Tom Hopeland.

"As a last resort, we can shoot a random woman in the street. I have no problem with that," said Tony

"We do," said everyone else.

Then Maria intervened for the first time. "We need someone that is sick, destitute, addicted, and tired of living. And I believe I know such a person. I will bring her to the ranch, but I would not kill her. One of you must do it, but not me."

"Fair enough," said Tony. "I can accept and respect the lady's feeling.

"I can certainly do it, but I would not be at the ranch, and I do not think my friend Tom has the stomach for it either. That leaves only you, Carlos You will have to do it."

Carlos reluctantly agreed to do the killing, and then said that he and his men would oversee procuring the vehicles, the radio, the weapons, and the bikes.

"It is settled then. There is only one last thing before we go our separate ways. Ms. Kruger and Maria need passports to travel to Mexico. I will not have any problem having someone make them in less than a couple of hours, but I do need pictures.

"You, Maria, can go to *Photo Serra*, which is just around the corner on Sixth Avenue, and have your photo taken for less than ten Quetzales. Just make sure it is for an American passport, I believe they are of a different size than the ones for a Guatemalan passport.

"Captain Kruger here is the treasurer of the group; he can give you the money to pay for the picture."

"I do not need your money. I have some of my own and certainly I can afford to pay ten Quetzales. Thank you very much."

"Sorry Maria, I did not mean to offend you. I apologize."

"If we also need a passport for Ms. Kruger, and one for me because the FBI took mine. But Ms. Kruger cannot walk to *Photo Serra*. How can we solve that?" said Tom Hopeland.

"I hope she has a passport somewhere in the house. It does not have to be a recent one, right?" said Captain Kruger.

"No, it does not need to be a recent one. My forger will need to make some alterations on her picture anyway. The only thing is that we need them today, and as soon as possible, so, as soon as you have the pictures you can bring them to the *Camino Real* and leave them at the front desk. 'To be delivered to Professor Hopeland.'

"So, if there is nothing further to discuss and no further questions, we can now go our separate ways."

"One more question," said Maria. "How are we going to know the date when the commandant is going to be traveling to Fort Matamoros to meet her dad?"

"I shall continue visiting her at the hospital, and hopefully I will be able to place a listening device somewhere in her room. And I will also keep my eyes and ears peeled. Also, I have other ways.

"You Maria and Carlos, will check with Juan, at the Hotel bar, or with me, Professor Copeland, or Captain Kruger, couple of times per day we will leave messages at the front desk of the hotel, simply saying 'meeting tomorrow' and the approximate time."

"Ok, fine, hope will see you again soon.

# THIRTY
## The Temple of Santo Domingo
## September 30, 1938
## Guatemala City

Maria's first stop was at *Photo Serra* to have her picture taken. After that she went to change her clothes for more casual ones.

Thereafter she looked for a liquor store and bought five bottles of *Indita Quetzalteca*, the cheapest, but also most popular clear rum, in the Country.

Her quest was to find a surrogate for Tanya, someone to take her place on the grave. It had to be Claudia Gonzalez, aka "Stinky."

Maria had a vague idea where to find her, therefore, she drove around the area of the General Hospital, *la Capilla de El Señor de las Misericordias* (The Chapel of the Lord of Mercy's), the *Cathedral Metropolitana*, and eventually the Church of Santo Domingo.

The latter was because she remembered that the next day was the beginning of October, the month of the Rosary, and there would be a heavy pilgrimage to that church for the whole month. Long ago, Maria visited that church daily during October with her mother and prayed the rosary together.

Maria had not been to Church since leaving her nursing position at the hospital and becoming a member of the FAR. She felt a strong desire to go inside, but she felt so guilty and dirty about what she was about to do that did not dare to see the face of the mother of Christ or that of her son, Jesus, for that matter.

Maria found "Stinky" there, passed out on the dirt at the side of the church main gate. Exceedingly dirty, smelling of alcohol, urine, and vomit.

Maria was strong and Claudia was mostly skin and bones, so it would not have been a problem for her to lift her up and carry her to the car, even though she had parked a couple of blocks away from the church. Yet, perhaps for the first time in her life, and indeed for the first time in her nursing career, she felt nauseated by the smell and dirt coming from the woman.

She did not know what to do.

Maria was no longer wearing the dress she wore at the lunch meeting, a day earlier. She was wearing an old T-shirt, jeans and sneakers. But still…perhaps if she had brought gloves, or an apron, the only thing she was sure of was that she was not going to let this feeling of repulsion interfere with her mission.

She stood there, watching the shred of humanity that the drunk woman snoring at her feet had become and thinking of what to do, when a couple of beggars, dirty and reeking of alcohol, came to her, asking for some coins.

Maria had an idea.

She gave a twenty-five cent coin to each one of them and offered two Quetzales a piece if they helped to get "Stinky" to her car. They would not have to go all the way to where she was parked. Maria would drive around, park in front of the atrium of the church and all they had to do was to carry her to her car.

The beggars knew "Stinky," and they became curious and protective, asking questions like "why" and, "where are you taking her" and "who are you?"

But Maria was very convincing. She told them that she was a distant relative and a nurse, that she had just found out about the misery that Claudia was living in and was going to take her to a rehabilitation place to cure her illness, sober her up, clean her and hopefully rehabilitate her.

The men were hesitant initially, but when Maria added to their reward the promise of a bottle of "*Indita*," they happily agreed.

It was done as promised, and the two men went away happily to drink themselves to oblivion at the nearest park while Claudia Gonzalez was slumped in the back seat of Maria's car on her way to meet death.

But first she had to be cleaned, somewhere, as she was stinking the car. There was no way she was going to drive out of town to the ranch in Escuintla, with that stink on it.

So, Maria decided to stop first at the safe house behind "*El Cerro del Carmen*," in Zona 6

Once there, she sprayed Claudia down with a garden hose, burned down her clothes and dressed her in clean ones.

Yes, that certainly took some time, but she had some to spare, the big event would not take place until the next day and there were only a couple of hours of driving from the city to the Kruger Ranch.

It was beginning to get dark, at about 6.30 in the evening, Maria was not concerned about driving at night. There was nothing suspicious about two women driving alone to the Northwest Coast of the Country. Sure there were the robbers and the corrupt police, but Maria had been dealing with those for years and knew how to properly handle them, either by cunning or by force.

The only thing Maria would try her best not to do was to bond with her passenger and she knew that the best way to do that was to keep her stone drunk.

The downside to that was that Claudia's body was limp like a rag, and she had to drag her out of the car, hose her down right there in the patio, cut down her clothes, burn them in the back yard, and give Claudia another bath. This time using soap and shampoo and then dressing her in clean clothes.

The hair and the makeup would be done at the Ranch later.

Nevertheless, Maria felt pity for the poor woman, who naked did not appear to weight more than seventy pounds.

She is already dead, was Maria's conclusion, consolation, and justification.

She has been dead for years. We will be doing her a favor. Her death will serve to save a life and perhaps will redeem her of her sins.

After all, Claudia had been tried to kill herself many times before, often, and for many years, and always failing.

This time, she will be liberated! This time, she will be set free!

Despite these thoughts Maria had tears in her eyes thinking about the pitiful wasted life that this poor wretch of a woman had endured

Maria was involved in these thoughts when she heard a car coming and the front gate of the house being opened. Maria reached for her gun and was ready to fire when she recognized the driver of the service truck that was pulling in.

Carlos was the one driving it.

"I see you found a substitute for the commander, Comrade Maria. It sure is skinny. I guess you could not find someone with more skin and fat over the bones…that woman is a walking skeleton… If she can walk at all".

That Was Carlos's greeting.

"Thank you, comrade Carlos, but I guess you know that there are not too many expendable females with the looks of Commander Tanya unless we were to kidnap one of the blue-blooded ladies from the Club Guatemala or the Country Club."

"Of course not, Maria. I was just joking. This woman will have to do, same as this truck, wagon, or whatever you want to call it would have to do. Both will look different when we put some makeup on them."

"Indeed, I am leaving tonight with her, so I will have some time to try to transform her so she will have some resemblance with the boss."

"Good luck with that. Just make sure that nobody looks closely at this pitiful creature."

"And good luck to you with the transformation of the van. Seems you got a bakery delivery truck. What are you trying to convert it into?"

"A van from the electric company. It actually has a guy inside. The driver."

"Oh my god, Carlos! That is not good or clever. Hope he is alive and you are not planning to harm him."

"He is alive, all right and I promise I won't hurt him; We will just keep him here until we finish the job."

"Ok, I believe you. Now, please, help me to finish cleaning this woman and getting her dressed, then help me to put her in the back seat of my car."

"Sure. But it seems like she is waking up, also she still smells pretty bad. You help me to take this guy, the driver of the van, inside and lock him up in a room then I will help you with her."

"Be glad to help. You kidnapped the driver, you deal with him. Is he hooded, I hope? "

Maria looked inside the van and after taking a glance, she said: "Of course, he is. I should know that you do everything by the book. As far as the woman is concerned, you should have smelled her before I hosed her down and gave her the first bath."

Carlos just said: "Let's give her some more booze, so she may go back to sleep."

"She had enough of that to last a lifetime, but you are right, I need her quiet and asleep."

Claudia was waking up and becoming restless and aggressive. To the point that Carlos thought that may be best just to put a bullet on her head right there and then. Maria opposed that and gently and with a soothing voice she talked to woman just coming out of a drunken stupor.

"Claudia, Claudia. Listen! Do You remember me? I am a nurse. I am taking you to a place where you can be cured and cleaned. Yes, I know you have been there, but this is different. We are not going to take the alcohol cold turkey from you.

We will do it gradually and meanwhile you can drink all you want. See, here is a bottle, I will open it for you, and you can have a drink. Just trust me and calm down. Ok?"

Maria put the clear rum in a glass filled halfway and handled it the woman who swallowed it in one gulp. Then she took another and passed out again.

Maria and Carlos put her in the back seat of the car and took three more bottles with her, in the hope that three-and-a-half bottles of booze would be enough to hold her until their arrival to the Kruger Ranch.

But just in case she would stop at the nearest pharmacy to buy some Valium pills, she would put some of it in the next drink for Claudia.

# THIRTY-ONE:
## *CASTILLO MATAMOROS*
## GUATEMALA CITY
## OCTOBER 2ST 1968

Tanya was still dazed and sleepy, mostly due to the sleeping pills and painkillers that she was giving quite regularly. The Pills she needed, because without them she was unable to sleep and, although no longer needed Morphine or Demerol by injection to kill her pain, she still was given some opiates in a pill form.

It was barely daylight when the Nurse Sergeant brought her breakfast. She was not hungry, but she told the nurse to place the tray on the small, wheeled table where she used to put her food every day.

The breakfast consisted of the usual, scrambled eggs, two pancakes, milk, two pieces of toast, small glass of orange juice, and coffee, she only nibbled on the toast and pancakes, drank the coffee, and asked for help to go to the bathroom to wash her teeth.

The female nurse, although a male-looking woman, named Laura, said: "Make yourself pretty, young lady. I will help you to take a shower, then comb your hair, apply makeup and put on a pretty dress. We are taking you to see your father this morning."

"How come, nobody told me, and why only me? How about my brother? Is my brother coming? The General is his father also."

"I don't know anything about your brother, young lady. My orders are to get you ready only. And let me remind you, spoiled pretty brat, that this is not one of those fancy hotels you are used to lodging in. In fact, I do not know why you are in this private and expensive hospital at all.

As far as I am concerned you should be in the military hospital or in the infirmary of the jail. That is where terrorists like you should be. So, get on with it."

"Well, you may be right about that, Nurse Laura, but meanwhile, tell whoever gives you orders that I am not going to go anywhere without my brother. You can shoot me if you want, but I would not go anywhere without him."

Seeing her determination, the nurse gave up and spoke softer and gentler. "Ok, just because I like you, I am going to call my superior and ask if it is ok to include your brother in the party. He would not be too hard to locate, that brother of yours is in the hospital almost 24/7 since the day you arrived."

"That is my dear brother, and I remind you, Laura, that my brother is your superior officer and so is Doctor Garcia, you can ask them."

"Sorry, I was ordered not to take orders from your bother, as for Doctor Garcia, I have not seen him this morning, he comes later in the morning usually.

"So, let me help you to the shower and then I shall call my superior officer and see about including your brother in the trip."

Tanya agreed and, with the support of the nurse, managed to get in the shower. She took a cool shower followed by a hot one and felt much better after that.

She was able to walk by herself, with the help of crutches, out of the bathroom, walk to the small closet without the help of the nurse and put on a pink, almost red dress that she had no idea who placed in there, or how, but she guessed that her brother had bought it.

She was unable to wear high heels and almost fell trying, therefore ended up wearing an old sneaker on the healthy foot only. The other had a cast on it.

Nurse Laura returned to the room and, after eating the rest of the breakfast that Lily Marie had not eaten, she was in a happier and friendlier mood.

"Good news, young lady. My boss said that it is ok for Captain Kruger to ride with us to see your dad."

It was almost ten in the morning by the time the party finally boarded the ambulance on which the Kruger siblings were going to ride.

Lily Marie was seating on a wheelchair and wheeled to the back of an army ambulance while handcuffed to the left wrist of Nurse Laura.

Captain Kruger, after having been stripped of his service pistol and frisked several times for other arms, was frisked once again by the soldier driving shotgun with the ambulance driver. Finding the flask, he opened it and took a sip, confirming that it contained rum and not acid or some other toxic substance. But he missed the additional container at the false bottom; the one containing the blood. It was not until the last moment that he was allowed to climb to be back of the vehicle to join his sister and the nurse.

The caravan was preceded by a Jeep with four, well-armed soldiers, the ambulance in the middle, followed by another Jeep, with three soldiers and a 50-caliber machinegun mounted in the back. Of the three soldiers, one was standing to be able to fire the 50 caliber, the other two being the driver and one seating next, all carrying M16 assault type rifles.

A total of nine soldiers, plus Nurse Laura, who although unarmed—from the fear of being attacked and disarmed by her patient—was a big woman and likely trained to fight in hand-to-hand combat.

Captain Kruger thought that the odds of rescuing his sister, and coming out of this alive, were slim. But he knew also that he would never forgive himself if did not try.

All in all, it was past 10.15 when the caravan left the front entrance of the hospital.

Captain Kruger knew that it was almost a straight shot from there to Fort Matamoros if they took 12 Avenue North, then a short drive around *El Cerrito del Carmen* (the El Carmen little hill) and a few blocks from there, standing tall, alongside a modern four lanes road and separated from the nearest neighborhood by a deep ravine stood the Matamoros Fort.

Maybe twenty minutes' drive from their current location, with the somewhat light traffic of that hour. The return might take a bit longer, perhaps half an hour, since it may take place at lunchtime when workers go out to lunch and traffic increases.

Captain Kruger proved to be correct with his previous estimations, exactly twenty minutes later, the first Jeep reached the gates of the fort.

It took another ten minutes, and another search, before they were ushered across the vast patio and through the old passages, till they reached the officers' room where General Kruger was held in detention.

The two soldiers guarding the door, saluted Captain Kruger and stepped aside to allow the Kruger siblings and the nurse inside the room.

The General, dressed in full military fatigues, and wearing all his medals, rose from the chair behind the small desk and approached his children with his arms open to embrace them.

His embrace was ignored by both siblings.

They noticed that there was an open bottle of Riesling, four wine glasses and a tape recording on top of the desk. The tape recorder was in the on mode.

There was also a well-dressed, spectacled, middle-aged man, with thinning white hair, sitting on a chair by the desk, the man was introduced to them by their father as "my lawyer".

The general asked, "Why, Lily Marie? Why?"

Lily Marie spoke next. "Although you know why because I told you why at the house when you gave me the briefcase with the ransom money, I am willing to repeat it all in detail."

"If you really do not remember General? Your lawyer here will argue that it is perhaps because the bump in your head made you forget part of it. So, if you want to hear it again, here it is, this is why all this shit is happening."

Lily Marie stop talking and said, "However, I am not going to tell you anything unless that fucking tape recorder and all these fucking people are out of this room. This is a private family matter, not a family circus, nor a deposition, which I have already given".

"But Lily, I need your testimony to exonerate me. To show that I did not do any of those things they are accusing me of."

"If that is what you expect me to do, you are totally wrong and, if anything, I am going to tell you, and tell them, that, yes, you planned the whole thing, as I have been saying all along. "

"But why Lily. Why?"

"Want to know why? I know you know why, but I will repeat it. So, get everyone out of this room except you, me and Mario, and I will repeat to you over and over the reason why"!

"Ok, you heard my daughter, everybody out, and that includes you Richard (addressing the Lawyer) and you, nurse, whatever your name is."

"We also want the soldiers to move away from the door. There may be some shouting that we do not want them to hear." said Captain Mario Kruger

"Do it, Richard please go wait in the visitor's lounge, and tell the soldiers to move twenty feet from the door. My daughter is not going to try to escape from this fort. She is too weak for that, and this is a fortress with over 300 soldiers in it."

Nurse Laura reluctantly removed the handcuffs from Tanya and walked out of the room.

The General poured a generous amount of wine, from a bottle behind his desk, offered some to his children, who refused it, and drank the whole glass in one gulp. Then sat behind the desk while offering seats in front of the desk to his children.

"Ok, now are you going to tell me why?"

"Because you killed our mother, Dad, and because I did not have the guts to kill you myself dear father.

"Oh, I did try! For a couple of nights, I was at the foot of your bed with a gun ready to fire, but I could not do it. So instead of killing you, I decided to kill your image, prestige, pride, your goddammed Nazi pride."

"I did not kill your mother, she killed herself. I was not even in town when she did it. The Police found the note she left."

"We know you did not pull the trigger, but just the same, you killed her. Do you remember what that note said, Father? It said I CAN NOT TAKE IT ANYMORE"

"Your mother was sick, she was depressed. She could never get over the death of her mother. I had nothing to do with it."

"Stop lying to us and to yourself, Dad. Lizzy found Mom's diary. It tells all the horror that she suffered from you," said Mario Kruger.

"Like I said, she was a sick woman; she imagined things. She made stories in her mind "

"Oh really! Stories like you abusing her physically and verbally, more so after grandma died. Stories like forcing her to have sex under threats to her life, and all while telling her about the horrendous things you did to the poor souls you put in the dungeons?" said Tanya.

"Yes dad, you even had some of those poor guys drop down from helicopters into the crater of active volcanoes" said the General's son.

"Those you refer to as poor souls and poor guys, were rebels and traitors. I was just doing my job, as you should Captain Kruger. There are still a lot of rebels out there to catch and bring to justice and you should be busy doing that."

"Justice? Why don't you admit that you are a sadist, a sick man who enjoys inflicting pain and watching people suffer?"

"And what about cheating? The womanizing, and the child abuse? Some of those girls were as young as 13 years old, mostly peasant girls from the ranch. I wonder how many you impregnated and how many brothers or sisters we have over there."

"You even gave mother an STD, chlamydia, she talks about that on her dairy."

"I am a man, a man has needs, most of those women came to me voluntarily or were given to me by their parents. And now most of them have husbands and own small houses at the ranch or in the nearby towns, all given to them by me."

"Of course, they will come to you, who would say no to the mighty general Guillermo Kruger? specially a mighty general with the bloody reputations that you have made for yourself.

201

"And what about the others, the ones who gave themselves to you in exchange for the lives or freedom of their children, husbands or brothers?

"Did you at least have the integrity to comply with their requests after you were done with them, or you laughed on their faces and send them away? Or perhaps you put them in prison or killed them as well.

"You are a real monster. You even had mom's chihuahua dog Nena killed."

"Nena was a nasty, little beast, who hated my guts I should have shot her in the head sooner, instead of paying the vet to put her down painlessly."

"You are a sick bastard, Dad. And to think that at some point in my life I wanted to be like you," said the general's son.

Tanya added, "Also, you are a thief, and a traitor. You betrayed President Arbenz, who was your friend, and you sold him and our country to the gringos, getting in payment for your deeds his ranch, just as Judas got his coins."

""The government confiscated that ranch, because it had been bought with money stolen from the people. They auctioned it and I bought it with my own money," said the general.

"That is a lie; that ranch had been purchased with Arbenz's wife's money, as she belonged to one of the richest families from El Salvador."

"We don't know how you can sleep at night, Father. Don't you have nightmares?"

"Assuming that some of those absurd accusations are true, how does all that relate to the situation I am in right now?"

"You still don't get it, do you, Dad? Mom killed herself because she could not take it anymore. She knew divorce was not an option as she was such a fanatic Catholic, and also because she knew you would never let her go."

"I loved your mother. I still do. She never mentioned divorce… I don't know if I would have let her go."

"Bullshit! Dad, you are not capable of loving anyone but yourself."

"I love you guys. I really do."

202

"I hope so, that is why I first joined FAR. I was hoping to get caught knowing that that would be a public humiliation and a low blow to your ego.

"But gradually, I began to realize that those FAR people really believe in what they are fighting for. They believe that they can make a difference, a better Guatemala via an armed struggle and by destroying the old institutions all ruled by people like you, and they are willing to die for it."

Tanya took a breath, got a glass from the table, put water on it, took a sip, then continued:

"While you thought I was still at Berkley, I was training in Cuba. I learned fast and became a good fighter and leader.

"When I returned, I returned home while conducting operations for the FAR on the side.

"Soon I was promoted to commander of a cell. We were responsible for robbing banks and kidnapping rich people for ransom. I tried very hard not to kill anyone, and so far, I am proud to say that I haven't."

"Oh, no? How about the many men who died at Avenida Elena?"

"That is different, Father. That was a battle; they could have killed me the same as we killed them.

"I guess you do not know that. After all, you, the mighty General Kruger, descendant of Germanic warriors, never been in an actual battle. You gave yourself and your country up to the CIA in 1954, without firing a single shot...shame."

"Arbenz and his government were communists, we were patriots defending our country, our faith, our families against the Russian infiltration."

"That is total bullshit, and you know it. That was exactly what the CIA, the right-wingers, the cowards in the army, and the Catholic church wanted the people to believe. But I know that you knew back then, that there were no communists in the Arbenz government and that the only Russian in Guatemala was the Vodka."

Tanya took another sip of water and continued. "And you also know that all the repression, which followed the so-called

Liberation, all the killings, all the false imprisonments, all the exiles, and all the selling of Guatemala to the United Fruit Company, and other foreign corporations, all that took place with your complicity, and with your help. Those are the reasons why we are fighting this war again."

"You will lose, and you all be dead".

"Wrong again, Dad. We will win. I may be dead by then, but we will win. We will win because we are right."

"What about the US Ambassador"?

"The death of the ambassador was an accident. We were supposed to kidnap him and get some of our comrades free, plus some cash in exchange for his release, but the stupid guy had a John Wayne complex. Instead of surrendering, he came out shooting and almost killed one of my men, who fired back in self-defense and, most unfortunately, caused a mortal wound to Mr. Mein."

"Now, little sister, tell us how you concocted the plan to get the General blamed for the kidnapping and killing of the ambassador."

"That came to me after we were ordered to kidnap Mr. Mein. I figured that if his government or his family were willing to pay a ransom, I would have it delivered to my dad, while I take money from my own bank account to give to the FAR. That is why I was willing to negotiate a reduction on the amount of the ransom. You know the rest."

"Ok but now that you had your revenge. You will tell them the truth, won't you honey?"

"You think? Dad, as far as I am concerned you should rot in jail, before roasting in hell. No father, I am not going to recant my story, on the contrary, I am thinking on adding some more to it, like the Arbenz Ranch part perhaps."

"That Ranch will be yours someday, I do not know if you are stupid enough to throw that away. You little ungrateful pieces of shit. I have always been a good father to you both. I have given you all you ever wanted." The General said this while approaching his daughter with the arm raised and ready to slap her in the face.

Captain Kruger got in between them and held his father's arm.

"Don't you dare to hit my little sister, Dad, don't you dare."

Mario Kruger was tall, and leaner and of course younger than his father, so the grip on his arm was very strong.

"*E tu Brutae?*" the General said, quoting the words of Julius Cesar as he was being stabbed by Brutus and other members of the Roman Senate.

His son let go of his arm.

"I tried to make an officer and a gentleman out of you, it seems like I failed."

"No, Dad, you tried to make me a man like you, and at some point in my life I wanted to be. But not since reading Mum's dairy. You are not a man, you are a psychopath, a monster.

And I do not want to be like you.

In fact, I never wanted to be in the Military, and now, more than ever, I don't think I want to be part of this military establishment, who represents and protects everything that is wrong with this Country and creates individuals like you."

"You are blaspheming now son, the military represents law and order, without them there will be chaos in every society."

"That is the Nazi way, and do you remember what the Nazi way did to Germany and to all Europe, not to mention the six million Jews that were gassed and burned.?"

"There was law and order in Europe under the Nazi, the Jews were parasites."

"Your mother was a Jew, remember?"

"Yes, she was, but she converted to Christianity, and we were not raised in the Jewish faith. Your mom was a devout Catholic."

"Great deal that did do to her, it did not even save her from a devil like you. Do you know what the priest told her when she told them about her life with you? They told her to be patient, to carry her cross humbly and willingly.

"The priest advised her to bear the brutish punishment, the abuse, the cheating, in the name of God, and she did that until a

205

moment came when she could not bear it anymore and found the fastest, but by no means easiest way out."

"You guys have been brainwashed, you both have become communists, terrorists, revolutionaries, the kind that I was committed by God to eliminate, but I can't because you are my own children, that is punishment enough." Then he stopped and asked again, "So, you are not going to recant your story?

"No Father, I am not going to recant my story."

"Fine, there is enough evidence to prove that you have not been telling the truth, and soon enough I be out of here and back to being General Guillermo Kruger. Then, I will pay back to those who put me here, including those who think they can take my place and fortune."

General Kruger paused, took another glass of wine in a single gulp and continued, "Now both of you, ungrateful pieces of shit of children, you can get the hell out of here and do not come back. You will regret this, Lily.

"I could have been the only man in this country who could save you from the firing squad. And you blew it, you blew it badly, girl, and this time I hope you would not blame me for your death."

"I would rather face the firing squad than be your daughter or owe my life to you. Goodbye forever, Dad."

"Guards, come, we are done here."

As his children left, the General sat behind the desk, put his head between his hands and, maybe for the first time in his life, cried.

As the General cried, he drank the rest of the bottle of wine and called the guard to request another one, plus a bottle of rum.

He always asked for corked bottles, to open them himself and this time he did the same as well but failed to notice the small holes that had been perforated on the cork of the wines and on the cap of the *Zacapa Centenario* rum.

# THIRTY-TWO
## *Centro Medico de Guatemala*
## October 1ˢᵗ, 1968

It was the last day of the month of September. The rescue was going to take place the following day, as Doctor Garcia had reported that was what he heard via the small transmitter he had given to Tanya.

Before Maria left the hideout with the semi-unconscious Claudia (Aka: stinky), Carlos started to work on the van that he had stolen.

First, he opened the door and got out the most frightened driver, who had his head covered with a black hood.

The two of them took the man into the house, took the hood off, and told him to be quiet if he wanted to live. Maria gave him a sandwich and a Pepsi. Then put him in one of the rooms, made a fake bomb from a wood stick painted red and connected some wires to it, put it on the door of the room and told the guy that if he tried to open would be blown to bits.

Then Carlos went to work on the van.

It was a commercial van, from one of the largest bakeries in the city and Carlos's goal was to convert it and make it look like a van from the Electric company.

He estimated that the work probably would take a good part of the night, unless he got help.

Help soon arrived.

One by one, few minutes apart, Efrain, Ricardo and a fellow known as Octavio, a guy that they borrowed from another cell, because he was supposed to be an excellent marksman.

He was so good that he was known by the moniker of "Bullseye"; all of them came in and went right to work along with Carlos.

207

Thereafter all went over the plan and received their own assignments for the following day.

"Bullseye" aka Octavio, was supposed to drive the van and park it in front of the building from the roof of which Tony was going to shoot Tanya.

Then, He was supposed to go inside that building, wearing an overall from the electric company, and leave a similar one, for Tony to change into, in the bathroom of the building.

Then both were going to climb to the roof and wait for the caravan to return from Fort Matamoros and then to do the shooting.

After the shooting, they would leave, ride the same vehicle, if possible, or use another vehicle parked nearby.

Unless Tony missed and killed Tanya, in which case Octavio was ordered to shoot and kill him.

Carlos was going to ride a motorcycle to Fort Matamoros, wait from a distance watch the front of the gate of the Fort, observe it from a house across the ravine, and report by radio the time at which the caravan conducting the Kruger siblings left the fortress.

Then Carlos would ride the motorcycle at high speed back to Centro Medico, leave the motorcycle on a side street, south of the Clinic, go to the restaurant across the street from the hospital and wait.

Then, as soon as the shooting started, he would run from across the street, get the driver of the ambulance and his partner out of the vehicle, and get into the driver's seat.

Once the Krugers were in the ambulance, Carlos was supposed to drive at full speed, and out of there.

Right after that Efrain and Ricardo would drive, either a bus or a truck, to block the nearby exit streets intersections to slow down the persecutors.

One of them, the one on the South side of the Medical Center, likely Efrain, would use the motorcycle left by Carlos to get away.

Ricardo would have to procure his own getaway motorcycle or other vehicle.

Efrain and Ricardo assured them that they had located the perfect place to obtain all the vehicles that they needed, and more, if necessary, but they required a person to drive a vehicle and leave it for Ricardo to get away. They decided that the best person to do that would be Tom Hopeland.

On the second day of October, at seven-thirty in the morning, everyone was up and running.

Captain Mario Kruger got the family station wagon out of his garage and drove it to a still semi deserted parking lot at the Oakland Mall.

He left the car there with a key well-hidden on top of the rear tire. Then, he hired a taxi to get him to the Hospital where his sister was.

Efrain and Ricardo, after paying a small Brive, got into the local police impoundment motor vehicles yard. Where there was an immense plethora of cars, motorcycles, bicycles, trucks, and buses to choose from.

After making sure that they were drivable, Ricardo chooses a flatbed truck, long enough, but not too tall, so it was able to carry a motorcycle on the bed.

Efrain chose a school bus.

They both drove to an empty parking lot and waited to hear from Carlos. It was only 9.30 am. But they were not worried, because the robbery of the vehicles would not be reported until much later, if not until the next day.

They were not concerned about finding a parking space near the hospital, because Carlos was supposed to tell them when the motorcade was approaching and to start driving towards the hospital.

Tony, in his character as Doctor Jaime Garcia, did not arrive until about 10 am. Just at the time that the ambulance carrying the Kruger siblings was leaving the hospital.

Garcia pulled into the parking garage of the hospital, as he always did, and left his car there. There was a duffle bag with his rifle in the trunk, but he would retrieve that later.

First, he had to check on Doctor K and Tom Hopeland, make sure they were still with the program.

Then he would go to the restaurant across the street, have breakfast and wait for the message from Carlos.

From the window of the restaurant, Tony saw the van from the electric company park in front of the building that they had selected to do the shooting from, and only few minutes later his beeper went on, indicating that the Kruger's were leaving Fort Matamoros.

Tony paid his bill, went across the street back to the hospital parking garage, got the duffle bag from the trunk of his car and unhurriedly walked the 100 meters, or so, which separated him from the building from which roof he was going to shoot Tanya.

Tony walked into the building, went to the bathroom, found the overalls, put them on and walked to the stairwell, he found Octavio already wanting on the roof.

Since they did not know each other, a password was needed, *"Malo mori"* he said. It was a password from a Classic Guatemalan novel entitled *Los Nazarenos* (The Nazoreans) written by a famous Guatemalan author, Jose Milla y Vidaure.

The novel did not have anything to do with the Passion of Christ; the Nazarenos was the name of a secret Society from colonial times, plotting to obtain independence from Spain.

Much like the FAR was now, striving for freedom from the military and the oligarchs.

*"Quan fedari"* was the correct response. Followed by a handshake and an exchange of names:

"Jaime", said Tony.

"Octavio," said the other man.

Both kneeled behind the wall, at the edge of the roof, and opened their respective duffel bags, from which they removed rather similar sniper rifles.

Octavio also removed a 9mm Beretta and tucked it on his belt.

"Just in case," he said.

He meant not only in case they were discovered before or after the mission was accomplished but also in case Doctor Jaime missed and killed Tanya.

If that happened, Octavio was supposed to kill Tony right there and then, in that very same spot.

Thumbs up from either Carlos or Captain Kruger meant Tanya was ok; thumbs down, he would put a bullet in Tony's brain.

"Nice tools" was the only comment that Tony made.

Inside the ambulance, Captain Kruger told his sister several times, in English, so the nurse won't understand, to keep always facing north when they got out of the vehicle.

Tom Hopeland had left the hotel, early that morning, driving a rental car, which he parked on a side street very near the hospital.

The car was to be used as an additional getaway if something went wrong.

He took his photo cameras out of the trunk of the car and walked to the hospital to join the other journalists who were gradually congregating there.

Good! He thought, there be plenty of witnesses and a plethora of pictures. Although he had no idea how they found out about Tanya leaving the hospital.

Tom hope there was no shooting, other than from Tony, and also that nobody got hurt.

Earlier, inside the hospital, Dr. K was extremely nervous, pacing and sweating, while carrying the concealed 9mm Smith Wesson that he was supposed to give to Captain Kruger.

Dr. K knew that there would be at least a need for a wheelchair to carry Tanya, or Nurse Laura, as the case may be, and he thought that the best place to hide the weapon was inside the bag on the back of a wheelchair.

As the first Jeep pulled into the side of the hospital building, followed closely by the ambulance, all the reporters came running towards it, forcing the soldiers to get out and stand close together with their rifles held on a horizontal position, making a human barrier, to push the journalists and curious people alike away from the prisoner.

Nothing could have been better for the rescuers' plan.

Dr. K. brought the wheelchair outside, as the rear doors of the ambulance opened, and Captain Kruger, getting out first, got the wheelchair, pushed it towards the ambulance, and helped his sister to get out of the vehicle.

Kruger did not have any problem fetching the gun from the bag of the wheelchair.

Tanya was handcuffed to the Nurse's left wrist, and she did have, or faked, some problem walking but got out, always looking North.

Then it happened.

A shot rang, and the side of Tanya's head started bleeding.

She collapsed and fell to the ground, almost bringing Nurse Laura down with her.

Captain Kruger cried: "My sister has been shot in the head; I think she is dead. She needs a doctor.".

All while pouring the blood from the flask over the head of his sister.

Dr. K immediately kneeled by her and said also rather loudly. "I am sorry Captain Kruger; it seems that your sister is dead."

Almost simultaneously a second shot shattered the left forearm of nurse Laura, who started to bleed copiously and screamed loudly.

Doctor K, once again said, "There is not much we can do for Mis. Kruger, as she seems to be dead, but this woman needs medical attention. Bring her inside and get those freaking handcuffs off her"!

Nurse Laura, who was about to pass out handled the keys to the Doctor who helped her to get on the chair and be wheeled inside the hospital.

The members of the media, who at first panicked and took shelter, were now coming back towards the fallen Tanya, taking pictures, and screaming.

Several more shots rang out, one hitting the shoulder of the soldier manning the 50-caliber followed by another shot, which blew the tires of that Jeep.

The other soldiers took cover while telling people to get down on the floor and out of there.

They saw Captain Kruger picking up the body of his sister and yelling to the crowd. "I am taking my sister's dead body with me, to give her proper burial. You people are making a circus of this tragedy, shame, shame, fuck you all bloodthirsty dirty bastards."

The soldiers from the ambulance tried to stop him, when, apparently out of nowhere, a young man came running, graved the driver by the collar of his shirt, and then pushed him to the ground.

Then, he took the man's weapon and pointed it at the other soldier, while telling him:

"Get out, get out, and leave your weapons on the seat, or I swear I put a bullet through your head. Let the Captain take his dead sister to give her a proper burial".

The man complied and, in less than ten seconds the ambulance was peeling tires and running out south at full speed.

As the soldiers were recovering from the initial surprise, they tried to board the Jeeps that were functional, only to be surprised once again, when a large truck came from the side street South of them and totally blocked the intersection at the south end of the avenue.

The driver of the truck threw something out of the window and thinking it was a bomb everyone took shelter.

It was not a bomb, it was a rather large string of cherry bombs, at least a yard long. (those called "machineguns" by the locals.)

A similar event took place on the North side intersection where a school bus, coming out of the side street, blocked the North side exit.

Another large string of firecrackers came out of the window of the school bus.

Nobody could identify the drivers of those two vehicles, who disappeared from the scene without leaving a trace.

The blocking of the streets was supposed not only to stop any would-be pursuers but also to allow Tony and Octavio to get out safely from the place from which they fired the shots.

The firecrackers were Efrain and Ricardo's own smart idea.

Octavio had gotten a thumbs-up signal from Carlos.

All was cool, the commander was alive. And hopefully free.

# THIRTY-THREE

The ambulance took off at full speed, with the sirens blaring at full blast thus making all traffic give them the right of way.

Carlos and Captain Kruger knew that it was just a matter of time before police patrol cars started chasing them, or worse yet, that one or more helicopters showed up in the sky.

Besides, Lily Marie, who was unconscious, and bleeding very heavily from the wound on the side of her head, did not look too healthy to her brother.

The bullet had caused only a laceration on the side of her scalp and took off a small chunk of her ear, but it may have also caused a concussion.

Her scalp wound was a large and nasty gash and although it appeared to be just a nasty laceration, since the scalp has a large number of blood vessels it bleeds easily and heavily. Plus, there was the blood her brother had spilled on her face.

Nevertheless, the temporal artery runs along that area, and it could have been lacerated by the bullet.

Frantically Captain Kruger was putting pressure on the wound, to try to stop the bleeding but was not being very successful as his hands were getting soaked with blood seeping through the towel that he was using to press on the wound.

Lily Marie was regaining consciousness now. She brought her hand to her head, and immediately got wet with her blood.

"Shit," she said.

"Welcome back to the world of the living, Sis. Unfortunately, you have a nasty wound on your head, and it is bleeding like a son of a bitch. How do you feel otherwise?"

"I am a bit dizzy and have a killer headache. You need to stitch up this wound, bro have you done that before?"

"Not on my own sister, but yes, I was being trained in jungle warfare, and they teach you how to do that and more. This is an army ambulance, and I am sure that there is a first aid kit, with suture material in it."

"You better hurry to find that, Captain. We are approaching our destination and changing vehicles as we speak," said Carlos.

"Here it is, I found it. An emergency kit and yes, it does contain suturing material. Sis, we are moving you to the family car. I will carry you there, just keep pressing that towel against the wound".

"Hurry up brother, it is beginning to hurt and still bleeding like a son of a bitch."

"I will stitch you up as soon as we move you to the other car and start getting the hell out of here. But you have to be brave because I have to stitch your wound cool turkey as I do not see any local anesthetic here."

Carlos parked the ambulance nearby and walked back to the siblings. It was the first time he had seen his commander since they both jumped off the roof of a house after the battle of Avenida Elena. Carlos was not a very emotional guy, but he almost burst into tears seeing his boss again and seeing his boss again bleeding.

"Glad to see you, my commandant. Are you ok? You are bleeding heavily from the head."

"Well, Carlos, I am very happy to see you again. And I have been better. As it happens, I am bleeding because I have been shot in the head, without my consent, warning, or prior information."

"Sorry, Sis. We had so little time and few opportunities to talk about this and get your consent. Besides, I was afraid that you were going to refuse to go along with the plan."

"Who was the shooter anyway?". "None of our guys can shoot like that."

"Believe it or not, it was Doctor Garcia. Who I believe is neither a doctor nor Garcia. I will tell you all on the way to the ranch."

"We are going to the ranch? The ranch will be the first place where they would be looking for us."

"Not if they think you are dead, and as far as we know, dear sister, as of right now, you are considered deceased."

"And you will have a proper funeral first thing tomorrow morning at the ranch," said Carlos.

"Empty casket, I assume," said Tanya.

Captain Kruger had finished stitching his sister's wound, and the bleeding had stopped. He exchanged glances with Carlos and preferred not to answer that question.

As Tanya insisted the captain said, "Well, not exactly."

"What exactly do you mean by not exactly?"

Another silence and then Carlos responded. "We found a surrogate."

"You mean a woman's corpse?"

"Yes, something like that," said Carlos again.

"You do not worry about anything, Lizzy. We have everything under control. Just close your eyes, take this pain pill, and try to sleep the rest of the way. We have at least an hour and a half before getting to the Ranch". Said, Captain Kruger

And Lily Marie relaxed and went to sleep in her brother's arms.

The rest of the ride went without problems.

# THIRTY-FOUR
## The Kruger family Ranch
## October 2, 1968

The Kruger ranch was in the department of Escuintla, about five miles from the actual capital City of Escuintla, in the northwest of Guatemala, near the Pacific Coast.

The Ranch had indeed been the property of the Arbenz family and was then named *El Cajon* (The Big Box).

When President Arbenz was exiled after a CIA and United Fruit Company-orchestrated coup, the government of Carlos Castillo Armas confiscated all his properties, including the ranch.

Never mind that the Ranch had been purchased with Arbenz's wife's money, her being a member of a very rich and prominent family from the 1% wealthy elite of El Salvador.

General Kruger, through treason, menacing and dubious dealings, was able to purchase the ranch and thereafter added a couple of smaller ranches to his, using his wealthy wife's money, and renamed the place as "Kruger Ranch", which now had over one thousand acres of land and hundreds of cattle heads, horses, and fruit trees.

In addition, General Kruger had placed a rather large black metal K over an enormous arch at the ranch's entrance, when remodeled the place, and built a lavish mansion there, leaving the old ranch house as a guest house.

Therefore, it was relatively easy for Maria to find the ranch. Maria and "stinky" Claudia arrived at the Kruger Ranch the previous night and stayed at the mansion.

Maria had had a good night's sleep after giving "Stinky" another bath and keeping her quiet by administering large amounts of alcohol, sometimes laced with Valium.

Coming early in the morning, Maria got up and gave Claudia another bath, the fourth one since getting her from the Church of Santo Domingo grounds.

Then Maria proceeded to trim Claudia's hair, comb it, change its color it, and apply makeup to her face to make her resemble, as much as possible, the woman that she was going to replace at the grave.

Once she finished bathing Claudia, with the help of a trusted woman, a servant of many years at the ranch, they dressed her in a dress belonging to Lily Marie Kruger. A dress of the same color as the one Tanya was wearing when she was shot.

The woman servant had been told that the person they were taking care of was an old acquaintance of the Krugers and would be there just for the night, to be transferred to a hospital in the morning.

The maid asked no questions.

Claudia almost looked pretty after all that work and from a distance, and if there was not too much light, perhaps she could be taken for Tanya Kruger.

Then Maria waited for the call from Tom Hopeland, informing her that it all had happened according to plan, that the Kruger siblings, and Tom himself, separately of course, were on his way to the ranch.

The Krugers were perhaps twenty minutes behind him, so they would be arriving anytime.

The siblings were going to drive directly into the garage of the guest house, the old ranch, which was located about two hundred yards from the mansion. This was to keep Lily Marie from being seen by anyone from the Ranch or the reporters who surely would start arriving soon.

As soon as they get to the entrance of the Ranch, Carlos would change places with Captain Kruger, letting him move into the driver's seat and taking the wheel.

The captain would stop the van, very briefly, at the ranch's entrance, which was about a mile from the houses, just to allow Carlos to get out and walk unseen the rest of the way to the mansion.

He would enter the main mansion through a back door and find Maria and Claudia. Shoot the girl in the head, help clean the blood, and place her corpse in the coffin.

Tom Hopeland would take pictures of the body and make them public as soon as possible.

Then, there would be a wake, lasting the whole night -as it is customary in most Latin Countries- the following morning, the body would be taken to the funeral home in Escuintla for cremation, returning the ashes to the ranch for burial.

The next day it would be a Saturday, the last day of the week on which funerals were allowed in Guatemala.

It was Maria's duty to call the Funeral home and order a casket for the wake that would take place overnight. It would be a closed casket because the shot had so deformed poor Miss Kruger's face, that she, being so young and pretty, would have chosen not to be seen looking like that.

Maria guessed that the casket would arrive almost simultaneously as the Krugers.

She hoped and expected that Tanya would not be seen alive again in Guatemala.

On the other hand, Maria tried her best not to become attached to Claudia and prayed for another way out other than killing her. She would not do it. She could not do it, but she knew that Carlos or any of the others would.

Tom Hopeland, left the Hospital after taking as many pictures as possible of the events at the *Centro Medico* and after making sure that the nurse and the soldier hit on the shoulder were okay. Once the military cleared the place and gave permission, he simply walked to where his rental car was parked and drove to the Kruger Ranch.

He had a funeral to attend and an airplane to fly.

Octavio and Doctor Garcia walked out calmly from the building from where they had fired the shots, boarded the van from the electric company, and drove away unmolested.

"Where to, Doctor?" asked Octavio.

"Please leave close to the American Embassy; I have to see someone there," was the answer.

The American Embassy was less than five minutes from where they were, so it was not necessary to make a U-turn to go there.

On the way, both were primarily silent, and only as Garcia got out of the vehicle Octavio said: "Nice shooting. Never seen anybody shoot like that before."

Tony simply answers: "Thank you. You are not so bad yourself." He had shot the nurse and the Jeeps.

Octavio stopped the van several yards from the embassy gates, and as Tony walked towards it, he drove away. The rear mirror showed Tony talking to the Marine guarding the door, showing some sort of credential, and being ushered in.

That is nice Octavio thought, and proved that Dr. Garcia was not really a doctor, nor a Garcia but an agent of the Americans, probably CIA. But why would a CIA agent help free the commander of an anti-government armed group?

Perhaps they did they have other plans for her?

And did the Krugers, Carlos, and Maria know about this guy's affiliation? In case they did not already know, he would inform them and call the Ranch as soon as he was able to get close to a telephone.

So, he did, as soon as he pulled the van inside the gate of the safe house, he called the ranch.

Fortunately, Octavio was reassured by Captain Kruger and Carlos himself that although they weren't sure, they had long suspected that Dr. Garcia was CIA, but as long as he was willing to help rescue his sister that was okay with them. Even if they had only trusted him as far as they could throw him.

Nevertheless, if he was willing to help to rescue Tanya, they would use his skills and connections and deal with whatever later.

Once reassured, Octavio sprayed the van with blue paint, hiding the lettering of the Electric Company. Then he went inside the house, opened the door of the room where a most scared bakery store driver, had been held for the night and half day, and pretended to dismantle the fake bomb that Carlos had put on the door of the room, then put a hood on the head of the frightened prisoner and, after assuring him that he was not going to kill him, putt two hundred Quetzales into the man's pocket, pushed him into the back of the van, closed the gates and drove away.

Once reaching a street near the area where he had been abducted initially, Octavio stopped the van, warned the guy to count slowly to 100, and then got out.

Octavio then took the first city bus heading downtown and disappeared.

Meanwhile, Carlos opened the mansion's back door and walked in; he was on the first floor, near the kitchen. Nobody was there, so he climbed the stairs and went up to the second floor, finding tearful Maria in a parlor next to the master bedroom.

"Where is the girl?" asked Carlos.

Maria just pointed to the door of the next room, the one connected to the parlor, and asked Carlos: "Is there another way, comrade?"

"You know it isn't Maria. It must be this way". Carlos said as he fitted his gun with a makeshift silencer and walked into the room.

Claudia was sitting on a chair with a bottle on the table before her, looking totally disconnected from the world. She looked at Carlos with a stupid smile on her face and failed to realize that she was about to be executed.

Carlos stood about four feet facing the woman and, extending his arm, fired his gun. The bullet hit Claudia right in the left eye, and she collapsed face first into the table, knocking the bottle on the floor and staining the table, floor, and clothes with large amounts of blood and pieces of bone and brain.

He called on Maria to help him clean, but she refused to come saying "I am not going to help you. That is your mess, you clean it."

"Dear comrade Maria, I want you to know that I am not happy about doing this either; I do not enjoy killing people. I do not enjoy killing anything, but you know this was necessary, and you said that this woman was tired of living."

"Still, I am not helping you, Carlos. I will sit here and pray a rosary for the repose of her soul and for your salvation. Call me when she is clean. The coffin is in the living room downstairs."

Carlos fetched some towels from the bathroom and started to clean the blood. Realizing that the towels were not enough, he ripped the sheets off the bed and continued to mop off the blood.

When he was finished, he bundled the blood-soaked linen and asked Maria where he could burn it.

Maria said that she had seen a giant oven in the kitchen, one of those old ovens people use to bake bread. She would go downstairs and start the fire while Carlos would carry the body of Claudia to place it inside the casket.

"Don't close the casket, the American reporter be here soon to take pictures of her. I do not want to see her."

"Fine Maria do not worry; I shall do the dirty work for you. And, for the record, I repeat again that I do not enjoy this, but it is part of the job. Part of the path you and I have chosen."

Maria felt like saying that she had not chosen to murder innocent people, but remained silent remembering that it was her, the person who procured the sacrificial victim.

She just cried silently and prayed another rosary, this one for the salvation of her own soul.

# THIRTY-FIVE
## Matamoros Castle
## October 1st 1968

General Kruger, after the stormy confrontation with his children, was left with mixed feelings. The strongest of which were the feelings of betrayal and rage. The second was his desire for revenge.

The General summoned his lawyer back and told the guard at his door to tell whoever was in charge that he wanted, in addition to more wine, and rum, the lavish dinner that Oliva, Zelaya, Camacho and Benitez had promised.

He would dine with his lawyer while discussing his case, his options, and his revenge.

Richard Kaine was a very rich and sleazy lawyer, he was Jewish, but was not a practicing Jew. Kaine was the kind of lawyer you want to have on your side when you are in trouble but never want him to litigate against you. The kind of lawyer, without scruples nor ethics, the kind who could make the dead talk when it was convenient for him or his clients.

The most important aspect of Richard Kaine was that he looked like a very honorable person. Well dressed, a bit pass middle-age, greyish white sideburns, gold rimmed spectacled, soft-spoken, pleasant, nothing on his outward appearance would indicate the kind of snake he was.

And Richard Kaine was going to be in charge of defending General Guillermo Kruger-Larrave, a person very much like him, against the accusations of his own daughter.

So, Kaine sat in front of Kruger and the later poured him a generous amount of German wine, while saying, "My dear Richard, I hope you can stay for lunch, or perhaps dinner, whichever it is because is well past noon.

"I have ordered fillet mignon and lobster, stuffed mushrooms and potato salad, and as much wine as we could drink, so let us enjoy while you tell me your plan of action."

"Well, General, let me tell you first, that I believe we have a strong case in your favor. Your daughter can be discredited as being insane and brainwashed by the FAR. Her actions were not very rational, to begin with. Sending the ransom money directly to your office was an obvious indication that her intentions were to implicate you in the kidnapping of the US Ambassador.

"Second, motive. Although there were accusations that you hated the ambassador, there is no evidence of that other than your daughter's words. And let us not forget that the amount of the ransom money was so ridiculous that you could wipe your ass with twice that amount."

"So, you do not think that we have to go to trial, Richard"?

"I do not think so, William. In fact, I am going to request both the civilian criminal court judge and the military judge to dismiss the case against you."

"Wonderful, let us drink to that! And let us eat to that! Of course, that is only if you can do it being today a Friday, which, as I understand is a Sabbath preparation day for Jews."

"You know that I do not observe the Jewish customs, Willy, let us drink and eat without remorse."

It was about 4.30 in the afternoon when the general and his lawyer finished their meal. Both were drunk, but the general wanted to keep drinking, the lawyer had enough, so he called his driver and asked to be taken home.

It was then that a soldier came to announce to the lawyer that he had an urgent phone call at the front office. Mr. Kaine, still with a wine glass in his hand, excused himself and went to answer the phone call.

About 10 minutes later he returned, somewhat pale, sweaty, and nervous.

"General!" he said.

"I have one good news, a good but not great news, and one bad news."

Kaine paused for a couple of seconds.

"The good news is that I will probably be able to get you out of here by Monday. The not so good news is that we have lost the main witness against you. The bad news is that that witness is your daughter, Lily Marie and she was shot in the head about an hour ago, and I am afraid she is dead."

"What? Lily Marie is dead. How did it happen?' Who did it?"

"We don't know, Willy. I am sorry. All I can tell you is that as she was getting out to the ambulance, right in front of the hospital, a sniper shot her in the head. A doctor from the hospital said she was dead. But then your son Mario took the body with him and drove off."

"Oh, the little sneaky bitch! She is not dead at all, Richard. I am sure she is not dead.'"

"Why do you think so Willy? You sound so convinced that she is alive."

"She and little Willy probably found a way to get her out of the hands of the authorities by faking her death. You see Richard, my kids are very smart.

"However, you are absolutely right, Richard. Both are good news, because dead or alive she can no longer testify against me."

"Then I, hope you are right about your kids, Willy, let's drink to that."

"Yeah! And as soon as I get out of here, I am going to track them down and punish them properly."

Thereafter the lawyer left, rather drunk but uplifted.

At about 7 pm, the General started to feel nauseous and dizzy, so he went to bed thinking that it was because all the booze and the food that he had ingested was making him feel ill.

At 7:30 p.m., he had the first abdominal cramps and vomited for the first time. Again, he blamed it on the booze and food and asked for an Alka-Seltzer.

Then, the cramps became stronger, the vomiting more severe and frequent, and the diarrhea started.

At 8.30 pm the diarrhea became bloody, the vomiting increased, and he felt faint.

226

The guards reported the general's condition at 8.35, and he was transported to the fort infirmary at 8.40 p.m. The medic of the fort infirmary started an IV at 8.45 and administered medication for nausea.

At 8.50 pm Coronel Ricardo Oliva was informed of the General's condition. At 9.00 Oliva called a meeting, at his home, with his friends Zelaya, Camacho, and Benitez.

"It is working folks! it is working!

The son of a bitch is sick as a dog, in the infirmary hooked on IV's. And you know that the daughter, the self-proclaimed Tanya, was shot to death earlier, don't you?"

"Yes, we have been informed, and we have questions about that whole shooting issue, but that can wait, let us now take care of our friend Willy Kruger, first."

"I suggest we give him an extra dose of the 'medication,' best if intravenously, just to make sure that he does not rebound. If comes back, he will immediately realize what had happened and who did it, and we will all be as good as dead," said Zelaya.

"That is right, and we had to do it before they send him to the hospital where the doctors may diagnose the real problem," said Camacho.

"If we do it, it must be done by one of us. I do not trust the medics or the nurses," said Benitez.

"Ok, I will do it," said Oliva. "After all, I am the one who sent him the food and the wine, and the one that most consider his closest friend. Besides, I have poison here in my house. Plus, I hate the bastard much more than all of you."

"Zelaya and I will make sure that the bottles and whatever is left on them are destroyed."

"Excellent, I will drive there to check on the condition of my good friend General Willy Kruger and also to deliver to him the news about his daughter's demise." He said this with a sinister smile.

General Oliva visited his friend and colleague at 9.30pm and, after injecting more poison in to the IV tubing, ordered the nurses to transfer the general to the hospital, if he was not better in the next fifteen minutes.

General Guillermo Kruger died at 10.13 pm, in the ambulance on his way to the hospital. The doctors diagnosed severe dehydration due to food poisoning and a heart attack due to fluid loss and drop in blood pressure.

Richard Kaine was found death on his bed the following morning.

# THIRTY-SIX
## Langley, Virginia USA
## CIA headquarters
## October 2, 1968

The phone rang. Agent Smith answered.

"This is Tony, reporting about my vacations in Guatemala, I would like to talk with your boss, Mr. Helms."

"It is Friday afternoon, the boss is playing golf. Can I give him a message?"

"Just tell him that the mission has been accomplished. I could write a report, but I know that is against protocol. Morton has the details."

"It surely took you a long time to do it Tony, usually you are not this slow, perhaps you are getting old and rusty."

"Rusty and old is your mother, Smith."

"I was just saying that it took you a long time, and that it is not like you Tony," said Agent Smith in more conciliatory terms.

"Sure Smith, it is easy for you to criticize when your job is just sitting behind a desk kissing the asses of all those around you."

"My job is as important as yours, or more Benedetti."

"Sure, Smith. Just tell Helms that I shall be at the hotel should he wants to hear the whole story before reading tomorrows papers."

And Tony hung up the phone.

First, Agent Smith thought that the news from Tony could wait until Monday. But then, thinking about it, decided that it was best to let the boss know right now.

He called the club where Helms was playing golf and was told that he was still on the seventh hole, having been committed to playing 18 holes. So, it was at least one hour before Helms was available.

Then Smith called Richard Morton, the acting ambassador of the US in Guatemala, and obtained the story of the recent events.

The story smelled a bit fishy to Agent Smith who surely was a complete asshole, but he was by no means stupid. So, Smith decided to drive to the golf course.

He just waited for Helms to play up to the 18 hole and approached him as he reached for the bar.

Tony received the call from Helms as soon as the boss got out of the Club's shower.

"This is Richard Helms, Tony. I was informed that you finally eliminated the target assigned to you over three weeks ago. Why did it take you so long, Tony? Usually, you conclude the business assigned to you in a matter of a few days. What went wrong in there?"

"The package was extremely well guarded, sir. I had to wait for an opportunity to make an offer to purchase it."

"I see, so, you are sure that the package is secured now, at everyone's satisfaction?"

"Yes, sir. I assure you that is the case. There will be pictures send to you, via Mr. Morton, sir."

"Excellent, Tony. Good work. Take few days off now and rest. You have earned a paid vacation."

"Thank you, sir. I appreciate it. I believe that I would do just that. This country is beautiful and I would like to stay a bit longer, or perhaps I would go to Mexico".

"You do that Tony. Have fun, talk to you later".

After hanging up the phone, Helms asked Agent Smith to connect him to the acting US ambassador in Guatemala.

Mr. Morton described again in detail what went on at the medical center, without omitting the fact that there had been two unknown individuals driving vehicles meant to block the exits of the streets leading to the hospital, and that the driver of those trucks threw long strings of firecrackers at the soldiers guarding the place.

"And you said that the brother of the girl rode on the back of the ambulance with her? Then, who drove the ambulance, and where they took her body?"

"Unknown, sir, however, as to where the body went, there are strong rumors that they drove to the family ranch, where they will have the wake and burial of the girl."

"You know what, Mr. Morton, I want you to contact the Guatemalan authorities and make sure they send someone to that ranch to confirm that the girl is dead and is being buried."

"So, sir, you suspect that the girl is not dead"?

"I am just saying that the whole thing looks a bit suspicious, and it is my job, to investigate things that look a bit suspicious. I just want to make sure that they are not burying an empty coffin. I just want to make sure that there is a corpse inside of that casket.

"Pull some strings, Morton. Call some people. Bribe some people. Threaten some people. Ask them to send the police or an army patrol to that ranch to open the fucking coffin and look inside."

"I will do my best sir, but you know it is Friday afternoon here and most people be out of their offices now."

"Well, Morton, call them at home. Call their favorite bar. Call their favorite whore house or call at their mistress's places, but get this going and done before she is buried.

"Oh, and make sure that Tony Benedetti does not find out about this."

"Yes sir, Mr. Helms, right now. I'll start making the calls right now."

After he hung the phone up Helms said:

"You are right, Smith. This looks extremely fishy."

"I feel the same, sir. That is why I took the liberty of calling you at the golf club."

"To me, the whole thing looks more like a rescue mission than an assassination scene. Let us look at the facts: First, why did Tony take such a long time to eliminate the target? Second, why did he not do it quietly at the hospital?"

"Tony said that she was heavily guarded, sir."

"I know he said that she was heavily guarded, but we know that he was present at the hospital and entering her room disguised as a doctor. He must have several opportunities to finish her off."

"Tony said that he wanted to do it in public, and before the press, so there would be no doubt that she was dead."

"And he did have to involve the girl's brother and other men? Tony said that he made those people believe that it was going to be a rescue operation rather than an assassination.

"Well, either he did it or did not, the matter would not be settled until I received word that Lily Marie's corpse is indeed inside that coffin."

"Even if she is sir, don't you think that by performing such a dramatic action, Tony jeopardized his security and even that of the agency."

Helms was fully aware that Agent Smith did not like Tony Benedetti, most likely because he was meek, short, and not very good looking, which was the opposite of what Tony was. But he was smart and usually right in his appreciation of people. Helms was not going to take Smith's opinion lightly.

"Indeed, Smith, perhaps it is time to retire Mr. Tony Benedetti from the Agency. However, there is no rush to do that. Let us see what news that idiot Morton will have for us"?

Morton first called General Oliva and could not reach him, as he was conferring with his cronies Zelaya, Benitez, and Camacho. Morton called those three individually as well, but none was available. He left messages for them to call him back, as soon as possible.

Zelaya was the first one to receive the message but decided not to return the call right away because he had just been informed of General's Kruger demise. Zelaya called his friends first and informed them that "the acting head gringo" wanted to talk to one of them.

At first, He was somewhat scared thinking that the call had something to do with the murder of Kruger, but then it thought that even for the Gringos, it would be impossible to find out about that, not this rapidly anyway.

Oliva was the one who returned the call and received the request from Morton.

"The Acting Head Gringo thinks that the Kruger girl may not be dead and wants us to send someone to their ranch to make sure that there is a body in the coffin that the brother is going to bury. Remember, we had questions about that ourselves; some details in the whole situation do not fit well."

"Let us call the military post in Escuintla and ask them to send a patrol to the ranch to investigate. Let us also call the funeral home, so, they can retrieve the body of our dear friend Willy Kruger and notify the first of kin. In this case Captain Kruger, the only officially surviving relative".

The funeral home picked up the body of General William Kruger and called the ranch to inform the son, Captain Kruger, about his father's demise. They told him that, as far as the death certificate said, his father had died suddenly of a severe heart attack. And Captain Kruger added in his head, "after he had a confrontation with his children and had a lot to eat and drink."

Captain Kruger felt a jolt of guilt, but surprisingly he did not cry nor feel sorry for his father. However, he felt responsible for his death.

Yet, he kept the news from his sister. At least for the time being.

He requested the caller to take the body to the funeral home, select an expensive casket and send the body as soon as possible to the Kruger ranch.

The wake of the General would take place at the same time as that of his daughter, and his casket would be placed alongside that of Lily Marie.

This one open.

Captain Kruger had driven his sister to the old, smaller, ranch house, leaving her there, requesting Maria to go keep her company, bring her clean clothes, and, if she asked questions, to tell her that they were going to bury an empty coffin.

She did not need to know that an innocent woman had been murdered to save her life, nor that probably both of them, had caused the death of her father.

Carlos had already dressed the dead body of Claudia in a clean, off-white dress and placed her in the coffin, in such a way that the ugly wound on her face be quite visible.

Tom Hopeland arrived half an hour later, took pictures of the girl's face, and then closed the coffin, nailing the cover shut, so nobody could open it and see Claudia's face.

The corpse of the General arrived sometime later.

One of the funeral home caretakers gave a note to Captain Kruger, telling him the following:

"As we were about to leave the city, this note was given to me by a man whom I had never seen before. He gave me 10 Quetzales and told me to give this letter to you personally and in your own hands."

Young Kruger opened the note who simply said:

*Don't feel guilt. It was not a heart attack. He was poisoned by the generals.*

The captain wondered who could have written such a note but suspected it had been Tony. Nevertheless, it made him feel lots better. Then, he placed the note in his pocket and prepared for the most important wake and funeral this area of Guatemala had ever seen.

Town's people, people from the ranch, people from nearby ranches, family members, and media people started flocking to the Kruger's ranch for the double wake of the general and the general's daughter.

About three hours later, a detachment of about six soldiers from the nearby city of Escuintla garrison arrived at the ranch. The leader of the group, a second lieutenant, asked in a very commanding way, for the owner of the house or person in charge. Upon learning that the person in charge and owner was his military superior, his attitude changed and became more polite.

"What is the problem, lieutenant? We are mourning two deaths in the family, and you come here with a bunch of soldiers, hopefully, to pay honor and respects to a general of the glorious Guatemalan Army?"

"Sorry, sir, I was ordered to come here and make sure that the person being buried as your sister, is indeed your sister. Therefore, I respectfully request that you let us open her casket and confirm that. Then, we will be out of here."

"Sorry, lieutenant, there is no way that I am going to let you defile my sister's body as she wished to be buried on a closed casket because she was shot on her pretty face."

"I apologize, sir, but I must insist. I am just following orders, and I do not wish to be forced to pass over you to carry them."

"Unless you show me a judicial order, you are not going to do any of that lieutenant. You get an order from a judge and come back when you have it. And please retire peacefully. There are many people here to witness your actions. Some of them may be armed; who knows? So, certainly I hope that you are not considering using force. Are you lieutenant?"

The lieutenant indeed considered the situation and decided that it was best to retire peacefully, obtain a judicial order and return later.

"Very well, sir, but nobody can leave this ranch, and please, do not move the coffins. I will leave several of my men to guard the entrance of the ranch. People are allowed to come in but not to leave. Not until I returned to check inside of those coffins."

The soldiers left but, as their officer had said, he left five soldiers guarding the entrance of the ranch.

Captain Kruger called the rest of the team apart, informing them of the recent events and the need to get rid of the coffin containing the remains of Claudia Gonzales.

Tom Hopeland produced an idea.

"If you have that airplane fueled and ready to fly, I can take the coffin to the nearest airport, and dispose of it."

Mario Kruger liked the idea. "That is a great idea. There is a small airport in Escuintla. You could fly there. I am going to call the funeral home, ask them to bring an unmarked van to meet you. And then take the body to the funeral home to be cremated as fast as possible. Then, when the lieutenant returns, tomorrow or later tonight, he will find only an urn with ashes:"

"Do you think that the people at the funeral home will agree with that? It may be risky."

"They will if I offer an extra thousand Quetzales for their services."

Kruger made the call, and after that he said: "everything has been arranged."

"A van will wait for you at the Escuintla airport. They will take the coffin, burn it, and return a similar coffin with an urn with the ashes inside. You will bring it back and we will continue with the burial, as planned, tomorrow morning."

"I will go with you professor. You will need help to carry the coffin and perhaps to fend off the hostiles, should they show up at an inconvenient time," said Carlos.

"Ok, fine, hopefully there would be no confrontation with anybody. So, let us go, people."

At this point, Maria, who was dressed in a long, faded black gown and covering her head with a black shawl, just the kind of outfit the local women wore at funerals, and who had been observing from the background intervened:

"Wait a minute, comrades. Don't you think you are ruining everything by doing that? All the effort which went to mount this show, and the murder of poor, innocent Claudia, and for what? So, at the end, still people will not be one hundred percent convinced that Commander Tanya is dead?

"Many people, including reporters, did witness and hear what the officer who just left said. So, there will be a question on their minds as to whether that officer's statement had any truth, and many, if not most, will question whether there was a body in that coffin.

"The only proof that we would have that there really was a corpse, are the pictures that professor Hopeland took early, but the reality of those they can easily be questioned."

"Comrade Maria is right," said Tom Hopeland. "Some people and some of the media will believe that the death and burial of the commandant was a hoax, and that will put the commandant's life at risk again." said Carlos.

"What shall we do then to convince everyone?" asked Captain Kruger.

"I only see one answer to that," said Maria.

"And what is that answer?" they all asked.

"Open the casket and let them all see the corpse."

"You mean make this an open casket, after we emphasized that Lily Marie, would not want that?" said brother Mario.

"Plus, that would be very foolish. What if someone realizes that that body is not Tanya's," Carlos said.

"Hear me out guys. I am not crazy enough to suggest an open casket, but how about a two-minute opening? Just lifting the cover to let them take a quick pick, even snap some pictures, all done from certain distance, and then proceed with the cremation." said Maria.

"Maria's idea makes sense. Someone could give a speech explaining our change of heart, considering the questions raised by the officer earlier," suggested Professor Hopeland.

"You have been a professor, Tom, I am sure you can give a speech to the crowd?" asked Mario Kruger

"Yes, I probably could, and I certainly be honored to do it, but I am a Gringo, and my Spanish is far from perfect. I believe that the most indicated to do this is the brother of the deceased."

"Ok. I will do it, let us go, we do not have a lot of time." - Said Captain Kruger.

So, everyone except Maria walked into the mansion's main hall, where the two coffins were displayed, guarded by six giant candles and multiple flower arrangements.

The place was packed with people when Captain Kruger stood in front of the crowd and spoke.

"Dear family, friends, neighbors and members of the press. In the middle of my grief for the loss of two close and dear members of my family, both on the same day, I am comforted and grateful for seeing so many people here gathered to pay the last respects to my father, General Guillermo Kruger-Larrave, and my beloved and beautiful sister Lily Marie Kruger Beltran.

"I am sure that it has not escaped to most of you, that my father lies on an open casket, while my dear sister has a closed one. I know that also most of you know the reason for that.

"The reason is that my beloved sister was shot in the face and her pretty features have been severely damaged and I know for a fact that she would not have liked to be seen looking like that.

"Unfortunately, tonight we have witnessed some events which put a question mark in to whether my sister lies in that coffin, or if we are burying and later burning, an empty casket."

"I know that most of you would not believe such fallacies... but we are human, and I am sure that some of you will have at least some doubts and questions. It is for that reason that I have decided, as the only surviving member of the Kruger family, to allow you to have a very brief view of my sister's face.

"All I wanted to do was to keep her wishes, but at the same time I feel that I must dissipate any doubts that you may have. Therefore, with a heavy heart and regret, I will open the coffin for only three minutes to allow those of you who wish to look at her to do so and I will also allow the members of the press to take pictures, if so they wish.

"Subsequently, and mostly, to keep the military from defiling her corpse, as they probably would want to have a coroner perform an autopsy, my sister's body will be temporarily removed from here. It will be taken to be cremated and her ashes will return here, to be buried alongside our father".

"Meanwhile, and through the night, coffee, hot chocolate, soft drinks, Beltran's distillery best *Zacapa Centenario* along with sandwiches, tamales and pastries shall be served to all of you. All these will be available right here, right now, and if all goes well, the funerals shall be tomorrow morning as previously planned.

"Oh, and one more thing, I just learned that my dad did not die from a heart attack. He was poisoned, most likely by those he considered his friends.

"Thank You very much for being here, for your support, understanding, and attention."

After that speech Captain Kruger was assailed by the press seeking more information about the poison, but he said that the only piece of information he had was the note he received and showed it to the reporters.

"I guess that what comes around goes around." Said Tom Hopeland to himself.

It all went as the captain had said and after only about three minutes, over which, most of those present did not come close to look at the body, because by then, in addition to the ugly deforming wound, Claudia's whole face had turned purple and was very swollen making her look repugnant and scary.

Thereafter, the coffin was closed, placed in the back of a pickup truck, and taken to the hangar where the four-seat Piper aircraft was stored; the casket was loaded in no time by Tom and Carlos and thereafter piloted by Tom Hopeland to the Escuintla airport to be taken from there to the funeral home and be cremated.

The return flight was equally uneventful, and the plane returned to the ranch only about two hours after taking off.

Since the body and the coffin were burned together, they loaded a similar coffin, inside of which was an urn containing the ashes of who it this life had been Claudia Gonzalez, aka "Stinky."

Needless to say that, hours later, when the military returned, this time with a Colonel in command and with a court order, and the coffin was opened, they were disappointed and angry.

However, they calmed down and pretended to understand the reasons behind the brother of the deceased's actions, more so after all the attendees who had seen the body's face swore that they had seen the body of Lily Marie Kruger inside that coffin.

The media even showed them pictures to prove the point and the military became much more friendly after having some drinks, eating some food and each one received an unopened bottle of the famous *Zacapa Centenario* rum.

Nobody paid much attention to the two women dressed in black clothes, with heads covered with long black shawls. Who all the way in the back of all the mourners, were on their knees, most of the time, praying one rosary after another.

Nor were they seen when silently left and walked, accompanied by Tom Hopeland, towards the place where the aircraft was stored and quietly boarded it.

It was the first time for Maria to be in an airplane and, needless to say, the woman who had battled in the city and the jungle was highly nervous and shaking like a leaf.

Tania was not nervous, she was sad and depressed because she knew that that night would be the last time, probably for the rest of her life, that she would see her beloved country Guatemala, her Guatemala, "the county of the eternal spring," the country for which she fought and was willing to give her life for.

She was also sad for her father and realized that although she was alive, both Lily Marie Kruger Beltran and Tanya, the warrior, had really died that day.

As a tear rolled down her cheek, she asked Maria, "Who was the person on that coffin?".

Silence, Maria did not answer.

"Maria, who was the person who died in my place"?

"She was a nobody, Commander."

"Did you kill her?".

Maria, still shaking as the plane was gaining altitude, only said: "No, I did not kill her, not directly anyway. She was someone who had been dead for a long time. Someone for whose soul I shall pray for every day of my life."

Maria started to pray another rosary and refused to say anything more.

# EPILOGUE

The plane landed in a small airstrip near Guadalajara because both Tom and Tony had decided ahead of time that it would be less conspicuous and harder to track if they landed there rather than at the main Guadalajara airport.

Also, they were unsure if there was an airport in Puerto Vallarta.

The trio spent a day in Guadalajara buying clothes for Tanya and Maria, finding an orthopedic doctor to remove the cast on Lily Marie's ankle, and considering if it was best for them to drive or ride a bus for the 190 or so miles to Puerto Vallarta. They bought a car since they had plenty of U.S. dollars and figured they would need transportation in Puerto Vallarta.

It was a brand-new Volkswagen Beetle, for which they paid just over two thousand American dollars.

After dinner and after giving the girls extra money, passports, and guns, Tom had them drive him back to the small airport to fly the plane back to Guatemala.

Once they reached Puerto Vallarta, it was easy to find Tony's apartment. It was a small flat on the second floor of the building, with only two bedrooms, but with a beautiful view of the Pacific Ocean and only a few yards from the beach.

Tanya took some time to recover from her wounds but eventually healed and became as solid and beautiful as before. She let her hair grow and used it to cover the missing part of her right ear and the scar from the head wound. She also dyed her hair blondish.

She changed her name to the one on her fake US passport and officially became Claudia Maria Gonsalves, born and raised in Los Angeles, California, USA.

During her stay in Puerto Vallarta, besides swimming in the ocean and going to a local gym, she wrote a book about

241

Guatemala's socio-political situation. With a pseudonym, different than Claudia Maria, of course.

And continued secretly lobbying for the cause of FAR.

Despite the beauty of the beaches of Puerto Vallarta and her delight for the Ocean, Maria was getting gradually homesick, perhaps more so due to guilt, so, she announced that she would return to Guatemala in January, right after the new year of 1969.

Tanya's pleas to her to stay were unsuccessful.

By then, Tanya had decided that if Tony or Tom Hopeland were going to visit her, as they had stated many times that they would if it was possible and safe because they might still have CIA eyes watching their movements, therefore, it would be safer for all, if she moved elsewhere, so she rented an apartment in another building located a few blocks away from their current location.

With men or without men, the two women would have a Christmas and New Year's party at her new apartment. Both Tom and Tony attended, and there was a lot of partying and drinking, so for a brief period, both women forgot their guilt and sorrow and had fun. Tanya ended up having sex with both of the men... although not at the same time. Not a threesome.

It was not until after Maria left that Tanya found out she was pregnant. The problem was that she was pregnant and did not know if the baby's father was Tom or Tony. There was no DNA testing readily available to the public in 1969.

So, she kept her pregnancy a secret, moved to Guadalajara, and had a baby boy there.

When the baby was six months old, she decided that her lifestyle and future plans were incompatible with being a mother. Besides, her true identity could be discovered at any time, and both she and her baby would be eliminated.

So, one day after calling her brother, she drove with the baby to the Guatemalan Mexican border and, with tears in her eyes, gave the baby to her brother.

She also told him to look in their house for the key to her safe deposit box, go to the bank in the city, open it and take the two hundred thousand dollars that was in it, and use it for the education of baby Mario.

Thereafter, Claudia Maria, returned to Guadalajara, enrolled at the medical school there, graduated with honors, became a doctor, and joined *"Médecins Sans Frontiers"* (Doctors Without Borders), traveling to all the troubled spots in the world.

Tom Hopeland, who eventually tracked her down, accompanied her, often.

Tanya never returned to Guatemala.

Not even after the peace treaty between the Army and the Guerrillas was signed in 1996.

While working in Africa, she contracted medication-resistant malaria and suffered attacks of fever, chills, and excruciating body aches, often and on for about two years, finally succumbing to the Ebola virus in 1998.

Doctor Lily Marie Krueger, AKA doctor Claudia Gonzalez, AKA Tanya, was only 55 years old.

Her body was immediately cremated, following the protocol of the WHO, and her ashes were returned to Guatemala by Tom Hopeland, and given to her brother to be buried at the Kruger ranch.

Her tombstone simply read, "Lily Marie Krueger AKA Tanya. Born 1943. She lived and died fighting for what she believed was right."

The name on the next tombstone where Claudia Gonzalez remains had been buried, was changed to her real name, and simply read: "RIP, we hope in God that you finally found rest and peace."

Maria, after two months of accompanying and caring for Tanya, and once she was sure that she was one hundred percent recuperated, from her wounds and fracture, and despite the pleas from Tanya to stay, returned to Guatemala to keep fighting with the FAR.

Perhaps she wanted to redeem herself and get rid of her guilt. So, Maria requested her superiors allow her to work only as a medic rather than a combatant.

One day, while in the mountains near Rio Hondo, she was called to assist a woman from a small village who was having trouble laboring and difficulty in delivering her baby. Despite the pleas, advice, and orders from Carlos and others who were aware of the Army being around in large numbers, Maria went to tend to the woman.

Right after delivering a healthy baby boy, an army platoon arrived and saw Maria's rifle lying against the wall at the hut's entrance. The soldiers come in, shot the woman, shot the baby, and after beating Maria badly, they attempted to rape her.

As two soldiers held her arms, the sergeant in charge dropped his pants and was about to mount her. Maria managed to get one of her arms free, yanked a grenade from the sergeant's belt, and pulled the pin off, killing herself, the sergeant, and the two other soldiers.

When Carlos arrived minutes later with a handful of men and killed, the remaining members of the army platoon it was too late for Maria. Carlos cried over what was left of Maria's body.

Maria's remains are buried right there in the mountains near Rio Hondo Zacapa, Guatemala.

War is hell.

CARLOS: Survived the war and his wounds, and after a peace accord was signed on December 29, 1996, the FAR became a political party, He ran for Congress and was elected and then re-elected. He remained faithful to his ideas.

TOM HOPELAND: Continues being a writer, returns to Guatemala, after some time, returns to the USA, then flies back on a regular flight to Puerto Vallarta.

Proposes and confesses his love to Tanya, but he is rejected.

He loses track of her for several years after the Christmas party but eventually reconnects with her in Mauritania, where she was at the time, working for *Médecins Sans Frontiers*.

He follows her all around the globe as their work allows them.

Tom writes very successful books about his experiences during the Guatemalan Civil War, about Tanya, and about Tony Benedetti.

TONY takes a short vacation to Puerto Vallarta after the events in Guatemala and has a brief fling with Tanya.

Although he tells her that he loves her, she rejects a formal relationship.

Tony reconnects with her briefly at the Christmas party, and becomes convinced that, for the first time in his life, he is truly in love, planning to return and woo her into his arms.

However, the CIA had other plans. The CIA no longer trusts him as his boss Helms is still skeptical about the shooting and death of Tanya, so they seek a way to eliminate him.

Therefore, he is sent to Cuba, to participate in one of the thirty-some CIA attempts to assassinate Fidel Castro. The covert mission fails, maybe because the CIA informed the Cuban Secret Police of the plot, or perhaps not, but Tony is captured by the Cubans and never seen again.

CIA reports that Tony was killed in a Cuban prison.

CAPTAIN MARIO GUILLERMO KRUGER BELTRAN:

Captain Kruger is arrested, accused of kidnapping the corpse of his sister, plotting against the government, and interfering with the authorities. He is condemned to six months in prison plus one year of house arrest. Captain Kruger resigns from the Guatemalan army and becomes the CEO of the family's liqueur factory and the Kruger Ranch.

He distributes nearly five hundred acres, about half, of the Kruger ranch total land, among the ranch workers. Keeps the rest to raise cattle and grow sugar cane, primarily to give jobs to his tenants and to provide sugar to the booze factories.

Mario Kruger builds a school and a medical clinic at the Kruger ranch, and visits his sister as often as it is safe for both of them to do it.

Eventually he marries the daughter of a neighbor rancher and raises a family. The oldest boy is actually his nephew, who was given to him by his sister Lily Marie when he was only a baby, and he adopted him.

Captain Kruger's wife never knows the full story. She believes that he is the product of an affair that her husband had before they met and that the mother is dead.

They lived happily ever after and had two girls and one boy.


DOCTOR K: was never discovered as being part of or helping the FAR, however, he was under suspicion by the paramilitary and his life was in danger.

Therefore, he took a government job far in the countryside, where he lived with his family for two years. Then, as things got worse in Guatemala as the military started wiping out entire villages, gunning down people in the streets, and making many people just disappear.

Nobody was really safe, university students, political leaders, union members, professionals, and many more, under the suspicion that they were in some way connected with or helping the guerrillas.

As more and more people in the cities started disappearing after being captured by the secret police, the military, or the paramilitary, Dr. K and his family decided to migrate to the USA.

Dr. K got his car back, but it never worked as it did before the crash.


All the GENERALS RICARDO OLIVA, RAMIRO ZELAYA, MARIO CAMACHO, and BENITO BENITEZ were gunned down at different times and at different places, presumably by FAR, the paramilitaries loyal to General Willy Kruger, or even perhaps the son of the General ex Captain Mario Kruger, or friends of his.

Those responsible for the four generals' assassinations were never found or identified.

# A BIT OF REAL HISTORY

I have been asked if there are any actual facts in this story. The answer is yes, some.

Although most of it is fictitious, as are the characters (there was no Kruger Family, no Tanya, no Tony, Tom, Carlos or Maria, and no battle of Avenida Elena), other historical names and facts are real.

There was indeed an American Ambassador by the name of John Gordon Mein, who was assassinated in 1968 during an attempt to kidnap him.

And for sure, there was a Civil War in Guatemala, a bloody war that lasted 36 years, from 1960 to 1996, and claimed between 140,000 to 200,000 human lives, between combatants, collateral damage, and those who simply "disappeared."

Untold atrocities were committed by both sides but mainly by the Guatemalan Military and the rightwing paramilitary forces supported by them.

Yet, after the peace treaty was signed in December 1996, none of those responsible were brought to trial.

Sadly, most of the conditions conducive to that war still prevail in Guatemala.

You are invited to Google GUATEMALAN CIVIL WAR and open Wikipedia for more detailed information.

# AUTHOR BIOGRAPHY

Percy D. Kepfer is an 85-year-old retired physician (Pediatrician and Family physician) who lives on the Treasure Coast of Florida with his wife of 58 years.

Dr. Kepfer has written previously several novels, including: "The Homeless Veteran," "Symbiosis," "The Smell of Power," and a children's story (this one jointly with his granddaughter Allison)

"Mud flower, the barefoot princess".

Plus, a compilation of poems written in Spanish since his youth.